Fantastical Summer

R.J. Catlin
Lucy Grecu
K.Ann
Vella Karman
Adara King
Vannah Leblanc
Noah J. Matthews
Juli Ocean
Gregory O'Donnell
Brad Pauquette
Alli Prince
Sarah Sax
Hannah Stiff
Faith Tevy
Thirzah

Fantastical Summer

Developed by

Vella Karman

THE PEARL

PEARLMAG.CO

The Pearl Factory, LLC
303 N. 7th St.
Cambridge, OH 43725
PearlBooks.co

PRODUCER
Brad Pauquette

EDITOR
Vella Karman

COVER
Jessica Ostrander (Artwork)
Brad Pauquette (Design)

LCCN: 2025938053

Paperback ISBN: 978-1-960230-15-7
Ebook ISBN: 978-1-960230-16-4

1 3 5 7 9 10 8 6 4 2

Contents

*To every Christ-follower who loves good clean fun,
especially the girls who want their own beach read.*

Foreword

Christians should be the most fun people in the world.

The worst thing that can happen to me today is to go to heaven. What could I have to worry about?

I've been working with authors for a long time. I can tell, just by reading something, if an author was having fun when they wrote it.

It's just like in a movie. Even if the movie is sad or scary, I think you can still tell if the actors are having a great time making it. There's something wonderful and unmeasurable that changes in the way the actors perform.

Within these pages, I think you'll find a lot of authors who were having fun when they wrote these stories. That's a special thing.

It's an invitation to you, too. When you come across someone having fun, you have a choice to make: scoff or join.

And just because we're having fun, it doesn't mean that we can't also be saying something serious.

If you want to learn a lot about someone: play a game with them. (If you want to learn very little about someone: fight them.)

It's been a privilege to work with Vella Karman to bring this book to life. I heard her heart in the beginning of our planning process to create a fun, lighthearted book, but one that still meant something. A book that might be silly and funny but nonetheless touched on the hard truths of life and invited more Jesus into our readers' lives.

I think she achieved that.

Through the selection process, the editing, the design, and the marketing of the book, I've watched Vella continue to hearken back to that vision and correct the course.

Thank you for reading this book and supporting a new generation of Christian writing.

May you join in on our fun, may you learn something about yourself, and may it be a *fantastical* experience.

Brad Pauquette
Supervising Editor

Introduction

The first time I understood that the sun sets every day was when an EF3 tornado destroyed my neighborhood.

That night, I climbed the still-intact stairs to my room. It was dark in the hallway without power. I opened my bedroom door and there—through my window, over the scene of destruction below, was the most beautiful sunset I'd ever seen.

I dropped to my knees in wonder and awe. Just seeing that sunset was a prayer. I tried to capture the moment in a journal entry before the light faded, kneeling at the windowsill, scribbling as twilight fell.

And I thought...maybe it wouldn't have been so beautiful if everything hadn't been trashed.

Was destruction necessary for greater beauty to emerge?

The sunsets in these fantastical stories aren't intentional. As the editor, it surprised me to find that almost every story included a sunset in some way or another.

I didn't plan it—just like the characters in these stories didn't plan for their lives to change. Shell didn't plan for her mermaid colony to cast her out, Kali didn't plan to buy magical sneakers, and Cassava didn't plan to be affected by gravity.

You're about to discover fifteen whimsical worlds, each with a different magical element.

Some feature classic creatures like werewolves and fairies, while some feel more like sprinkles of magic dropped into a world with drive-throughs. One's technically sci-fi, but they all left me excited.

Thankfully, fun stories can also be meaningful.

Even without the raw power of a tornado or the aching beauty of a sky raised red over destruction, these fantastical stories have moved me.

I hope you read and fall to your knees at the power of our Almighty God.

I hope you read and can't stop thinking about deep questions.

I hope you read and appreciate the simple beauty of typed words on a page describing a sunset.

They happen every day, after all.

Vella Karman
Managing Editor

The Beast

NOAH J. MATTHEWS

I was sitting on a rock next to Mom's sun umbrella when it happened. It was your perfect West Michigan get-out-on-the-lake day—the sun was glistening off the foamy waves, tourists and locals alike were strutting about the sand in their underwear listening to the seagulls and pretending this was California.

I wore sweatpants cut off mid thigh and a T-shirt from Dad's garage band years while my newly-teenaged sisters splashed in the water in teal one-pieces. I couldn't remember the last time I'd worn a swimsuit—Mom was all "your-legs-will-make-the-men-stumble" and everything, and as much as I hated it, I agreed with her. Well, sort of.

I didn't believe that my legs were sexy enough to knock out any straggling male who crossed my path (though they were pretty dazzling, I must say). But I did believe I needed to be hidden. Whether or not I *wanted* to be was a different story.

I *wanted* to be swooning over some God-fearing, homeschooled stud—but those were rare, maybe extinct.

As the gulls squawked and the breeze blew my dyed-hazel hair about my face, I knew I was just kidding myself. I wouldn't find a guy. I knew the truth. I had been three when it happened—the bad thing.

I knew what color my hair actually was. I knew what happened when the moon came out to shine its bald face over the Michigan lakeshore. And I knew that it was my fault.

I sighed and hugged my knees to my chest. I scanned the crowd—absently, you know, just to see if something good turned up? I wasn't allowed on dating apps, anyways.

A tall guy in a black swim shirt and polka-dot trunks caught my eye. He was good-looking, you know, nothing crazy, but nice. His black curls were pulled back, held together with a rubber band. As he walked up, dripping from the water, I saw his shiny dark skin and bright smile. I hid my eyes in my knees. This was stupid. I could already hear my mom in my head: "Melinda Walters, you're only seventeen—what would your father say?"

Then it happened. The thing. The thing this story is about.

The guy walked up to me. I looked up, and there he was, hovering over me dripping with PureMichigan™ water, exuding confidence and sweat. Gross. But also…nice.

He smiled down at me, his hands easy at his sides. "Hey, I noticed you from the water. Have I met you somewhere? Third period science, maybe?"

I blushed, buried my face in my knees, the sun hot on my hair. "I'm homeschooled."

"Oh." But he didn't sound disappointed.

I slowly lifted my head to look at him.

He had a good strong jawline, and something about his eyes sent a shiver through my arms—like he'd been a fairy godmother and suddenly zapped me with pixie dust. I'd never felt more beautiful.

"I'm David, by the way," he said quickly, extending his hand to me. I uncoiled a little and shook his hand. Good firm grip.

"I'm, uh, I'm Melinda." I grimaced at the sound of my own name.

"Melinda." David smiled. "That's a pretty name."

"It's my grandma's name." I wiggled my toes in the sand.

"I like it." David stood there in the sun and the silence passed a moment between us. But it wasn't awkward. It was—I don't know what it was. The kid was magic, that was for sure.

David toed the sand—still with that carefree confidence. "You wanna hang out sometime? I'm here swimming every second I get a chance—you like swimming?"

My lungs, which had been filling with air and butterflies as David talked in his almost musical voice, quickly deflated. I tucked a strand of hair behind my ear. "I can only doggy paddle."

David chuckled and I pretended to laugh too, but my insides had coiled up in a knot. And I could hear it growling.

Hide. Stay safe. Be still, idiot. Remember what you did?

And that was it. That was enough to push the tears to my eyes so I apologized to David while wiping my face on the sleeve of my gray tee.

I think he was trying to comfort me, saying things like "hey, the doggy paddle is a good start," and "I can teach you sometime, if your parents are okay with it," and "it'll be okay—I love you."

And then he was walking away, lending an understanding smile as he trotted through the sand and into the water.

And then his words registered in my mind and it was all I could do to keep from screaming. Had he said that? Was that creepy? As a homeschool girl, I didn't know the first thing about romance. (I did know the second, though—*marriage.* That happened in there somewhere.)

Oh, come on! He was just being nice. Just wait till midnight. Start hiding, baby—it'll be midnight in ten hours!

I wrinkled my nose, felt the anger build within me. "Shut up—ten hours is a lifetime away."

Oh please. A lifetime of loneliness...

"You're hopeless."

Oh, come on—I'm not the one sitting in a gray T-shirt in the middle of a Michigan summer, seventeen, alone...

"Yes you are! We both are!"

Yeah but I have fangs, though.

I stared off into the wind, glancing over the lakeshore at the gulls dipping in an awkward dance over the water.

Very slowly, so soft and quiet I didn't feel it till it was over—a tear fell from my eye. I didn't wipe it. I just stared. Stared out at the freshwater lake while that beast inside me bragged about its fangs.

"I know," I whispered. "We both do."

That night when the rest of the family had gone to bed in our cute-as-a-button lake house, I tiptoed down the grass and dunes to the beach. Dad had bought the lake house back before the millionaires escaping Detroit bought 'em all. Not sure what they were running from, but whatever it was they thought they could escape it in the soothing fresh water of Lake Michigan. Not likely.

I glanced back at the house standing all alone on the top of a grass-covered dune. All the lights were still off—even Mom and Dad's. I nodded—I was still undetected. Quietly, I marched on toward the beach.

The sun had set about an hour ago and the moon was trying to push its head over the water, bald and sweating like an old man climbing stairs. No offense to my lovely grandpa.

I strolled down to the water, my bare feet making soft impressions in the white sand. I stuffed my hands into the pockets of my blue sundress (*all* sundresses should have pockets) and stared out at the moonlight creeping over the sapphire water.

The beast inside was growling and whimpering to be let out, but I ignored it. I thought back to David, how he'd said the magic words ("I. Love. You." For any of you who didn't catch it before.)

I sat down on the sand, pulled my knees up to my chest. Three-year-old Melinda Walters. Mommy said: "Now Melly-Belly (that's what she called me then), you leave those gray berries alone. They look poisonous."

You don't say? Well, I liked gray, so I decided they would be delicious and amazing and magical.

Magical. Yep. That's what they were alright. And I'd paid for eating them.

I had my own room for keeping up appearances, but I slept in the basement—caused less destruction there. I wasn't allowed out after sundown (hence my silent and dastardly escape), and I had completely given up all hope of getting into a relationship.

Well, not all hope, I guess.

I watched the moon rising over the water—it had most of its head out now, and I could feel the beast (metaphorically) flipping tables and breaking vases inside me in its impatience.

I secretly hoped that the beast was different from me—some demon of the underworld sent to annoy me and destroy my luck with boys. But something inside me wondered—wondered if *I* was the beast, if it wasn't just a part of me but a part of *me*—and if it wasn't, could it become so?

I shivered, listening to the hush of the waves, the gentle swish of the lake. The lake had always calmed me, even though I (and the beast) hated swimming.

And then the moon was out of the water and I could feel it happening. My stomach went hollow a moment…and then I shut my eyes and let it take me.

Fur grew rapidly down my arms. A chill raced down my spine and I could feel the tail sprouting.

I tensed, felt the beast writhing in my chest as its form consumed mine. Tremors worked through my fingers and I shut my eyes against the slight pain of them lengthening, the claws forming, the snout stretching my face, my nose turning wet and wrinkled like a dog's.

There were tears streaking down my face. It was like with each passing second, with each new beam of the moon, with each new piece of fur, my *self* was being eroded like sand before waves, like a carcass before the mouth of wolves.

I felt the brush of my fur against the inside of my sundress. As the wind stirred my whiskers, I knew the transformation was complete.

I opened my eyes.

A few seconds ago, a normal(ish) seventeen-year-old West Michigan girl sat on the beach in a sundress (with POCKETS). Now, an anthropomorphic wolf sat on the beach (still in a sundress with pockets), and she was crying as she howled at the full moon hanging over the lake.

I sat there in the moonlight, listening to myself howl while the breeze rustled my fur. The beast had overtaken me and I could feel it doing happy dances in my head as it finally shared control of my body. There was always a rush of adrenaline when it took over, and there was a comfort in letting it have its way, you know?

But it was also awful. So, so awful.

Slowly, I rose to my feet, staring dumbly at my gray paws gripping the sand. It was late. I should go home—to my miserable basement—and forget it all.

Which is just poetic. There was no way I could forget that I turned into a wolf at night—it's a *pretty* dramatic thing.

I took one last look over the water, took that Pure Michigan™ freshwater smell in through my snout, and stopped cold in my tracks.

David—that sweet dark-skinned beauty—trotted along the sand toward the water. The moonlight glistened off his hair as he stopped, turned toward me—

Oh, no! Panic set in. *Run? Stay? Hide?* The moment he saw me as a wolf—I was done for. He'd call the police—I could already hear it. *"Yes, officer? Yeah there's a wolf walking upright in a sundress. Danger. Insanity. Definitely should put the country into DEFCON 1."*

I tried to calm my breathing, tried to tuck my hair behind my ear. But there were no long dyed-brown locks—all my fingers brushed was gray fur. Gray. My real hair color ever since the stupid berry.

Why had I been so stupid? *Why—oh no, he's looking at me. No, no, please, David, stop it—stop running! Help!*

David was running toward me, padding across the sand on bare feet. In the darkness I couldn't see his face—what was he thinking, running after a wolf in a sundress?

But if he got close—ughhhh I'd die. In the moment, the possibility of him recognizing me even as a *wolf* didn't seem unreasonable. The kid was magic. I'd felt it.

I took off running—an awkward stumble across the sand into the night. I'd be able to run faster if I got on all fours—but that would rip the dress and Mom would *kill* me for that.

So I hobbled away, half skipping on my tiny paws as David sped after me. It must have been a funny sight—the moonlit lakeshore of Lake Michigan, a wolf in a sundress hobbling over the sand, trying to avoid any rocks as a sleek young dude chased her, clods of sand flying elegantly behind him.

Then I tripped and fell sprawling snout-first onto the sand. The sand was cool under my body and for a moment I just wanted to rest—to stop running and just *exist*, you know?

But I pushed myself awkwardly to my feet, taking in big gulps of air through my snout, trying to catch my breath.

David called out from behind me. "Hey—hey are you alright?"

I tensed, listened to his soft footsteps as he came up beside me. *Run. Stay. Eat him. Don't—wait, EAT him!*

Yeah. Why not? I like meat.

I put a paw to my snout. I couldn't believe what I'd just thought—or what the beast had just said—I didn't know which anymore.

I turned toward David. Here, the moonlight hit him just right so that I could see his face. His eyebrows were knit, his lips pursed like he was thinking. His hands were clasped.

Silence passed a moment. My muscles flexed and unflexed spasmodically—the beast trying to get control. I knew if I let it, we WOULD actually eat David. I could barely live with myself as it was.

I smoothed the front of my dress with a paw, then paused. The blue really looked good against my fur color.

Suddenly David spoke. "What happened to you?" It wasn't an accusation.

I clenched my jaws together, looked at the ground. "Nothing. Nothing happened."

Silence except for the hush of the waves. Then, softly, David whispered, "I was a wolf too, you know."

A chill went through me as if someone had poked me with an icicle. My hackles went up and I looked into David's face.

David's lips were pursed, his eyes glistening in the moonlight. He stood straight, but I noticed his hands were in his pockets. There was less confidence flowing from him.

I cocked an eyebrow—or at least, that's what it felt like. I have *no* idea what it looked like on my wolf face. "What's up?" I asked.

David toed the sand. "I ate these berries when I was three."

Suddenly a really weird feeling expanded in my chest. It wasn't quite compassion, but it wasn't jealousy, either. I wasn't sure what it was, but I spoke the first thought that came to mind: "So you—um—how? Like…?"

David let out a chuckle, smiled down at me. "Only God."

I looked down at the ground, toeing the sand with my paws. "Really."

As good a Christian homeschool girl as I was, I'd never seen God do anything except guide the hands of doctors...sometimes. If he was in the mood. And you prayed really really hard.

David took a deep breath. "I was a wolf for years—every midnight..." He shivered. "My parents had given up finding a cure. Therapy didn't work. I finally got to the end of myself." He glanced off over the water. "It was on this beach. I was sitting, crying, didn't know what to think. Then—I don't know. God started fixing me. Bit by bit, but it happened. The beast—the beast *wasn't* me."

David put a hand to his chin, squinted at me. "That make sense?" A smile worked its way onto his lips. It wasn't a creepy smile, or a patronizing smile—it was...I don't know. A good smile. A genuine smile. An I-wanna-help-you kind of a smile.

Hope fluttered like a dying sparrow in my chest—I wasn't sure what to think. Mom and Dad had already prayed for the beast to go away—and it hadn't. I liked David's story, but I wasn't sure it'd work on *me*. I knew what I was.

"I'm Melinda, by the way," I said abruptly. *Time to exit the situation.* "The girl from the beach. In the T-shirt."

"I never forgot you," David said, his hands at his sides.

I squirmed inside. *EAT HIM!* screamed the beast. I trembled—I just—could it be true? *Could* this nightmare end? My thoughts stirred up a metaphorical dust fight in my mind.

"Melinda—are you alright?"

I laughed reflexively—stopped as I realized it sounded like a wolf's howl. I wrapped my arms around myself, took a step back. "Sorry."

David knit his eyebrows together. "Don't be sorry. You have a beautiful laugh."

I coughed—choking on his compliment like water down the wrong pipe. Was he stupid or something? Was he *deaf?* My laugh was anything but beautiful—even without the wolf-howl part. I looked up at him. "Why are you so nice?" It was all I could do to keep myself from shouting it.

David held his hands out like Mom would when one of us kids *really* wasn't getting the point of what she was trying to say. But there was confidence in the way David used the gesture, like he wasn't pleading so much as declaring. "Melinda, I love you! Like—I did from the moment I saw you; love at first sight, you know?"

I tried to shrink. "You...*love me?*"

David said nothing.

I held out my paws to him. "*Look* at these paws—these claws. David, I have *fangs!* I'm a *wolf*—a *beast!* You can't—"

"That is *not* who you are." His arms were crossed, and he stood still as the statue of some ancient god.

I clenched my teeth, shut my eyes. "You don't know who I am..." I whispered. "It's *my* fault I'm like this..."

I felt his hand on my arm. Slowly, I opened my eyes, found myself looking up into his brown-eyed face.

He bit his lip, and I thought I saw a tear in his eye. "Melinda—you are *not* your mistakes. You are *loved. That's* who you are. That's what God showed me, and I *know* it's true about you."

"But—"

He put a finger to his lips. "I love you, Melinda—exactly as you are. You are *not* alone."

My hands were shaking. "But how? You barely know me—you—"

"I know enough. I'm not going to turn you away—no matter how furry you are." David smiled, a bleary-eyed, gentle smile.

Tears were slipping from my own eyes and sinking into my fur. I tried to open my jaws—to say something, but no words came.

And then he wrapped his strong arms around me and held my wolf-ish head against his chest. I slipped my furry paws around the small of his back and I shut my eyes tight against the tears. David's chest was warm and I could hear his heart beating. I held onto him tighter, feeling some of that twisted, wolfish weight slip from my back.

"Please don't leave me. Please don't let go." I didn't realize I was saying it out loud. And when I did, I suddenly wasn't embarrassed.

I was loved. Beast and all.

I leaned into his chest and David stroked my fur. My tail started wagging beneath my dress. I didn't mind.

In that quiet, tingly, moonlit moment, I heard David whisper—his voice so soft it was only because of my wolf hearing that I caught the words: "I love you, Melinda—*that* is who you are."

A warm feeling expanded in my chest, like an oven had just been opened and the smell of fresh bread was wafting out. I'd never felt safer—so completely at home.

I hugged him tighter, that funny, weird feeling you get when you stay up too late running through my body.

Whether my beast would shrink over time like David's, I didn't know. But I did know this—even though the beast was a part of me, I was *not* the beast.

I was loved, and that was enough.

Beachcombing

SARAH SAX

Teaching is a lot easier said than done.

"You can only use each shell once," I say. "That's why no one cares about scallops." I pick one up to show Ashley. "They end up on the beach broken more often than not, and if you happen to find a whole one you'll either damage it while trying to get it open, and thus waste a perfectly good portal, or sit it in your china cabinet—"

"We don't have a china cabinet," Ashley says with her mouth. Her face says more. It has a saltshaker's worth of freckles all over it, it's framed by windblown black hair, and it says: *Just how old-fashioned do you think we are?*

Well, Mr. and Mrs. Sellers aren't exactly young, but I don't say that. Ashley's had enough reasons to glare at me as it is. At least she feels comfortable enough to do that, and interrupt me, and other…fun, unwelcoming things.

"Fine, on the kitchen counter or by the bathroom sink or wherever things go to rot while you watch and dream of the possibilities. It's just not worth it."

Ashley shrugs and (very deliberately) shoves a scallop in her pocket (it's only half a scallop, might I add). She's definitely my daughter.

It's a pretty shell though—pink fading into yellow, like a sunset. I think about commenting on that, then decide to skip the small talk and go on with the lecture. After all, there are portals to find.

"Olives are better, cowries too. Conches are best, but they're hard to find in one piece. You can get away with a slightly damaged olive or cowrie as long as there's no big pieces missing. I never bother with coquinas—they're about as satisfying as, uh, a drop of water. To someone dying in the desert. Of thirst, you know?" *Yeah, I fumbled that metaphor, kid, stop staring at me.*

Her eyes make me so uncomfortable, it's not even funny. They're hazel like mine, but they're shaped just like her dad's, and I can only ever think of them in that regard. Maybe that's why I don't spend much time looking at them. Ironically, I realize I've been staring at them for some time now without speaking. I clear my throat and go on.

"So. Yeah. Where do you find these shells? All around us. But where's the best place? Here at the tide line." I gesture at where we're standing, between damp and dry sand. At our feet and stretching down the beach is a thick black line of shells—pretty crushed looking, but a beachcomber knows this is a treasure chest.

Of course, Ashley doesn't yet know this, which is why we're here. I still find it hard to believe that she can't identify an olive to save her life and that she needs to be shown where the tide line is. *I* grew up by the beach. *She* is my child (even if I haven't seen her for twelve years). Therefore, *she* should have all beach knowledge—fish scales in her tears, the swimming agility of dolphins. That sort of thing.

I sit and run my hands through the shells. "You can find so much here if you have the patience to look. I've found baby conches and things that are perfect for traveling, they just get missed. The tiny ones are surprisingly hardy—hey, a shark's tooth!"

Ashley actually looks interested until I hold it up. Then she frowns again. "That's a shark's tooth? I thought they were supposed to be bigger than your hand."

I take a second look. Yeah, to someone *not* raised at the beach, this must not look great. It's no bigger than my pinky fingernail. Actually, it might be smaller. "Not all of them are big. The biggest one I've found was half the size of my thumb. It's still cool though, right?"

Ashley shrugs. *Fine, girl, have it your way.*

"Can you do anything with it?" she asks.

"With a shark's tooth? Nah. They're just cool. Oh, and here's a piece of sea glass. You *can* travel with that, sort of, but I usually don't bother." I'm about to explain the merits of jingle shells (there actually are a few) when Ashley interrupts again.

"Why don't you bother with the sea glass?"

"Eh, I guess I could. But they're not strong enough for traveling, at least not in my experience. You can see things all right, but it's like watching a video rather than being there. I want to do the traveling. Though there's this one story of a girl who collected enough sea glass to make a giant portal."

"And?"

"And she stepped through it and was never seen again. It broke her up, more than likely. Sent little bits of her to different worlds. I don't know if it's true, but if that's your style…" I shrug, trying not to laugh in Ashley's face. "I wouldn't recommend it."

I can't believe how nostalgic this feels. I grew up by the beach (or on the beach, you might say). My grandma introduced me to beachcombing pretty much the same way I'm introducing Ashley. I've traveled lots of places and loads of times, but I've never done it with my daughter.

"So how do we do this?" This girl sure has my knack for interrupting and for general impatience. I'm surprised she hasn't driven me crazier than she has. But hey, anything's good as long as she doesn't take after her dad. She already has his eyes. And his nose. And let me tell you, only one of us ever freckled the way she does, and it's not me.

I pat the sand and Ashley gives me a "seriously?" face.

"C'mon, you've got to sit, or you'll get major back pain from bending over these shells. Plus I tied my hair back and you didn't, so it'll get in your face." She takes after me in this regard—we both have very thick, very dark, very long hair.

"Sit in the sand?"

"No, in a bushel of thorns. Seriously, Ash—"

"Don't call me that!"

Worth a try. "Seriously, Ashley, it won't hurt you. And we're wearing bathing suits, so it's not like your clothes are getting dirty or anything."

"It looks wet."

"It can't be *that* bad, it's been low tide for a while. Just sit, will you?" I stare her down until she sits. Grudgingly. And trying to touch the sand as little as possible.

Was I that weird as a kid? I mean, obviously not about sand, but about other things. I decide it doesn't matter because here is a little girl who needs to learn about beachcombing and seashell portals.

"Shells are awesome, and not just because they can take you different places. There are *so many* different kinds. Like, jingle shells? They're thin and pretty flaky but also these lovely metallic colors— usually silver or white, but sometimes gold or copper. And with those you don't just travel *to* places, you travel to their parallel realms. If that makes sense." I don't think Ashley's quite ready for that though.

I settle with a moon shell. Those are the best option for beginners. Plus they're pretty. This one's the color of dolphins, with a hint of lavender. "You can tell moon shells are fresh if the very center of the spiral is blue," I say. "It's like an eye. This one's very blue, so it's good and fresh. Now here. Hold this up and look inside it. Imagine yourself *going* inside it." I try to remember how my grandma put it. "Visualize it as vividly as you can—imagine the cool smoothness of shell sliding around you." Now, *that's* using a metaphor. "Do you feel it?"

Ashley, to her credit, tries. I was afraid she might be uncooperative and waste the shell completely. After ten seconds of screwing up her face, she starts to move the shell away.

"No, no, no!" I screech, then remember she already doesn't like me. "Sorry. You'll waste the portal if you do that. Keep trying. It's kind of hard at first."

"You don't say," Ashley snaps.

"I *said* I was sorry. Focus, okay?"

Ashley focuses, glaring, but slowly the glare smooths out and I wonder…I really don't want this outing to be a bust. Ashley already thinks I hate her, which is fair, considering I almost killed her *before* she was born and gave her away as soon as she *was* born. Even if you change your mind and track your kid down, just deciding to be a part of her life doesn't make it automatically happen. Of course, Mr. and Mrs. Sellers didn't make it easy. I guess I'm lucky to get this afternoon at all, considering how far away they live from the beach.

I kneel beside her, wishing I could see what she's seeing. "Anything happening?" I try to sound patient and nice. It sounds squeaky, like I'm talking to a baby, but (wonder of wonders!) Ashley doesn't glare at me this time.

"I see something," she says, her voice strained. "It's—clouds? No, a castle! There's a castle in the clouds!"

Clouds? That's a new one, and I've been to some weird places. "In the snow you mean?"

"No, it's definitely clouds." Ashley almost turns to look at me but stops herself in time. She learns faster than I did. Faster than I do, I guess. "It looks like a fairy-tale castle. It has these big sparkly white towers and—hey, wait, I'm moving!"

"What do you mean, you're moving?"

"I think I'm flying," Ashley says, very seriously. "Oh! It's a dragon! I'm riding a dragon!" The look on her face, the astonishment in her voice, it's all *priceless.* "It's...*yellow!* I didn't know dragons could be yellow."

"Really?" I'm pretty excited myself. "What else?"

"We're flying toward the castle." She laughs and ducks a little. "There's these big flags on the towers, one almost brushed me. Oh, there's another dragon! It's purple. I've never seen a purple dragon before either." She's never seen a dragon before, period.

"Anyone on it?"

"No, I think I'm the only one around. Is this real?"

Amazing how quickly she goes from astonished to skeptical. Like me when I found out I was having her. "It's a portal, that's all I can tell you. I think some of the worlds are definitely real, but I have no idea which ones. And the ones that might not be real? I can't explain those either. It's—Ashley? What's wrong?"

She just went stiff. Like, scary stiff. Like, I'm-afraid-she-might-keel-over stiff.

"Make it stop!" she shrieks. "I can't stop it!"

"Okay, calm down." I feel a little panicky myself, which doesn't help. "What's happening? Make what stop?"

"The dragons! They're going for each other! I don't know what to do!" Ashley's voice gets increasingly higher pitched as she talks.

Well, this is not good. I imagine what Mr. and Mrs. Sellers will say if I tell them their daughter was killed by dragons. I don't know if they believe in the portals. They'd probably say I kidnapped her, or worse.

"Uh, all right. Try to calm down, Ash." (I tell myself there's no time to waste on her full name. She doesn't correct me, so maybe she agrees.) "Are there any reins? Any way to control the dragon? Anyone you can call to for help?"

Ashley doesn't answer. She's entering full-blown panic mode. I find myself getting frustrated, which isn't fair because this isn't her fault at all. I'd probably panic too. "Do you want to get out?"

This time she responds, or rather nods frantically, which is enough for me. Feeling only a *little* regret over the portal, I put a hand on her shoulder. "Okay, then listen to me and listen carefully because if you don't, you could get lost in there." She definitely hears *that,* and it does *not* help her relax. "Sorry to scare you, but those are the facts and they're important. Right. Imagine that shell again, just like you did at first, but imagine crawling backward out of it. You *really, really, really* need to block out everything around you, even if the dragon's about to roast you alive." Again, poor word choice, but there's no time for that. "Come on, you can do it."

The hand I have on her shoulder is shaking, I'm surprised to see. I *shouldn't* be surprised. Just because you give up your kid doesn't mean you can't care about them. But I guess you get used to being told you don't care. Hunting them down be—

"Ashley!"

She screams, jerking away from the shell. I'm not sure what she saw—maybe the dragons clashed, maybe the one she was riding threw her off, maybe she really is being roasted alive—but whatever it was, it was enough. She goes even stiffer than stiff, then goes totally limp, then falls over face down on the sand.

"Ashley! Oh, my God!" Mrs. Sellers would say that's taking God's name in vain, but she doesn't know everything. Because right now, I truly mean it. "Oh, my God!"

I roll her over and start pinching her arms, flicking and then slapping her face, anything to get a response. Nothing. I peel her eyelids back. Her eyes are staring at nothing, and since they're spinning in circles, "nothing" must be a carousel. It makes me dizzy. It also freaks me out.

"Ashley! Ashley!"

I've never actually been in a situation where someone got stuck in a portal. There's been close calls, certainly, but nothing nearly this close. This previously-happy fact means I don't have the faintest idea of what I'm doing. Or what I should do. I've heard a few things in stories—some people swear by dunking the shell in rough water but the ocean's having a flat-as-glass day, unfortunately. The tide should come up soon, though not soon enough.

I really only have one option, and it probably isn't going to work. But what else can I do? I can't leave Ashley in there. And if the tables should turn…well, better me than her. Or so I try to convince myself. It's not like they can accuse her of murder.

Her hands are locked in tight fists, which scares me all over again and also costs us precious time, since I have to unpeel her fingers from around the shell. But I get it, finally, and before I can waste any more time, hold it up to my eyes and go inside.

I've never rescued someone from a portal, but I *have* peeked in fresh-used shells, so I'm not surprised when instead of dragons and castles I'm greeted with gray. It's like I was plopped inside a storm cloud. It's also really hard to move forward, but I pride myself on being something of an expert at shell travel.

Plus I'm stubborn.

Ashley is in the center of the portal, which is beginning to swirl in on itself like a hurricane. She looks like one possessed—levitating upright, head tipped back, mouth open as if screaming. When I tell you I tear that portal apart getting to her, that's very nearly true.

"Ash! Ashley, honey, can you hear me?"

She doesn't respond verbally, but she flinches when I touch her shoulder. Good sign. Now to get out of here.

If going in was hard, getting out—with a barely-conscious twelve-year-old—is even harder. To make matters worse, the portal (that was beginning to swirl on itself, remember?) is going faster and faster. Walking against it is like swimming against a current or trying to get out of a riptide. And I have to move slowly or else I might trip. The chance of us getting out of here is slim—if I stumble, it gets even slimmer. If I fall…we might as well start the paternoster or The-Lord-Is-My-Shepherd to get ahead of the pastor.

The dark humor part of my brain thinks: *Hey, Mrs. Sellers, you've been wanting me to pray!* It also notes the almost rhyme of "noster" and "pastor," for what reason I don't know, since I'm no poet. Brains are strange places.

Ashley comes to life out of nowhere and starts kicking and screaming. I don't exactly stumble, which is good for us, but I come scary-close to it and say some words Ashley really shouldn't hear. Fortunately, she doesn't seem to.

"I want out! I want out! I want out!"

"Calm down, Ash! I'm trying to get us out of here!" I really want to yell with her because it's true, and because I could probably out-scream her. An interesting experiment, for which we have no time. I can't even cover my ears.

One foot in front of the other. Except my feet aren't working right. They're carrying me back instead of forward, back into that [redacted for Ashley's sake] spiral. I kick with all my might, but it's like trying to go up the down escalator. My feet scrape against the sides of the shell…and then they scrape against nothing.

The portal is taking us away.

I don't say anything to Ashley, who is faithfully screaming her head off. (Though this news might be enough to shut her up.) It suddenly dawns on me that we're not getting out, we're going to be sucked into the portal's core, we're going to *die* the minute it goes out. And I don't want to die. I don't want to think of people finding our bodies on the tide line. I don't want this to be the end of my beachcombing career and the lovely nostalgic day I had planned and the relationship I thought I might be building.

I could drop Ashley and make a run for it.

After talking about relationships, I hate to say how tempting a thought that is. Because it is. Let's face it, things were never great between us—from cussing out the pregnancy test to going to the abortion clinic (only to chicken out). And then shoving her at the first pair of adoptive parents and heading for the hills. And *then* deciding a decade later: "Hey, it would be nice to know my kid…"

And then maybe becoming a stalker before popping *hey-presto* into said kid's life, much to the parents' dismay.

But here's the thing. We were making progress. They actually let me visit. They actually visited me. They actually gave me an unsupervised day with Ashley, who actually agreed to come. And it's been a few years since I was that girl who cussed out the pregnancy test. Maybe that girl hasn't changed *too* much, but she's changed a little. And she knows Ashley has a good life, a great one even.

It's called love, okay?

Yes, bring on the cheese platters and the Hallmark movies. Love conquers all. Which is why I shove my daughter toward the shell's entrance as hard as I can. She disappears and my last thought is going to be: *I have a daughter, and she's awesome, and guess what, I'm going to die for her.*

And then something slams into the shell like a semi into a Mini Cooper. I get thrown end over end as the shell is flooded with sand and salt. I take a breath and immediately regret it because salt water is not something you want to inhale. It always makes me feel like I'm going to throw up.

Then I realize I'm breathing.

I'M BREATHING!!!

GLORY HALLELUJAH!

I'm lying in what used to be the shell bed and is now being covered by the rising tide. I must've dropped the shell—and let me tell you (as a small wave goes over my face), the rising tide is a reckonable force. Capable of turning sharp shells into soft sand, and of washing out portals, and rescuing people inside those portals. Things like that.

I hadn't realized we were that close to high tide. I must be getting sloppy, unless miracles do exist. Well, I'm not going to complain. Instead, I roll around in the sand and shells and water, and straight into something that turns out to be a pair of legs, attached of course to a body. I look up, get blinded by the sun, and have to sit up.

It's Ashley, and she looks not only alive but well. Which is not profound, but it's all I've got.

I must look like a maniac, and what I do next sure doesn't help. I sort of stumble-crawl on my knees and launch myself at her, practically knocking her down. Oh, well. At least we're hugging. That never happened successfully before. I didn't even want to hold her at the hospital.

"You okay, Ash?"

"Uh-huh." Notably, she still doesn't protest "Ash." She does free herself from the hug, and I don't blame her because it is kind of awkward. We sit side by side, and if we're almost touching—well, I won't mention it.

"This is *not* how I imagined today going at all," I say. "Guess I should've known better, though. Shell-portals are dangerous. If you couldn't tell."

"You don't say," Ashley deadpans. Which cracks me up, which makes Ashley smile. "We should try again sometime though."

I was *not* expecting that. "You really want to? After what just happened?"

Ashley shrugs. "So, that was scary, but obviously you've done it for a while and haven't been killed yet." Profound, this one. "You could teach me. It *was* cool. I guess I just wasn't prepared for it."

"Fair." I stretch out, letting a wave rush up my legs. "I think my grandma had the magic touch, or else we just got lucky, because I didn't get a dangerous portal until three weeks after I started. By then I was pretty experienced, y'know?"

Ashley looks a little wistful. "Too bad we'll be leaving today. We don't go to the beach a lot."

"You'll just have to keep visiting, I guess. Or convince your parents." It's not so hard to say: *Your parents.* Even if we've had a little bonding experience, I don't think that's enough for Ashley to want to move in with me. And let's be honest, it's probably for the best.

So she'll just have to keep visiting me. I'll have to keep visiting her. She'll learn the portals like the back of her hand. Maybe I'll be able to call Mr. and Mrs. Sellers something other than Mr. and Mrs. Sellers (they do have first names, after all). Maybe I can learn to stop misusing God's name and avoid words Ashley shouldn't learn. Maybe I'll even start praying, who knows?

Love, amiright? Hallmark movies, amiright?

Whatever. There's a lot that could happen in the future. What I have right now is a lot more than I ever expected to get, so I'm going to watch the tide line disappear and the shells get pounded into sand and not even think longingly of the portals disappearing. So maybe that last one is a little much to ask, but otherwise…progress has been made. You can't deny it, and if you can, you simply haven't spent enough time with me.

My daughter and I sit side by side as the tide comes in.

Just look at how awesome that sentence is.

Soul Marks

ALLI PRINCE

I sat and watched the burning embers of the campfire, my legs pulled to my chest and my arms wrapped tightly around them. Chelsea and Derek sat on a log to my right. They had their arms looped around each other, their foreheads pressed together. I watched as silent whispers of devotion and who knows what else tumbled unburdened from their lips.

They were the lucky ones. Chelsea had a mark on the back of her hand. A tree and a river. Derek's mark was the exact same. They were soul marks. Little pictures or words like tattoos that you're born with. A tiny hint to help lead you along to the one who is destined to love you.

Everyone is born with them—well, everyone but me, apparently. They call people like me a variety of different things. Soulless being the most hurtful and markless being the truth. Only a small percentage of people are born without one. I guess that just made me unlovable.

I watched Chelsea and Derek from the corner of my eye as the rest of the youth group chatted and teased each other. The campfire crackled and burned in front of me, and Pastor Ryan's obnoxious '90s worship music blasted from his Bluetooth speaker. It was a late-night campout, one of many that the youth group at the local church hosted in the woods during the summer.

"It's a beautiful night," a voice from my left said. I looked up. Pastor Ryan stood behind my log, a cup of coffee in his hand. He scratched his graying beard with the other and stared up at the stars. Then he motioned to the spot next to me. "Mind if I sit?"

I shrugged and scooted over. A giggle reached my ear and I glanced over at Chelsea and Derek, then frowned. Beside me, Pastor Ryan snorted.

"Young love," he elbowed me and wiggled his eyebrows. "It's great to see soulmates find each other so young."

"Yeah." I rolled my eyes. "*Super* great. *If you have one.*"

I held up my blank forearm and sneered. "I'm *un*lovable, in case my mom forgot to mention it before *you* invited *her* to make me come here."

Pastor Ryan nodded his head slowly. Then he took a long sip from his coffee. I was just about ready to storm off when he finally spoke.

"So was I, kid."

I swallowed and glanced down to his hand where his soul mark was. "What do you mean?"

Ryan reclined back as far as he could without falling off the log and stared down at his hand. I knew his wife, Gracie. She helped out with the women's Bible study and served in the soup kitchen on Thursdays. She had a soul mark, same as Pastor Ryan's.

I gritted my teeth together and turned harshly away. "Listen—if you're just trying to make me *feel* better—"

"I'm not, kid…I'm not. Sorry, it's just…a hard story to tell, sometimes…" He leaned forward, clasped his hands together, and began. "I wasn't born with a soul mark. My body was completely and totally blank…until I met Gracie."

~~~

I wasn't too surprised I didn't have a soul mark growing up. My parents didn't have matching marks, and the way they fought, it wasn't hard to figure out that they didn't love each other, not really.

I'd been an accident. He and Mom had been young and stupid. They thought they could live life up until they'd meet their marks and then settle down. Well, one thing led to another. My mom got pregnant and their parents forced them to get married for propriety's sake.

As a kid, I'd watch my mom stare out the window, lightly tracing her soul mark, a single star that had faded with time. My dad got a cover-up tattoo. I never knew what his soul mark was. The tattoo wasn't an image or a string of words or anything. It was just a big black square. Big and empty and pointless.

Part of me wondered if he'd actually been markless, like me. I couldn't imagine my dad, the burnt-out semitruck driver who sat on his rump watching old college football reruns, ever loving anybody. Least of all, a scrawny-looking kid with curly red hair and a crooked nose like me.

He never came to a single graduation or baseball game, never showed up when it was "bring your parent to school" day. He didn't teach me to shave, how to tie my first tie for prom, or talk to me about girls. He just sat there, day in and day out, drinking a cold beer, his feet propped up on the ottoman. My school life wasn't much better.

Jessica Johnson was the first girl to ever break my heart. She was the pretty girl who sat next to me in my 8th-grade English class. We used to be best friends. We'd sit on the bus ride home with our shoulders pressed together as we listened to music from her Walkman. The day she broke my heart, we stood outside under the football bleachers. It had rained the day before, so we stood in the mud. She chewed on a glossy pink lip and held up her right hand—her soul mark was a kite with clouds around it. She looked down. "Listen, you're an awesome guy. You're funny and adventurous. But…I have a soul mark."

"You don't even know who that mark belongs to," I protested. "What if he's some—some old creep who doesn't even know you like to dip your fries in mayo, or…or…"

She just shook her head.

"Going out with you would be like cheating on my future, wouldn't it?" Jessica moved a single strand of gorgeous blonde hair behind her ear. She wouldn't even look me in the eye as she said it. "It's just wrong. I'm sorry."

I gave up on being loved. If I couldn't be loved, I'd be smart, funny, and everything else I could be. So I poured myself into my studies and got accepted into my top school by the time I was a senior. But, despite the hard work, I ended up attending the little state college in my hometown. I couldn't get a scholarship, and my dad wasn't going to pay for me to go to some fancy university. I stayed at home, worked a part-time job at the Dairy Queen down the block, and took mostly night classes.

That's when I first saw Gracie.

She was sitting by herself outside the university in the rain. Just…sitting there, taking the wind and the hail, her eyes closed, her body drenched. I watched from the library window as she sat there, shivering.

I saw her like that often, outside, no matter the weather, staring up at the sky. I heard whispers about her as I passed. Never anything I took stock in, but enough to keep my eyes lingering on her figure as I passed.

In the middle of January, I finally met the mysterious Gracie. I was on my phone, stopped at a crosswalk, when she walked up next to me. It was late—the sun had long since set, and my only thought was of my tiny twin mattress crammed into the back corner of my house, where I could finally rest my bones and sleep.

I glanced up as she passed me, her eyes glued to her phone as she stepped into the street without looking. I saw the headlights of the bus. I reached forward. My hands wrapped around her green satchel. I pulled with all my might. The bus honked. Gracie screamed. Together, we fell onto the sidewalk. I busted my knee on the way down. Pain flared, blood oozed, and the bus flew by. I sat on the ground, gasping for breath, adrenaline pumping through my veins. Then I turned to her.

"Holy *crap*—are you okay?" I ran a hand through my hair. "That was so close, you almost—"

I stopped as I noticed Gracie. She sat with her legs drawn under her, eyes wide as she stared at the street. I reached out and our fingers brushed. She gasped and snapped her hand to her chest. Then she met my eyes and tears freely fell down her big round cheeks, her dark-brown irises huge against the panicked white of her eyes.

"Hey," I held up both my hands. "Hey, it's okay. Here—I'm Ryan. Your name is Gracie, right?"

"I...oh my—" She slapped both hands over her mouth as sobs began to wrack her body. "I-I wasn't even *paying attention*, I just..."

Then she looked at me again and just wouldn't stop crying, so I scootched across the ground, careful of my knee, and held her hand as she sat there, sobbing. Finally, after she calmed herself, she wiped her eyes and stood.

"Gosh, I'm sorry." She smoothed out her pants and slung her bag back over her shoulder. I stood and winced, favoring my busted knee.

"Hey, no worries...like I said, I'm Ryan. You're Gracie, right?"

She nodded. "Yeah...that's me...listen, Ryan...would you...not tell anybody what happened today? If my parents found out, it'd be a nightmare."

"I mean…" I hesitated and glanced around. Nobody had really seen us. I shrugged. "Sure, but…why weren't you paying attention?"

Gracie looked down at her shoes—green Converse—and sighed. "Just…having a bad day, that's all. I'm a bit…preoccupied."

"So you have *one* bad day and nearly walk into oncoming traffic?" I snorted. Gracie squared her shoulders and held up her hand. "My mark…he…he's dead."

I stared at the faded mark on her hand—it had at one point been three distinct musical notes with little sparkles around them. Marks were usually full of life, of color. Now this one was faded and gray. Barely visible in the waning sunlight. I swallowed.

"Oh…I'm…" *Sorry?* Did saying that actually help anything? I shook my head. "That must be hard for you."

Great. Not much better.

Gracie shrugged and fidgeted with the strap on her bag. "Well, it certainly isn't fun…"

I scratched the back of my neck. "Well, if it makes you feel any better…I was born without a soul mark, so…"

I held up my blank right hand. She stared at it, her eyes wide, the big brown irises swirling.

"Oh…I'm…that must be hard," she echoed.

I laughed. "Certainly isn't fun…"

The corners of her mouth turned up and I noticed her dimple—uneven and only on her left cheek. My heart skipped a beat and I coughed and looked away.

"So…uh, I'll see you around, then?" I asked. Gracie nodded. The crosswalk light turned on.

"Yeah," Gracie said. "See ya."

I find I didn't so much mind my busted knee because every time I thought of it, the thought of Gracie's smile quickly followed.

The next time I saw her sitting out in the cold, just outside campus, I joined her. I learned she loved God, like I did. That she'd never actually met her soul mate—just woke up one day with her mark faded and gray and never to be. She learned that I tried to teach myself guitar multiple times, only to give up every time I tried to learn a bar chord. Eventually, winter turned to spring, and spring turned to summer, and the semester was over.

I stood at the crosswalk, eyes closed and head hanging forward. I needed to decide if I was going to take summer classes and graduate on time or if I could take another semester and graduate just a little bit late. Footsteps approached from behind me and I heard Gracie's familiar lilting greeting.

"Hey, you."

"Hey." I grinned. "Ready for summer break?"

"Oh definitely." She nodded. Then she leaned over and lightly bumped me with her elbow. "You?"

I scratched the back of my neck. "Eh, I'm not sure. I haven't really decided if I'll take summer classes or not."

Immediately, she frowned. "Aww, but I thought we could hang out this summer."

And just like that I decided to graduate a semester late.

We chatted for a while until the crosswalk turned, and then, right as she was about to walk away, I grabbed the strap to her bag. She stopped, turned, glanced up…

"Uh—hey, we should exchange phone numbers." I felt my cheeks heat. "You know—so we can hang out."

She beamed. I looked at the dimple on her left cheek and then passed her my phone.

That night, I walked through the door, and the suffocating smell of cigarette smoke hit my senses. I coughed and waved a hand in front of my face. I could already hear the TV blaring from the living room.

"Hey, Dad," I called once I was in the door. He barely acknowledged me. Just gave a grunt, his eyes still glued to the TV. I kicked off my shoes and nodded. I was making my way across the living room, holding my breath, when my phone began to ring. I fished it out of my pocket and ducked into the kitchen.

"Miss me already?" I teased and pressed the phone to my ear. I held it between my shoulder and chin as I rummaged through the cabinets and grabbed the cereal. I heard Gracie laugh from the other end and I smiled.

"Hardly. Hey, so some friends and I were thinking of taking a weekend trip to the beach. Probably late June, early July. You in?"

My stomach flopped. "Uh—*yeah*. Yeah, that sounds fun. Just let me know when, and I'll take off work."

"Great! Okay, I'll text you the details."

We chatted briefly, then said our goodbyes and hung up as I finished making my cereal. I walked into the living room and paused. My dad scratched his belly. The TV blared a game from twenty years ago, the image discolored with static.

"That was Gracie," I found myself saying. "On the phone with me…I…I asked for her phone number today…"

My dad grunted. I swallowed and stepped forward.

"I think she likes me, Dad. Like, *really* likes me. And…I think I like her."

He grunted again. I narrowed my eyes.

"She invited me on a summer trip so, I'll probably leave for a weekend or two. I-I won't be around for a while."

Finally, *finally*, my dad slowly looked away from the screen. He stared at me, dark circles under his eyes, his mouth partially open. I stared at him. He took a swig of beer and let out a sigh.

"Did I *ask*?" He grunted and turned back to the TV.

"No." I whispered, my teeth bared. "You never do."

I stalked to my room and slammed the door shut. I didn't need his approval—I didn't need his love. Gracie would love me—and if she didn't, then I was going to love her better than anyone else ever could.

It went about as well as you could expect. I started doing everything I could think of for her. I opened the doors, let her decide where to eat when we hung out with her friends, and kept my phone on in case she texted or needed something. By our summer trip, I was exhausted. Worse, she could tell.

"Ryan, talk to me." She reached forward and squeezed my arm. I looked down at her hand—at the faded and worn soul mark. You could hardly see it now. She was nearly markless, like me. I turned my head away and stared at the ocean. The waves lulled and then crashed onto the beach. They scattered seashells everywhere, tiny granules of sand swirling in the swelling waves. Gracie scooted toward me. She wore a green summer dress. Her tan shoulders were exposed, light freckles dusting her back and forearms. I sighed.

"What are we, Gracie?" I asked. Another wave crashed. The sun was starting to set on the horizon. Gracie squirmed.

"Friends?" Her voice was tentative and quiet. I brought my knees to my chest and dug my bare toes into the warm sand. Gracie tugged at a strand of hair. "Maybe...maybe a little bit more."

"Why?" I asked. "What's the point? I'll never be better than..."

I looked down at her hand and she sucked in a breath. She moved her hand down to her side and turned away. Between us was a broken seashell. Half of it was missing. I scanned the beach around us. Who could find a missing half of a seashell on a beach with hundreds—thousands—of others just like it? What if the missing half wasn't even there?

"It's pointless," I whispered. "I...I'm markless. Unlovable."

She looked up again at this, her brown eyes glistening.

I shrugged. "And I can't love you like you *should* be loved...so what's the point?"

Gracie shook her head. "Love is a choice that you get to make, Ryan. It's not something that just happens. You have to choose it…I'm willing to choose it. Are you?"

Gracie leaned forward and placed her hand on my shoulder again. Her face was inches from mine.

"I…I'm not perfect." I whispered. Gracie's hand moved up to my hair. She ran her fingers through the brown strands.

"I never asked you to be," she whispered back. I swallowed the lump in my throat.

"We aren't soulmates…we'll fight, we won't love each other perfectly because we—" My voice hitched, and I swallowed. I tried again. "Because we weren't made for each other."

"We don't have to be." She shook her head. "We'll take it one day at a time. We can choose this—it's our choice."

And then her lips brushed mine and I scooped her into an embrace.

I was right, and so was she. We fought—we made up. We made mistakes, and we hurt each other, but then we came together again and chose to persevere.

Five years later, two and a half years after our wedding, I woke up to the sun streaming through the window. Gracie was curled up next to me, her hand on my chest. I blinked the sleep from my eyes, placed my hand over hers—and froze.

There, on my right hand…I sat up and rubbed my other hand over it. I leaped from the bed and dashed to the bathroom.

"Ryan?" Gracie slurred as she awoke, her hair tangled in her face. She yawned.

I flicked the bathroom lights on and stuck my hand under the water and scrubbed—I had to be sure it was real, had to make sure it wasn't dirt or my imagination.

It wasn't.

I stared at my hand and padded back to our bedroom. Gracie sat on her knees, her eyes wide, head cocked to the side.

"Gracie," I whispered—then cut myself off as I felt the lump in my throat. I held up my right hand.

There, clear as day, was the image of a dove. Gracie gasped. She looked down at her own hand. A laugh that bubbled up like a sob burst from her throat.

She had the same mark.

I sat, mouth open, as Ryan stared down at the back of his hand. Together, we looked at his soul mark in the dim campfire lighting. Then he looked at me.

"Love isn't something that just happens to ya, kid. Sometimes, love looks like patience and kindness. It endures forever, no matter what." He nodded to Chelsea and Derek, who had progressed from snuggles to quick little pecks on the cheek. Ryan shook his head. "They have a head start, sure. But that doesn't mean they won't have to work on their relationship. That they won't have to wake up every single day and *choose* to love each other."

Ryan nodded and then stared up at the sky. I followed his gaze, staring at the big empty cosmos. Everything I'd thought I'd known about the world had shifted. Part of me didn't want to believe his story—I'd spent so long feeling unlovable. What would life look like if that was no longer true? Then, just barely above the sounds of crickets and the crackling of the fire, I heard his faint whisper.

"Because love isn't just some feeling…love is a choice you get to make."

Oh Deer

ADARA KING

Hi, I'm Jaiden, the goat girl. If you find that statement confusing, allow me to clarify. No, I am not an actual goat; no, I do not own goats; and no, I am not obsessed with goats enough to earn a nickname for it. I am, however, a faun. Don't be too hard on yourself if you're drawing a blank: you're not alone. In fact, I myself had no idea what a faun was until my first year of high school.

My fourteenth birthday party was the first time I ever felt true embarrassment; or, more accurately, social-status-butchering humiliation. I won't get into the specifics of what happened, but "embarrassment" is the keyword here. As I learned quite painfully that day, whenever I felt ashamed from then on, I began to transform into a fuzzy, hoof-clomping, downright horrifying mythological half-goat. We're talking little baby horns, a tail, and fluffy goat legs with knees that bend the wrong direction: a human circus animal.

Like many teenagers, I now had something to hide. To that end, Mother insisted I make some changes. Leg-hiding maxi skirts, tail-hiding blousy T-shirts, and a thick horn-nub-hiding headband filled my wardrobe. Dressing for winter in the little beach town of Pass Christian, Mississippi, isn't necessarily conducive to fitting in;

but if I wanted to hide my—um—"problem," I had little choice. All I had to do was keep my head down and behave, and I'd be fine. Simple enough, right?

∼∼∼

"Jaiden Rivers, please make your way to the principal's office. Jaiden Rivers to the principal's office, thank you."

The intercom's gravelly buzz still burned in my ears as I stumbled down the hall toward Principal Clancey's office. My sneakers—laced extra tight in case of emergencies such as this—thudded inhumanly, barely muffling the clomp of hooves. *What on earth did I do to deserve the intercom?* I thought, my stomach roiling with humiliation and anger. *Everyone was giving me the "look who finally screwed up" stink eye back there.* I rounded the corner and nearly face-planted into the office door, catching myself just before my button nose smashed into a pig snout. Deep breath in, deep breath out. Deep breath in and out. In and out.

I waited until I could no longer feel the twitch of my confined tail before I grasped the handle and flung the door wide.

"Ah, thank you for joining us, Miss Rivers," Principal Clancey said, a professional smile curling her lips. She waved a wrinkled hand to the figure standing beside her. "This is Fredrick. He's new in town and will be joining your class next year. His mother requested he be given a tour of our facilities, and I found it prudent to recommend his class's president to act as guide." A quick glance at this Fredrick character told me everything I needed to know. He leaned against a bookshelf, hands tucked in the pockets of baggy black jeans. His long-sleeved flannel shirt was unbuttoned, revealing the faded band T-shirt underneath. Fredrick caught my eye with a smirk, nodded a greeting, and readjusted a plain black beanie that was fashionably styled and pulled over his ears.

Irked, I called up a professional smile of my own, "Of course, ma'am. Right this way, Frederick." Turning on my heel, I glided from the office, my new ward in tow. Situating himself directly next to me, he flashed a lopsided grin as he extended his hand, "Thanks for doing this, miss…"

I raised an eyebrow at him and slowed to a stop. "You're welcome?"

Frederick chuckled, emerald eyes glinting. "I was hoping for a name, to be honest."

"And I was hoping to finish class, so I guess we're both disappointed," I grumbled.

"What was that?" Frederick quirked an eyebrow.

Sighing, I pivoted and continued down the hall. "Jaiden Rivers. I am the junior class president; and, as such, it is my duty to ensure that you become thoroughly acquainted with the campus. If you would follow me this way, Frederick, we—"

"I'm gonna stop you right there."

The hairs on my neck bristled. "Pardon?"

He snorted, "Man, you even clarify stuff poshly."

My stomach prickled with burrs of irritation. "Your point is?"

Frederick grinned. Schooling my expression, I straightened my spine and flashed a mildly raised eyebrow at him. His lips twitched as he shook his head. "Yeah, no. I don't have a 'point' per se, just… lighten up, dude."

"What?"

"You're not in front of Principal Whoever–"

"Clancey."

"Yeah, her," he said lightly. "So you can cut the prim and proper act now. We're cool."

It took more willpower than I care to admit to keep my tone even.

"What the heck are you talking about?"

"Ooh, that's better already!"

"What—"

Frederick slid past me and strolled down the hall, his hands tucked in his pockets. "And you can relax on all that 'Fredrick' stuff. Fred's fine. Or Freddie, if you feel like."

Freddie? Seriously? He was halfway down the hall before I caught up to him. "Feel like what, exactly?" I sniped.

Frederick-Fred-Freddie grinned at me playfully. My stomach squirmed as I glared back.

"Feel like being more than my guide."

I eyed him warily. "Excuse me?"

He laughed and rapped me lightly on the head with his knuckles. Ducking, my hands flew instinctively to my headband as he continued unfazed. "I don't know what's going through that posh little mind of yours, but you're gonna get wrinkles if you keep scrunching your nose in disgust."

"Then hurry up and clarify so I can stop judging you for things you haven't said yet."

"Yes, ma'am." He sped up, placing himself directly in my path. Extending his hand, he bowed elaborately. "Miss Jaiden Rivers, may I have the honor of requesting your friendship?"

"Wha—?" I stepped back and gasped. My heel snagged on my skirt hem. The world went horizontal. I was falling. A single thought twirled in my brain. *So this is how I die. Great.*

In a flash, he was there, jolting my descent to a halt as he caught my arms. He grinned, small tendrils of jet-black hair dancing across his eyes. "I see you're falling for my lines already."

"If we're being technical," I huffed breathlessly, righting myself and taking a quick step away from him, "I tripped. 'Tripping for my lines' isn't a thing; therefore, you sound ridiculous."

Frederick-Fred-Whatever raised his hands in mock surrender. "Interesting conclusion. That may be the most creative 'thanks for that oh-so-daring rescue' I've ever heard."

Wow. This guy…. Huffing, I busied myself brushing imaginary dirt off my skirt, doing anything I could to avoid making eye contact. "Alright. Nice…reflexes, I suppose."

A hearty laugh tickled my ears, finally forcing me to glance in his direction. "Worse, but I'll take it."

Something about his grin was starting to tick me off. *Decorum, professionalism*, I reminded myself. "Shall we?" I asked lightly, slipping down the hallway before he could reply. The eventual thud of footsteps behind me filled me with relief as I quickly readjusted my headband. Two little horn nubs met my touch beneath the fabric. This was going to be a long day.

After several agonizing minutes of avoiding any attempts on his part to start a conversation, I paused by a door marked "library" and pulled up my professional smile. "The library is open from 7:30 a.m. to 3:30 p.m. I can recommend some study groups that meet here if you're interested?"

Frederick snorted. Crossing his arms, he replied, "I don't see myself as the 'study group type,' but thanks though."

Indignation fluttered in my gut. I had a feeling he was dissing more than just the "group" part of study groups. "Well, Frederick—"

"Uh, uh, uh," he wagged a finger in my face, mouthing the word "Freddie" with his smuggest smirk yet.

"Fine," I growled. "Fred." He fake pouted as I continued, "Study groups aren't for everyone. I myself prefer solitude when I work."

"Hmm," Fred hummed, still smirking.

What's this guy's deal?

"You care a lot about academics, huh?"

Startled, I glanced at him. He wasn't smirking anymore, just eyeing me with an air of insightful interest. "Of course I do," I answered, careful not to let my expression slip as my mouth formed the familiar words. "An impeccable academic record is essential to attending a quality university and eventually starting a respectable career."

"Hmm," Fred nodded. "I guess, but there're plenty of respectable careers that don't need a diploma."

I froze, nearly tripping on my skirt again. "Pardon?" I spluttered. What was this punk on about?

Fred paused a few steps ahead of me, his eyebrows raised. "Uh, yeah. Like artists, authors, craftsmen, trade school programs. It's not like college is pointless or anything, I'm just saying there's more out there."

I could feel my jaw literally drop at his words. How could he stand there nonchalantly dismissing the importance of higher education? "Are you serious? College is the next step. It just is. There's no other way to be taken seriously. Besides, half of those 'careers' you listed don't count."

Fred paused and glanced at me, eyebrows furrowed. "What do you mean 'they don't count'?"

My skin tingled as I shrugged. Something in his tone felt…off. "Fred, come on. Hobbies aren't careers. Be serious."

Fred's back stiffened. "That…is a very close-minded statement."

"Close-minded?" I asked. "Apologies, but I'm fairly certain I'm practicing basic practicality. The term 'starving artist' is a stereotype for a reason."

Fred scoffed and whipped around to face me. "You wanna talk about hurtful stereotypes?"

"Hurtful?"

"Yeah, and a bit offensive, actually. You're degrading thousands of people who've poured every bit of themselves into their art. They've achieved greater things with their 'starving artistry' than you ever will with this high-and-mighty teacher's pet act you've got going for you."

Indignation stole my tongue before I could stop it. "Are you serious? You want to talk about hurtful stereotyping? Fine! You have 'school dropout' written all over you. You were probably transferred here after your last school got sick of your frivolous class clown act and dropped your sorry butt down here with people who actually give a darn about succeeding in life."

Silence.

Harsh tension stole between us, taut like a rope about to snap. *High-and-mighty? Seriously?* Amid the boiling indignation simmering beneath my skin, a dark, heavy feeling crept up my spine. The moment the feeling touched my heart, I understood. *Oh no.*

One look at his face stalled the words brimming in my throat. His eyes were dark with...something, and it tied my gut in knots.

"Sorry," he murmured. His hand flitted to his beanie, tugging it further over his head as he backed away. "Thank you...for the tour." With that, I was left alone with the biting memory of my words and the faint whispers of a feeling I can only call regret.

I was trudging up the stairs to my home's covered porch by the time the clump of shame-induced hooves dulled to the normal tap of sneakers. I paused with my hand on the ancient Swiss cheese-like screen door. "What am I doing?" I whispered. Sighing, I dropped my backpack and sank against the chipped oak railing.

Groaning, I pulled my knees to my chest and tucked my head against them, making myself as small as possible. "You're such a fool."

My eyes burned, but tears didn't come: I wouldn't let them. Deep breath in, deep breath out. In and out. Each calming breath carried pressure with it until my eyes stung no more. I sat for a second longer, making sure my face lacked the telltale redness of sorrow before I snatched up my bag and went inside.

"Mother, I'm home." My voice echoed down the hallway, dampened by the lintless runner that ran the length of the floor. Photographs of Mother and I hung expertly spaced on either wall. As always, I ignored the identical practiced smiles grinning from each manicured moment as I made my way to the kitchen. Mother was there in a pressed coral suit, gathering various color-coded Tupperware containers.

She barely glanced at me as she worked. "Ah, good, Jaiden. You're late."

I flinched, familiar whispers of shame pricking the back of my mind. "Yes, ma'am, I know. The principal asked me to show a new kid around the school today. The tour ran long, and I missed the bus."

Mother froze and snapped her scrutinizing gaze to me. I stood straighter and willed the two little spots on my head to stop tingling. "You walked back?" she asked, her words creeping like lionesses set to pounce. "On the open roads?" Knowing her questions were not meant to be answered, I stayed silent. Her nose twitched as she took a step toward me. "That was stupid and dangerous. You're supposed to be smarter than this." My heart sank like an anvil, settling with a thud at my feet as I lowered my gaze. Unconsciously, my hand began to float toward my headband. She tensed.

With one fluid motion, she snatched my wrist and yanked off my headband, tearing a few hairs with it. I cried out, but Mother merely grabbed my shoulder and forced me to meet her eyes. "How long have your horns been out?"

"I—"

"How long?" She gave my shoulder a sharp shake.

"Since—since the—"

"Don't stutter."

I bit my lip and took a quick breath to unscramble my words. "Since Principal Clancey summoned me to her office. She used the loudspeaker in the middle of class."

"Ah," Mother released my shoulder. "I see. How many hours has it been?"

Shaking, I clenched the fabric of my shirt. "I'm not sure. I managed to get my emotions under control a few times, but the transformation kept getting triggered. No one noticed though, I swear."

Mother sighed, her biting gaze losing some of its edge. "You're usually more careful than this, but if you say no one saw, I believe you. Today was your last day of school, correct?"

I forced my lips into a weary smile. "Yes, ma'am. Some rest—"

"Good. Since you have nothing going on," she interrupted, gathering the containers she'd abandoned on the counter, "I need you to do me a favor." Thrusting the largest container at me, she began making her way to the door. "An old friend of mine moved here recently, but I haven't had the chance to visit her. Unfortunately, the company dinner is tonight, so I'll be at the office till late. Please take those cookies to her and say 'hi' for me. I wrote her information down." She nodded at the container in my hands. "Grab the door, will you, Jaiden? Oh," she paused at the top of the steps and locked eyes with me. Her gaze was stern as she spoke, "Be especially hospitable to her child…Ed? Yes, Edaline, I believe. She's around your age. Be her friend."

Dumbfounded, I followed Mother outside and helped her load the Tupperware into her white Toyota Camry. "Why friends? Can't I just go for 'polite acquaintances' like usual?"

She shot me a harsh look. "No, her mother is dear to me, and I would like our families to get along. Besides, I said so." She slid into the driver's seat but hesitated before shutting the door. "Remember, it's important to always put your best foot forward; and your best foot, Jaiden, is not a hoof." With that, she slammed the door and drove off, leaving me standing in the driveway, a gentle breeze nudging my skirt against my goat legs.

"Perfect," I grumbled. My social battery was drained to nearly the full extent, but as exhausted as I was, dealing with strangers for an hour or so would be easier than dealing with Mother if I disobeyed. Sighing, I dragged myself down the road. The coral Post-it note stuck to the container read simply: "Thalia Meadows, Cedar Ave. Look for the house with the navy-blue door."

"Thalia, huh? Please be nice." Ten minutes of walking and one traversed train track later, I found myself poised to knock at the navy door of a quaint one-story house. I rapped smartly and stood examining the exterior of the building as I waited. Pale yellow planks covered the walls like fish scales, punctuated by white shutter-framed windows. Snuggled against the house, a small flower bed overflowed with gently nodding black-eyed Susans. A single garden gnome stood sentinel among the stems, a chipped red and white clay mushroom his only companion. Over everything, a soft chorus of wind chimes chirped a melody that would have been obnoxious in any other setting. The house felt warm in a manner I was unaccustomed to, like a caring embrace.

CREAK.

Startled, I spun to see a thin middle-aged woman with a long, onyx braid thrown over her shoulder. She was wiping her hands on a ratty blue apron when she made eye contact with me. Her eyes went wide. "Cassia?"

A thin laugh escaped my lips. "Um, no ma'am. My name is Jaiden Rivers. I'm her daughter."

"Ah, I see," she tittered, shaking her head in amazement. "You're the spittin' image of her. You comin' in?"

I stepped inside the narrow entryway and recoiled, assaulted by the pungent odor of yeast. She took one look at my face and burst out laughing. "Sorry, dear. I'm on my fifth attempt at bread, and the house is starting to soak in the fumes. Give it five minutes or so, you'll get used to it."

She led me deeper into the cloud of bready fragrance to the source of the aroma. Blue subway tiles covered in snowdrifts of flour paved the floor of the kitchen. The lady danced around the mess and plopped on a yellow barstool next to the marble-topped island, patting the stool next to her. As I sat down, she started chatting. "I'm Thalia, but you can call me Lia. Your mother and I were young women together, and I have to say, she is one of the dearest folks I know. You really do resemble her; it's remarkable. Has anyone told you that?"

"Well, I—"

"Oh, I bet they have. You have the same eyes, same nose, same reddish hair. Why, if your locks weren't cut so short, I'd truly believe Cassia from way back when was sittin' right there. In fact, I think I did believe it for a second." Lia chuckled as I died a little inside. Where do people find this kind of energy? "So tell me, dear, what brings you by?"

I smiled politely and passed her the container. "Mother made you cookies: family recipe. She was unable to bring them herself, so she sent me."

Lia's smile doubled in size as she opened the container. "That Cassie, she remembered." Lia slipped a cookie from the container and took a bite, closing her eyes as if savoring the moment. "She used to make these for me whenever a boy broke my heart. Never had better. Here, take one."

I stiffened, staring at the offering. "Um, I'd love to, but Mother would prefer I didn't. Besides, I wouldn't wish to deprive the rest of your family of a treat."

Her eyes brightened. "Yes, my family! I have a kid around your age."

Here we go. "Yes, Mother mentioned her."

Lia's eyebrows furrowed slightly. "Uh, yes. One moment." She hopped up from her stool and scurried to the hallway. "Eddie!" she bellowed. I flinched in surprise, ears tingling. Was that necessary? It was a really small house. "Come to the kitchen. There's someone I'd like you to meet."

A door near the middle of the hall creaked open and a form emerged. "Ma, please, you don't need to shout. You'll give the neighbors a head...ache..."

A wicked swirl of emotions swarmed up my chest, choking the breath from my lungs. Leaping to my feet, I stared open-mouthed at the boy frozen in front of me, his bewildered expression a mirror of my own. We stood pointing at each other in horrified silence until his mother broke the stalemate. "Fredrick, you've met Jaiden before?"

Her words seemed to jog him out of his paralysis. He flashed a tight grin in her direction, never once breaking eye contact with me. "Yeah, we've met."

I flashed her a tight-lipped smile as well, eyes trained on his. "Indeed." If we'd been a few feet closer, someone would've thrown a fist.

"Fantastic!" Lia's chipper voice shattered the tension. Fred and I started as if lifted from a daze. She was grinning ear to ear as she looked between us. "I was so worried Eddie wouldn't make friends here, seeing as this is his first time in 'real' school, and he's a little... well..." She laughed and pinched his cheek. He looked away. "I'm just so glad he's got you."

"Wait, Ma—"

Quick as a flash, Lia snatched up our hands, led us to what appeared to be Fred's room, and flung us inside. "Have fun, y'all!"

"Ma!"

SLAM.

Crap. I stared at Fred's back as he in turn stared at the door, so still one could easily mistake him for a statue. We were trapped. I glanced around the room, scrambling for something to say. Every available inch of space was dominated by an ancient desk, twin bed, and bookshelf overflowing with spiral-bound books.

"Uh, nice room?" I ventured.

Fred spun to face me, flames practically pouring from his narrowed eyes. Instinctively, I stepped back with my hands raised. "What the heck are you doing here?" he hissed. "You shouldn't be here."

Rude. I glared back at him, hissing in reply, "I didn't get a choice in the matter, *Frederick*. Our moms are apparently friends, and mine sent me bearing cookies."

Sighing, he ran a hand through his hair and froze. "Where's my beanie?" Brushing past me, he began rifling through a pile of clothes in a corner I hadn't noticed.

Wrinkling my nose, I snipped, "I don't want *me* to be *here* either, just so you know. You were supposed to be a girl."

Fred barked out a harsh laugh and faced me. "Is that some kind of insult?"

I scoffed. "I wish it were, but no. Mother told me your name was Edaline, and your mom called you Eddie. What was I supposed to think? Believe me, if I had even heard the letter 'F,' I'd be halfway across the tracks by now."

Fred pulled the elusive beanie over his ears and plopped on the bed. "Alright, fine. You're already here, and since you're not running for the door, I assume my mother isn't the only one pressuring you to stay?"

I found a clean spot on the gray carpet and sank down. "You assume correctly."

"Right, so sit there for an hour, make both our moms happy, then leave. Got it?"

"Fine," I pulled my knees to my chest and looked away, combing the wall for something other than Fred to stare at. Tucked behind the desk, a small window offered a view of an oak tree. Its twisted limbs drooped with gentle weariness, lengths of Spanish moss dripping from them like lacy boas. There was beauty there, braided into every inch of bark and leaf. Scars too. *What hurt you?* I thought as my eyes floated along a particularly deep gash near the roots. Who's to say? What person can know the story of a tree when they're only present to glimpse a moment in its life?

With that thought, my lips began to mouth the words my selfish heart needed to say. "I'm sorry, Fred."

The faint rustle of fabric and creak of ancient mattress springs told me I had his attention, but I didn't look away from the view. He cleared his throat. "You're what?"

My tone remained level, earnestness slipping into my cadence. "I'm sorry for insulting you."

A soft quiet seeped into the space between us, heavy but no longer strangling. "How...do you think you insulted me?"

I glanced over and watched him struggle to maintain a passive expression. Was he seriously testing me right now? The audacity. I grinned. "Well, I'm not sure about you, but I can think of a few different ways. Shall I list them off?"

Fred crossed his arms across his chest and leaned against the wall. "If you must."

I raised my fingers and began ticking them off. "I implied that you were flippant with your future. I implied you deserved expulsion from your last school, which I wager hit a nerve. You were homeschooled, weren't you?" Fred clenched his jaw. "But the worst insult, I believe, was what I said about ...hobbies."

Standing, I approached the bookshelf and ran a hand over the spiral-bound books. The bedsprings squeaked. Fred was tense. "What are you—"

I pulled one down and gazed at the cover. *I knew it.* A fresh wave of guilt stung my throat as Fred leaped to his feet, clearing the room in a single stride. He backed me into the bookcase, towering over me like a dark pillar of fury. "Don't touch that," he growled, yanking the book—the *sketchbook*—from my hand.

Ice swirled in my veins, but I didn't budge, staring into his flashing green eyes. We stood there eyeing each other, barely a breath apart: then I saw it. A look: shame, mixed with a breath of fear. He sighed, adjusted his beanie, and looked away. "Sorry, just...please don't touch the sketchbooks. They're...my mother doesn't, um...just, don't, okay?"

He moved to step back. Without a second thought, I grabbed his shoulder, halting his retreat. His eyes whipped to me in surprise, but he didn't pull away. "Fred," I began, my voice soft. "I'm sorry I insulted your passion. I was thoughtless and..." I paused, studying his expression. "You didn't deserve that." His shoulder tensed beneath my hand. At that moment, he seemed fragile. "Can you forgive me?"

Fred sighed, staring at the sketchbook in his hands. "I...I owe you an apology too. I made some nasty assumptions and lashed out and...I shouldn't have." He turned to me with a sad smile, scooped my hand off his shoulder, and gave it a squeeze. "I'm sorry too."

We stood like that for a moment, smiling at each other, a new warmth tentatively blooming between us where our skin touched. I opened my mouth to speak when—"Hey, kids. I was wonder—oh! Am I interrupting something?" Fred and I flew apart as Lia's voice pierced the air. She grinned slyly and trotted into the room to give her son a playful elbow to the ribs. I could hear the thud from where I stood. Wheezing and clutching his side, he turned away. *Is it my imagination, or is his neck a bit red?* "And you, young lady." I came to attention, snapping my gaze away from him. My skull tingled.

Fumbling, I tried to subtly adjust my headband and skirt. "Yes, ma'am?"

Lia smirked and smacked me playfully on the shoulder. It stung. "You work fast, little Cassia. We've gotta keep an eye on you." Fred choked as I gawked at her. *What. The. HECK?!*

"Ma'am, no, I—"

"Ah, ah, ah," Lia tutted, wagging her finger in my face. "Come with me, dearie. You too, Eddie." She linked her arm through mine and dragged me, blustering, to the front door.

It appeared that no amount of "you've got the wrong idea" or "we weren't doing anything" or "I swear, I barely see him as a man" was going to be enough to stop whatever it was Lia had planned. At the very least, she didn't seem mad...maybe? Regardless of what she thought we were up to, it didn't stop her from gleefully tossing Fred and me out the front door. The two of us stumbled across the threshold, barely managing to catch ourselves on the porch railing. The splintery wood bit into my hands as I clutched it, praying neither of them heard the thump of hooves.

My storm of confusion was cut short by a soft pressure on my shoulder. "You okay, Jaiden?" I locked eyes with Fred, whose visage brimmed with a comical mix of concern and bewilderment.

I gave him my own mixed-emotion expression and nodded, "Yeah, you?"

He huffed. "Let's find out, shall we?" His hand slipped away as he spun to face the door. "What the heck, Ma—oof!" He doubled over, the impact turning him into a human taco. A pair of chucked sneakers bounced off his stomach and clattered onto the planks.

Lia, arm outstretched post-chuck, flashed a smile I assumed was meant to be an apology. She looked a little too satisfied for it to carry any real conviction though. "Sorry. You were supposed to catch those."

Fred's voice echoed faintly from his cowed position. "Then yell 'catch' next time so I know a projectile's coming for my spleen, Ma."

She laughed. "Noted. Now, straighten up and go away."

"Did we do something wrong?" I stuttered. "Because seriously, we didn't—"

"Easy, tiger." Lia waved her hand at me as if I were an unruly critter that needed to chill out. "Y'all aren't in trouble. If you were, I'd beat both your butts then send you packing. This isn't a punishment: this is what I call friend-shipping." She flashed exuberant jazz hands at us and scurried inside, slamming the door behind her. Her voice tripped in a sing-song cadence through the wood. "Go explore. See the world. Become besties! And be back before ten, Eddie. Have fun!"

We gawked at the door for a solid minute, unsure what the correct response was. Clearing my throat, I took a stab at it. "Okay, Fred. I'm going to say this, and I'm only going to say this once: what the flippy flap just happened?"

Fred exploded, a hearty cackle sending him doubling over again. "You did not just say that with a straight face."

Almost against my will, my lips twitched, an irresistible force pulling the corners upward. "I refuse to use the alternative, so yes. I think it's a perfectly reasonable question, don't you?"

Still chuckling, Fred scooped up his sneakers and shook his head at the door. "Honestly, I can't answer that. She's a bit of a loose cannon, but this is out there, even for her."

As he tugged his shoes on, I eyed his disheveled black locks, casual dress, and sharp eyes. Maybe it was the late afternoon light playing tricks on me, but he didn't really look like a punk anymore. He was just a boy with a crazy mom and a love for art. *I wonder what else he loves.*

"So," I ventured, hooking my thumb at the road, "seeing that both of us are stuck out here, would you maybe want to go for a walk?"

Fred scrunched his face in mock deep thought. "You know...I think I'd like that."

I smothered a grin. "Good, then let's go."

Within five minutes, we were walking along the main road that ran parallel to the beach, surrounded by silence broken only by the soothing hiss of waves against sand. All the while, I sensed the steady presence of his company beside me, and I felt…it felt…it felt nice. It felt like having a friend.

Confidence bolstered my tongue as I broke the silence. "So, art? Is that your only dream or are there other things you hope to do one day?"

Fred smiled. "Starting off with the deep stuff, huh? Someone's getting comfortable."

"Wha—I—hey—"

He chuckled and bumped me with his shoulder. My steps wobbled, but I was relieved to hear a marked lack of clomping as I rightened myself. I tossed him a playful glare and bumped him back, sending him into his own wobbly recovery. The fading glow of afternoon light glinted in his eyes as he laughed. "Chill, Jay." He hesitated, eyes uncertain. "Do you mind if I call you that?"

I bit my lip to hide my budding smile. He looked so unsure. It was kind of endearing. "I'll allow it. I'm not as high and mighty as you think." He winced at the reminder. I changed the subject. "And anyway, you haven't answered my question."

He brightened. "Right. Yeah, I want to be an artist in the future, hopefully something in graphic design or teaching."

"Teaching?" I interjected.

"I like kids," he shrugged. "But yeah, that's my main dream. I don't really have another, but…"

"But?" I tilted my head and raised my eyebrows, encouraging him to continue.

His eyes met mine. "It's more of a wish than a dream." He took a breath and laughed, the hesitation melting from his face. "Ah, screw it. I really love to dance. I want to join the team at school and maybe go professional someday. You know, competitions and the like."

I felt my eyebrows crawl up my forehead. "Competitions? You're that good?"

He held out his arms and flashed a grin, "I could tango with you right now and prove it."

Swatting his arms away, I giggled, "If you want your toes broken, be my guest. I'm about as graceful as a baby g-goat." I coughed and walked ahead, forcing him to jog to catch up. "Why not chase your dreams? Why not dance and paint and teach a bunch of kids in a cramped classroom?"

He chuckled ruefully. "Well, you kinda summed it up earlier: the arts aren't exactly the most stable career paths. Besides, Ma holds views similar to yours about the whole 'higher education' thing. She wants me in finance. And anyway, something came up a few years ago that made dancing a bit…complicated, so I guess the choice was kind of made for me."

"Ah," I bit my lip. A soft breeze stirred around me, pushing the fabric of my skirt against my legs. *Share,* a gentle voice whispered from the back of my mind. *Tell him.* Deep breath in, deep breath out. "Those aren't my views," I blurted, clapping a hand over my mouth in mild horror. Fred screeched to a halt, whirling to face me with his jaw practically skimming the pavement. Slightly deranged laughter spilled over the hand still clamped against my lips. The words were out there now: they were real. "Ha! I said it! All that uppity college-slash-career stuff, that's all my mom. I've never even heard of a trade school."

Fred laughed in disbelief. "Seriously?"

"Yes," I giggled. "I wanted to play soccer. Mother supported the cardio aspect of sports, so I was allowed to play all through elementary and middle school."

"You left out the most important bit."

I glanced at him. "Which is?"

"Were you any good?" he asked, cupping his hands as if he were aiming a camera at my face. "For all I know, I could be in the presence of athletic greatness right now. If this moment might end up in your future documentary, I'd like some proper warning so I can make sure to act all suave and charming."

I snickered. "I don't know about that, but I will have you know that we were quite excellent. A professional scout watched us play a few times and said we had real potential. We were ecstatic."

A small crease formed between Fred's eyebrows as he let his hands fall to his sides. "What happened?"

I shrugged and looked away. "A mix of things, really. Mother said my games were becoming too much of a distraction. And she was right: I didn't want to sit inside and study. I still don't, actually."

Fred moved as if to pat my arm sympathetically but paused, unsure. His hand hovered in space for a breath before he let it fall. Clearing his throat, he started down the road again and asked, "Do you miss it?"

I sucked in a quick breath, the skin on my arm tingling where his touch would have landed. I tried to sound carefree as I responded. "Yes, but, um, I wouldn't have made it anyway. I developed a condition in freshman year that kept me from playing; so, I guess it worked out?"

Fred chuckled. "I'm not sure I'd call that 'working out' per se."

"Maybe not, but that's how it played out. Might as well try to be positive about it, right?"

"I suppose so."

Infusing my voice with a lighthearted air, I quipped, "Glad we finally agree on something."

He snorted. "About time, huh?"

I bopped him on the shoulder, turning my head slightly to hide my smile. "Don't get cheeky."

He ducked his head as he laughed and adjusted his beanie, tendrils of hair falling into his eyes in the process. My pulse hiccuped. He tossed me a grin and retorted. "I think you're the first person to call me 'cheeky' and not mean it as an insult."

"You're welcome, I suppose?"

"*Pfft*," he turned away, an odd little smile on his face.

I blinked. *Was his neck that red a second ago?* "Hey—"

"Jay, check it out."

"What?" I looked where he pointed and smiled. To our right, a small playground jutted up from the wavy grasses of a field. Multi-colored slides and plastic swings sat quaintly waiting for the machinations of imagination to be exacted upon them. Fred turned to me, a wicked grin on his face.

"Um, Fred? What are you thinking?"

"Three little words, darlin'."

"What?"

He sank into a runner's lunge. "Ground is lava!" The words barely slipped from his tongue before he took off for the playset, a trail of shouted numbers in his wake.

"You have got to be kidding me," I muttered, but I couldn't frown. It was childish, of course, but…

"Seven, six, come on, Jay. You're burning up!" Fred shouted, posing atop the conquered slide. "What are you waiting for?"

Good question. "Nothing!" I shouted, taking off full speed for the nearest structure. My skirt whipped in the breeze as my thudding gait tossed puffs of dust behind me.

An hour later, the sky sported the tender orange of sunset. It was the final round: score tied, winner takes all. My legs hammered the earth as I strained to reach the swing set before time ran out. Wind found only at great speeds ruffled my hair, summer bugs ricocheted off my face, my muscles teetered on the edge of exhaustion, and I had never felt so free. With the last of my stamina, I launched myself into the air, barely landing on the swing's seat by the time Fred yelled, "Zero!"

My momentum yanked the swing forward, leaving me clutching the chains for dear life. The metal links dug into my palms, but I held on. Laughing like a maniac, I hollered over my shoulder, "Did you see that, you disbeliever?" I froze.

Standing there, jaws dropped in what could only be horror, stood my classmates. They stared at me, the class president, clinging to a bucking children's swing, hair disheveled and matted to my sweaty forehead. My headband lay between us, lost at some point during my hour of frivolity.

The world went white, all sounds dominated by a growing hum of terror. Heart slamming my ribs, I fell from the swing, numb to the bite of dirt and stones as I collided with the ground. An echo vaguely reminiscent of my name rippled at the edge of my awareness, but I didn't want to hear it. Reality tilted as I stood and fled.

Nothing existed, just shame: only shame. I was such an idiot. A frivolous idiot! And Fred…I was exposed. A fraud. I wasn't perfect. I'd never be perfect. I was worthle— *Jay.*

No.

Jay!

Please no.

"Jay!" Fred grabbed my arm, snagging me midstride. I stumbled, straining to escape, but he was stronger. Without a word, he crushed me to his chest in an embrace, one arm around my waist and the other hand cradling my head. Every inch of him trembled against me, and his chest shuddered as he panted. *Did he run after me?* "Easy, Jay. Breathe. Just breathe. It's okay." I tried to shake my head and pull back, but he held on. "If you want me to let go because you need space, I will; but if you're just gonna run and hide somewhere and torture yourself over something I think I'm beginning to understand, then I'd be doing you a grave disservice if I let you go now."

"But you couldn't…" I whimpered. Tears slipped from my eyes: I was too drained to impede them any longer. The throb of adrenaline escaped all at once, and I sagged against him. The tender pressure of his arms never relented: he didn't shy away or tell me to stop crying. Instead, he guided my head to his shoulder and stroked my hair as I wept into his flannel shirt.

"It's okay, Jay. It's okay. Nobody's judging you. Just cry for now. I've got you."

Slowly, very slowly, my tears began to subside. Chest heaving, I breathed. Deep breath in, deep breath out. Deep breath in, and out. In and out. As rational thought gradually returned to me, I pulled back, breaking his embrace.

His smile was gentle and honest. "You're safe with me, Jay. You don't have to hide anymore."

I opened my mouth to ask what he meant but choked. He was gazing at the top of my head, a look of quiet understanding in his eyes. What was he—oh! My hand flew to my head, but no fabric met my touch, just keratin. He saw them. He knew. Frantically, I tried to back away from him, scrambling in vain to cover the monstrosities with my hands. "Don't look at me. It's nothing. Stop looking!"

Hurt flashed across his face as he obeyed, closing his eyes. "I told you, Jaiden," he murmured. Something in his voice made me pause. Slowly, he reached out, felt around for my hand, and took it. "You don't need to hide anymore. I understand. I see who you are, and, news flash, that person is really cool."

"You don't mean that." He couldn't.

His lips twisted in a wry smirk. "Can I please open my eyes?"

My heart fluttered like a hummingbird in my chest, cold fear licking at my soul. I couldn't move, couldn't speak, and couldn't bear the way his beautiful features would contort if I let him see my wretched, monstrous appendages. I was ugly. I was a monster. I... *You're safe with me, Jay.* His words stirred in the back of my mind. *You don't have to hide anymore.* I peered at his face. His eyes were still closed as he patiently waited for my response. Not even a drop of disgust or revulsion twisted his face. Soft as a prayer, I whispered, "Okay."

As his eyelids slipped open, he grabbed my other hand and held them both between us. His expression shone with a warmth that made my knees weak. "I think I know what's going on: why you're so proper and composed all the time, why you spoke about your mother's views as if they were your own, why you always tug on that headband of yours when you start to blush."

"Wait, I blush?"

"Yeah, big time. You look like a rose petal. It's cute." I stared at him wide-eyed as he laughed. "Yeah, just like that. Look, Jay, I've only known you for a few hours, and I know this sounds insane, but I see you. Underneath that headband and floor-length skirt, you're snarky, adventurous, and trapped by something more than just expectations. Something mystical."

"How...?"

His expression tensed with apprehension, like a man about to trust his life to a sheet of fabric as he jumps from a plane. He pulled a hand away to rub his neck: his very *red* neck. "Because," he continued, "you're a lot like me." Without another word, he pulled off the beanie. I gasped. Buried among fluffy locks, two black and white cat ears twitched on top of his head.

Mindlessly, I reached up and stroked one. The fur was soft as velvet beneath my fingertips. It was mesmerizing, absurd, impossible, and real. Dumbstruck, I glanced at his face and giggled. The red on his neck had traveled up to his cheeks. "You're like me," I whispered.

He chuckled shyly. "Well, not exactly. I've got a cat tail under my flannel, and I suspect you're hiding something to do with your legs under that skirt; but yeah, basically. I just…I know what it's like to live like this, with parents and secrets and…yeah. I really do understand, Jay. So please don't hide, because…I think I need someone who understands too."

Warmth melted my heart and I squeezed his hand. "Freddie, thank you."

"Freddie?" There was a new layer in his voice that stirred tingles in my chest.

"Yeah," I replied, shooting him an impish grin. "Is your friendship offer still open?"

His eyes twinkled. "It'd be my honor."

We stayed like that for a moment, together as the sun dipped soundlessly beneath the ocean. I opened my mouth to speak but paused, confused. "Freddie, are you still embarrassed right now?"

Fred—now Freddie—cocked his head inquisitively. "Not at all. Why?"

Without a word, I reached out and poked his very real, very *present* cat ears. He froze, eyes wide with fearful understanding. His gaze whipped to my head. "You're not embarrassed either, right?"

"Oh my gosh," I breathed. My hand zipped to my head, coarse nubs meeting my touch. "They aren't fading. Why aren't they fading?!"

Freddie's face looked as horrified as I felt. "There's probably a logical explanation for this," he said, beginning to pace. "Maybe if… or…" He sighed.

I was right there with him. As someone trained to be aware of her emotions at all times, I knew for a fact that no part of me was ashamed. In fact, right then, I was more comfortable in my own skin than I had been in my entire life. My entire life...

Thoughtfully, I tugged up my skirt and gazed at my hooves. They looked comical stuffed into a dusty pair of misshapen sneakers with the laces knotted too tight. I crouched down, fingering them. My touch traveled up the shoe and came to rest at what used to be my ankles.

Auburn fur soft as dandelion fluff tickled my finger, its earthy tufts clashing horribly with the worn rubber and fabric of the sneakers. The shoes's walls bulged unnaturally as they strained to contain and hide my abnormality. The shoes, the hooves: they didn't match. My fingers began to work the laces.

"What are you doing?" Freddie asked, pausing in his panic to watch me.

I stood to face him, shoes in hand. "What if this isn't a bad thing?" I ventured. "What if this is actually good?"

"Where are you going with this?"

"Freddie," I dropped my sneakers on the road and stepped closer, "tell me honestly. How do you feel right now?"

He closed his eyes, brow furrowed. "I don't know, worried? Scared?"

I shook my head. "Not emotions-wise, deeper than that. How do you *feel*?"

He grimaced and scrunched his eyes tighter. After a long moment, his features began to relax. "I feel..." his eyes flew open, "Oh my gosh."

Happy tears stung my eyes as I smiled up at him. "Yeah. This is who we are now. And you know what? Thanks to you, I think I'm okay with that."

"I...think I might be too." We burst out laughing; joyous, bewildered, and free.

I offered Freddie my pinkie. "Let's not be afraid anymore."

He linked his pinkie with mine. "Only if you're with me. I think I'll need an ally going forward. We've got some mothers to face."

I giggled. "Deal." Blushing slightly, I offered him my arm, and we walked home in silence, listening to the gentle whoosh of waves against sand and the glorious clomp of my hooves on the asphalt.

Goodbye to Yesterday

HANNAH STIFF

Emmi forced herself upright from her slide into the sand. Her face was coated like a salted pretzel, hot and stinging. She rubbed her reddening cheeks and sand rained down on her white capris.

"When I say go for it, you don't have to do a faceplant." Kade snickered as he ducked under the volleyball net to grab her arm. He pulled her to her feet and reached down to scoop up the wayward volleyball. "Well, that'll be fun to watch later, eh?"

Emmi winced and fingered her necklace. "You think I'd like to watch that?"

Her cousin shrugged, his mouth hitching up in a lopsided grin. "I think you'll find it funnier when you do."

Emmi didn't reply. Still running her thumb and forefinger along the thick gold band of her necklace, she turned and let her gaze travel across the beach and its occupants. She picked out sun tanners, surfers, children in the heat of some argument over sandcastle dimensions. The evening sun threw gleams of gold onto the sleepily approaching tide, and metallic necklaces threw gleams of light across the sand. Most of the people in sight wore one.

"Emmi." Kade stood beside her again, concern and contriteness edging his voice now. "I'm sorry, I was just joking—"

"It's all good, Kade," Emmi interrupted, dropping her hand and stuffing it into her capri pocket.

He sighed and looked up at the pastel-streaked sky. "Sometimes you can fool me pal, but those occasions have been few and far between." He took a breath and continued. "I'm not saying you haven't enjoyed yourself, Emmi, but you haven't, aren't…well, can't…"

"Bravo sir, you're going to rock your english studies this fall," Emmi quipped, allowing a glimmer of a smile to show. It quickly morphed into a grimace, like someone had pulled the strings of a puppet. She sank onto the ground, clasping her knees to her chest and digging bare toes into the warm sand. Kade plopped down beside her and leaned back on his hands.

"I want to, so desperately, Kade." Emmi whispered. "I can't remember the last time I just enjoyed a day without thinking about how it would end."

That wasn't exactly true. She could remember the last time, the last hour even. It was the evening before the start of grade school. She recalled the anticipation during the car ride, bouncing in her seat, asking her mom if her necklace would look just like hers, or could she get a different color?

"It will be gold, like mine," her mother replied with a calm smile.

"You'll be a big girl now, Emmi," her dad reminded her, flicking his eyes from the road to peer at her in the rearview mirror. "There'll be no room for childish mistakes."

"Oh, cut it out, Dale!" her mom interjected. "No need to give the wrong impression from the get-go." She glanced back to see if their six-year-old was listening, but Emmi was calling out that she could see the Flashback service center.

The necklace was choker style, and Emmi tensed at the chilly thrill of it being placed around her neck and snapped firmly in place behind. She traced her initials and a set of numbers and letters that were stamped on it as the Flashback employee droned on to her parents about "memory capacity," "bi-annual maintenance checks," and "minors' Flashback material." She didn't know one word in twenty he said, but she didn't care.

It was after school the next day that Emmi understood what it all meant. As she chattered like a red squirrel over new teachers, Kade's glow-in-the-dark erasers, and her goal in soccer during recess, she stopped herself short as she saw her mom turn down a wrong street.

"Oh, we're just stopping quickly at the Flashback center hon," her mom explained.

"Why? My necklace..."

"Has a surprise hidden in it!" her mom exclaimed, lifting her hands off the wheel to clap as if in celebration. "We need to pull it out." She refused to answer any more questions, even when the service employee popped a small memory card out of a hidden slot of her necklace and stuck it into a laptop on the desk.

"The file has been sent to your email address, ma'am," he said after a minute, and slid the card back into Emmi's necklace.

"See you tomorrow." Emmi's mom nodded and led the perplexed child out.

Once the dinner plates were thrown into the dishwasher, Emmi's dad announced they were watching a movie.

"About a little girl we all know," he added with a wink. Emmi stared as he wirelessly connected their TV to her mom's phone and selected a file.

EMMI-DAY01-MONTH01-YEAR01 appeared on the screen, and suddenly Emmi was looking at herself eating breakfast.

"Hey, was Mom videoing me this morning?" she questioned, her eyes as large and round as her mouth.

"Don't be silly dear," her mom said. "Don't you see? Your necklace did."

Emmi touched her necklace and a shiver raced around her throat. "But, it sees all of me," she mumbled as she watched Past Emmi reach for more milk.

"It's omnidirectional," her dad corrected. "Which means it can expand its view to see your whole body. Pretty cool, huh?"

"I hope it's not going to record our entire breakfast hour," Emmi's mom muttered. "Why does it think…"

"Oh, you see—that's why!" Her dad pointed as Past Emmi's elbow hit the milk carton and dumped its contents onto the tablecloth.

Emmi cringed and saw her mom, in the past, shake her head at Emmi and wipe the white pool of liquid with a cloth. Past Emmi gripped her cereal bowl, dropping her gaze as her mother's reprimands began.

In a growing daze, Emmi heard her dad continue his explanation.

"Your Flashback necklace not only records your day, it uses your heart rate, blood pressure, and even nervous system signals in your brain to determine what portions of your day to keep in its memory."

As if on cue, the scene faded to a long line of kids jostling their way onto the school bus like migrating wildebeests.

"Your father means that any big emotions will trigger your Flashback to start saving the moment. Like this one dear." Her mother's eyes were glued to the screen now. "This is what I'm interested in," she murmured, sitting back on the sofa.

Emmi watched her life flash in front of her face, quite literally, for the next hour. She watched Past Emmi introduce herself to her new classmates and trip on the way back to her seat. She saw Past Emmi score her goal and make friends with Amanda Keach. She witnessed the blank look on Past Emmi's face when her math teacher asked her what ten take away three was.

Her mother raised her eyebrow and paused the video. "Really Emmi, what's ten take away three?"

"I…forgot." Emmi whispered.

"Now Angie." Her dad set his coffee mug on the side table and turned to Emmi. "This is an important step in your education, young lady. Your mother and I didn't grow up with this sort of luxury, and so it was harder for us to mature. Learning from mistakes means you have to remember them, right?"

Emmi nodded her head, a marionette compelled to move by its puppeteer. "That's what Flashbacks were designed for, sweetie. All your school friends got theirs yesterday too." Her mother rose and turned to face Emmi. "You must keep your necklace on all the time. We'll make a stop at the Flashback center every day to retrieve your file."

"Every day?" Emmi bit her lip and gazed up at her parents, her brown eyes wide and shining in mute appeal.

"Emmi!" Her mom's hands flew up in the air and then rested on her hips. "This is going to grow you in so many ways. And think, you'll be able to share your biggest moments with us, not one detail missing!"

Not one detail missing. From that day on, evenings after supper were "personal improvement time," as her father termed it. She sat between them, praying her Flashback would forget certain incidents and scenes. But it never did. They would dance across the screen in 4K: the piano recital with the botched entrance, her bicycle accident, the awkward conversation with a classmate.

Emmi pitched a sand dollar at the receding tideline as she thought of the night the necklace had so vividly captured her tenth grade debate team's defeat in the finals. Her parents had rewound it again and again, telling her to "pay attention! Here's where you lost your momentum" or "now tell us why your point was irrelevant to the topic." She spent the rest of the evening creating an entirely new script for them to prove that Present Day Emmi had learnt from Past Emmi.

"Hey, it looks like you were having your own little Flashback." Kade's voice drew her out of her mental meandering and back to the world of salty breezes and distant frying food.

"Yeah, glad those ones stay in my head," Emmi's laugh shook like shattering glass. She flicked a piece of seaweed with her toe and let out her breath slowly. "I wish I was you."

"Me?" Kade guffawed. "Straight Bs every year, doesn't make the football team, two-left-feet me? You're nuts. Every kid since first grade wishes they had your smarts."

"They're not smarts, they're survival!" Emmi's voice broke, then rose. "I work hard, compete, fight for perfection, 'cause I don't want Mom and Dad to see me fail!" A seagull overhead screeched in response to her outburst, and she lowered her head.

"They love you, Emmi." Kade's words stretched over her pain like a tiny bandage, well meant, but ill-equipped to cover a gaping wound.

"I know." The reply came out like a prerecorded phone message. "They're proud of my accomplishments, they brag on me wherever they go. If they only knew how hard their critiques hit me. They don't seem to realise how flustered I get when they come down on me after a misstep."

Kade cleared his throat. "Maybe I shouldn't say anything, but before we left, my dad tried talking with your dad. I think it was about you cramming for all those exams."

"I overheard the conversation," Emmi assured him, rubbing her temples and squeezing her eyes shut. "Dad said something to the effect that Uncle Brett didn't seem to realize my stress levels existed because I lacked confidence, my lack of confidence being a direct result of my lacking diligence…"

Kade punctuated the last remark with a snort.

"…and so," Emmi concluded, "Dad and Mom both told him he really should be more concerned about their nephew who had failed to take home a medal or certificate or award of any kind beyond a participation trophy."

"*Eee,* my heart!" Kade moaned, grabbing his chest in mock agony. Emmi smiled, then jabbed a finger in the direction of Kade's neck. "I envy you the most about that. Why didn't your parents ever get you one?"

Kade rubbed the bare skin thoughtfully. "They always told me they would rather I make that decision. Perhaps next year with college I'll…"

"Don't!"

Kade's head snapped up at the aggressive tone Emmi's voice had adopted. Her eyes were dilated, and she clutched his hand.

"Don't ever, Kade. Maybe you don't have parents who would use it for performance tracking like mine do, but you'll end up doing it yourself. It happens to everyone. You'll realize what it's capable of, and you won't be able to let it go, even when you loathe its very purpose."

Kade blinked and opened his mouth, but Emmi wasn't listening.

"This necklace has been a part of my body now for thirteen years! It's become an organ. If it were to come off suddenly I think I'd come apart." Her rigid fingers let go of Kade, and she cradled her head as it shook back and forth. "This is my normal, as painful as it is. At least I'm used to it."

She scrambled to her feet, staggering a little as the sand shifted underneath her, and Kade jumped up as well. "You haven't seen your daily files all week," he countered. "Hasn't that been…"

"Nice? I don't know. I've felt like…like I'm on some sort of a fun park ride. Besides, Mom and Dad have seen them. That was the deal. I send them my files every evening, and when I get home it'll be time for my seven-day recap of what I did wrong."

She shook loose hair away from her face and turned to leave.

"Which reminds me. I need to get to the service center before they close."

"You'll miss the sunset if you go now!"

Emmi's smile was pitiful. "Kade, I wish a sunset was high on my list of priorities."

"You're on summer break, remember?"

Emmi just kept walking toward the dunes. She heard sand squeaking behind her and squared her shoulders.

"I'm going alone, Kade," she warned, and the footsteps stopped. "But thanks," she added under her breath.

The Flashback service center was a mere five-minute stroll down the boardwalk, placed conveniently in the building where an old convenience store had once developed camera film. Emmi saw an early evening queue already forming just inside the door and took her place behind a group of loud college students.

"Oh yeah, the look on your face when he, like, dumped the slushie in your lap was priceless. Just wait till you see it!" A tall redhead gabbed to her equally hyped brunette friend.

"Oh my word, I can't even!" She waved her hands and covered her face in dramatic terror.

Emmi watched them with dull disinterest. Her phone buzzed. She dragged it from her pocket and the screen lit up with a text message from her mom: *Hey hunny, you @ the center yet? Dad and I are waiting.*

Emmi's stomach turned over with a sickening lurch. Her conversation with Kade! Of all the empty-headed things she had done, this would have to be one of the worst. She gripped the phone tightly, imagining her parents' faces as they heard her unguarded comments on the beach not an hour ago. "Immature whining," her dad would call it, her mom's eyes stern and disapproving. As she stared at the question, stupefied, a pathetic sniff behind her caught her ear, and she cocked her head like a sheepdog at a lamb's bleating. "Grammy, I don't want to see today. It's gonna make me sad again."

The child's whimper choked Emmi's heart and she turned to see a girl, still damp from her swim.

"But Ainsley," the elderly lady beside her consoled. "You'll get over it faster this way. It will help you go forward."

The child shivered a little under her pink towel. "Can't I just remember it in my head? It's in my head, I promise!" She caught Emmi staring and looked up at her, pleading.

"She remembers. And she doesn't need any more reminders," Emmi spoke slowly, unsure of anything save that she needed to speak now or regret not speaking for the rest of her life.

The lady jumped at the sudden addition to their conversation and goggled Emmi. "I—I wasn't saying she didn't," she began apologetically.

"And how can she go forward when others drag her back?" Emmi's voice rang out steadier now, her heart banging violently against her ribs.

"Drag her…drag her back?" The woman placed a hand on her granddaughter's shoulder and looked from her to Emmi with widening eyes.

"If you think replaying the letdowns in a child's day is going to help her 'get over' them, you're sadly mistaken, ma'am." Emmi stopped short as something sharp rammed into her throat and she blinked back threatening emotions.

The lady's mouth parted, but no words came out. Then she moved her hand from the girl's shoulder and patted her back like she was meeting her for the first time. "Well dear, Grandpa's waiting in the car, and you still need to dry off before we go to dinner," she said in a subdued voice, clearing her throat.

The child's face lit up, and she threw a glance at Emmi in juvenile wonder.

"Thanks," she breathed, and dashed to the door, flip-flops slapping the tiled floor as her grandmother followed behind at a slower pace.

Emmi's upper lip trembled and she expelled the pent-up air in her lungs.

"May I have your memory card, please?"

She whirled around and saw the service worker, his fingers impatiently drumming on the counter.

Emmi clutched her necklace and unconsciously took a step back. "Never again!" she gasped, the words tumbling out like an avalanche. She stumbled out of the entrance and made for the beach. She ran, knowing the second she slowed her pace her resolve would weaken and the fear would begin its noose-like tightening on her soul.

The cliff overlooking the bay was deserted save for some dozing cormorants, and they flapped off in confusion as Emmi came pelting up the crude footpath. She lowered her head, chest heaving, and rubbed her sweating hands down the sides of her capris. A minute passed and she straightened. She saw the sun, a melting medallion dripping slowly into the low-lying clouds. The sky blushed and shone with deep pinks and even deeper reds.

"I was going to miss this?" she asked the coastal breeze that had chased her up the slope and now tossed strands of hair over her shoulder like a teasing schoolboy. She didn't realize she was crying until a stray tear slid down her nose and hung there for a moment before splashing onto her shirt front.

"Emmi!" Kade's voice panted, and she turned to see him scrambling the last few feet to the top of the grassy bluff. "What's wrong? You came flying over that boardwalk and up here like someone was after you!" His eyes roved over her tear-stained face.

Emmi's laugh teetered like a seesaw, and she shook her head. "I'm fine Kade, really," she said with a smile, two more tears sliding over her cheeks and down her chin in spite of herself. She shook her head again and nodded at the scene in front of them. "The next time I tell you a sunset's not worth my attention, give me a shake, will you?" she murmured.

Kade's neck and shoulders loosened as Emmi's eyes glowed with the sky's melding and merging tones.

"I think I'll make this an evening ritual," she mused. "It can become my new 'personal improvement' part of the day."

"Say what now?" Kade glanced at Emmi with a line between his eyebrows.

"I'm not going back," Emmi answered. "I left before I got my file, and that's the last time I ever go to one of those places again." She paused and threw her shoulders back, the muscles in her neck quivering. "And today's the last day I carry this millstone around."

Her hands reached up and grabbed ahold of the gold band. She closed her eyes, her breaths becoming irregular and short. After a few seconds, she opened them up again and looked at Kade. "I could use a little help perhaps," she whispered with a trembling smile.

"It'd be a pleasure." Kade choked on his words. He grasped the necklace and pulled his hands apart in a swift yank.

Emmi flinched at the short snap, followed by the rank smell of battery acid filling her nose. She spun around and saw the necklace, limp and twisted, lying in Kade's palm. A few stray wires stuck out of one end and released a few weak sparks. Kade offered it to her and she took it, clenching it in her fist.

"Well then…" She walked to the edge of the cliff. "Goodbye to yesterday." Like a pitcher throwing a fastball, she hurled the necklace out over the water. Catching the fading light, it scintillated wildly, like a falling star, before plunging into the breakers with a splash.

Kade strode up to her side and placed an arm on her shoulder. "Prouda' you cuz," he muttered. Emmi just smiled, her grin widening and stretching like it was finally flexing its muscles.

"I bet your parents are wondering if we got carried off by the tide," she suggested, and the two turned and began the descent down to the beach. Emmi rubbed her neck with cautious fingers.

"How's it feel?" Kade asked.

"I bet I'm a sight now, a nice tan everywhere but 'round here." She smirked.

"We're at the beach," he assured her. "We can fix that problem."

Alone

R.J. CATLIN

Emily wiped sweat from her face with the back of her forearm. A blanket of gray veiled the sun, but the clouds didn't help much with the heat. She stepped off the ladder into the freshly-weeded flower bed. Well, it didn't have any flowers yet, but it would after she was done painting the siding.

She shaded her eyes from the early summer sun, squinting at the ramshackle cottage she had purchased last week. She sighed, a smile spreading across her face.

A pile of old fallen shingles and weeds sat in the gravel driveway next to her rusty gray station wagon, instead of littering the ground beneath the eaves. The missing shingles left the roof bare in patches like her mother's hair just after she began chemo.

Emily wiped her fingers on a rag, successfully smearing more light-blue paint on them, then wiped her hands on her pants. What was the point of wearing paint clothes if you didn't get paint on them?

The little house sat in the middle of a meadow with a speckling of maple trees throughout the yard. Butterflies flitted around the yard as Emily stretched the burning sensation from her arms. A monarch fluttered around her hair as she walked over to the tree where her water bottle and granola bar sat. It landed on her head and yanked a strand of hair. Emily yelped, swatting at the insect. She missed, so she rubbed her head instead, glaring at the creature as it fluttered away.

"Return to the muck you weather-bitten dewberry!" the butterfly shrieked at her. She stopped rubbing her head and stared after it, eyes wide. That couldn't be right; butterflies didn't shriek, let alone insults.

Emily picked up her water bottle and took a swig as she stared into the meadow beside her house where the butterfly had disappeared. Something thumped heavily on the ground behind her. She turned.

A stony creature, about the height of a Labrador, stood in front of her. His legs, his hands, even his head looked like stone covered in moss. A crack in the rock's head and two gray pebbly eyes constituted a face.

Emily inhaled, coughed, then spit out the water in her mouth as she stumbled backward.

"What in God's good creation are you?" she wheezed, then coughed some more.

The creature blinked and stepped back, his forehead dripping with water. Emily wiped her chin with the back of her hand.

"It's bad smell," he said in a gravelly voice, raising a rocky arm and pointing a pebble finger at the siding that Emily had just finished painting. "Rabbit's unhappy."

"Rabbits," Emily murmured, a bit weak about the knees. A fine layer of moss covered the top of the creature's head, like he'd recently gone to the barbershop for a buzz cut. She sat on the grass before her legs gave out. "What *are* you?"

The creature reached up and scratched his head, which made a grating noise. He tilted his head like a confused puppy, then said uncertainly, "Is Barroll?"

"What's Barroll?" she asked, her eyebrows pinching together.

"Me." He nodded his head proudly.

"I see." Emily didn't think "Barroll" was his species. Perhaps he was a troll, though he didn't look at all like the grumpy creatures that lived under bridges in picture books.

Emily introduced herself, supposing that even fairy-tale creatures deserved good manners. Barroll bounced happily from foot to foot at it, repeating her name and pronouncing it "A-Milly." When he finally calmed down, she asked him again what he wanted. He sobered at that.

"Rabbit not like smell. Bad smell."

"Well, I've got to finish painting, but if it makes you feel better, once it's done and dried, it won't smell so strong."

She stood, stretched her arms, then picked up her roller brush, dipping it in the paint tray. When she began painting the siding, she felt a tug on her pants. Emily looked down. Barroll held his round palms up to her.

"We help," he said. "Faster."

Emily found him a paintbrush and he began wiping paint on the lower four feet of the house. Once he was covered in paint splatters and done painting the parts of the house he could reach, Barroll disappeared with Emily's paintbrush into the meadow. The evening sun made the grass look like golden ocean waves.

Emily sighed and cleaned up her mess, the porch creaking as she crossed it and opened her front door. Dust motes drifted around the main room, devoid of furniture, catching afternoon sunlight from the broken windowpane like glitter.

"Don't let your life be empty without me," her mother had said.

Emily kept her shoes on as she crossed the dingy carpet to the kitchen. She went over to the sink, twisting the knob. The icy water that sprayed her paint-stained hands changed its mind, steaming the paint off her skin. The sun played through the leaves of the tree in front of the window. A pair of antlers popped up just above the field grass. Emily blinked, and they were gone. She wiped her wet pink hands on her shirt.

She had one more side of the house to paint. The rabbits could stand to be patient with their new neighbor.

The next morning, when she stepped out on the porch after breakfast, her foot squished right into a pile of rabbit pellets. If she hadn't been so busy shrieking *"ew!"* and wiping her shoe in the grass, Emily might have noticed the very large hare with antlers that laughed mischievously to himself before he disappeared into the field.

When she brought her paint things outside to finish the last side of the cottage, the paint from yesterday had been smudged by…were those tiny handprints?

Emily groaned and stomped her foot like a petulant child. She'd hoped to fill her life with house repairs and tending a garden, not pests.

She'd spent enough time fending off people who didn't like her when she'd lived in the city. She didn't need to fend off animals who hated her as well.

That evening, Emily sat with her peanut butter and jelly sandwich and glass of milk on the edge of the porch which creaked under her weight, her legs hanging off the edge. She had mowed the grass around the house yesterday, but it still smelled sweet. A stray blade tickled her ankle and she pulled her feet up, crossing them after scratching the itch.

As she watched the sunset, the emptiness that had been growing in Emily's chest since the day after she moved in became big enough for her to recognize it.

"A-Milly, where is more of you?"

Emily jolted out of her thoughts to find Barroll standing in front of her. She put her hand on her chest to still her racing heart, taking a deep breath.

"You startled me," she told him. She scooted over, patting the empty space next to her. "Wanna join me? I was just watching the sunset."

Emily had never seen anything tumble *up* stairs before, but that's what Barroll did. Once he situated himself next to her, he asked again, "Where is more of you?"

"What do you mean?" Emily looked down into his shiny round eyes.

"People always are many," he explained. "You're one. Where is more of you?"

Emily looked at the yard, the trees, the meadow. She looked at her beat-up car, the rabbit hopping curiously across the gravel driveway, the empty dirt road in the distance.

She was no stranger to loneliness. Emily grew up in the city with her mother as her only friend. Birthday parties with negative RSVPs. The bus ride home listening to the inside jokes in the seat behind her, and sometimes the not-inside jokes criticizing her clothes, her attempts at jokes, and her single mom.

"It's just me. Mama died a couple years ago," Emily said.

"Died?" Barroll gently patted her hand with his stubby round fingers. "Barroll is alone much time, too."

"Being alone isn't that bad." But the two-year-old knot in her chest tightened. "Then no one can make fun of you."

Barroll shook his head. He stated, "We will be friend."

Emily laughed under her breath. "All right, Barroll."

As Emily filled her kettle at the sink, she glanced out the window.

A pair of antlers disappeared into the grass.

She blinked. The grass wasn't tall enough to hide a deer. She must have imagined it. After a breakfast of Earl Grey and peanut butter toast, she filled the sink with soapy water. When she'd scrubbed two plates and a fork, the flutter of colorful wings at the window caught her eye.

An odd-looking butterfly perched on the windowsill. Frowning, Emily leaned closer, pretty sure it was the one that had pulled her hair when she was taking a break from painting the other day. The butterfly had a tiny, person-shaped body. The shiny black skin and hair reminded Emily of the shell of a black beetle and was freckled with white like a spattering of paint. The wings were burnt orange outlined in black, similar to the wings of a monarch butterfly.

The creature was sprawled on her hands and knees like she had fallen and was catching her breath.

Emily pushed the bottom half of the window up, propping it there with a wooden dowel. The breeze slipped in, tickling her cheek.

"Shoo!" she commanded, waving her hand at the butterfly-person as the thing stared balefully at her. "Get out of here."

The butterfly-person slowly stood, flapping her wings once, like she was trying to decide if she would heed Emily's warnings.

She suddenly jumped into the air and darted through the open window. She yanked on a strand of Emily's hair, screeching "nasty rude human!" in her ear. Then she fluttered around the kitchen, banging into things and making a racket. Emily grabbed the broom and, after a considerable amount of time chasing her around, finally got the creature to leave by the window she had come in through. She slammed it closed, trapping the creature outside and the hot summer air inside. The next project on the list would be to get screens for the windows.

Emily had barely caught her breath from chasing around the butterfly creature when someone knocked on the door and she scrambled for it. Barroll had a tendency to knock and then leave without waiting for her. She'd missed him entirely the first three times he'd come to visit her inside. Emily flung open the door and he was already toddling off the last step of the porch.

"Barroll! Come inside," she called to him as she tried to catch her breath. "I have lemonade and a question for you!"

He turned around and came inside. His stumpy little legs left dirt marks on the carpet she'd yet to replace. Emily pulled the pitcher from the old yellowed refrigerator and filled a plastic cup, dropping in a few ice cubes as well. He'd cracked one of her glasses and squashed a paper cup the last time she'd offered him a drink.

He slurped happily as she asked, "What are the things that look like butterflies but aren't?"

Barroll looked up from his lemonade, some of which was dripping down his chin. Rock lips weren't very flexible.

"Fairy," he said, then went back to guzzling the lemonade. He picked out the ice cubes and munched contentedly on them. When he was done, he said, "Like sweets and pulling hair," then hopped off his chair and toddled outside.

A few days later, the fairy appeared at the bedroom window to scowl and stick her tongue out at Emily as she was putting her socks on. She hopped over to the window and opened it, one sock half on her foot. "Wait!" she called as the fairy beelined for the trees. "Would you like a cookie? I made it myself."

The creature paused midair. She tilted her little head slightly, eyeing Emily, but nodded once.

"Come in and make yourself comfortable." Emily left the window open, hoping the flies would take pity and stay out. She went into the kitchen and found the container of cookies she had put in the cupboard above the tiny counter space.

The little creature flitted around the room, then settled on the little round dining table. She sat on the stack of paper napkins as Emily fetched the thimble from her sewing kit and cleaned it in the sink, then poured a few drops of lemonade into it.

The two of them sat sipping their drinks and eating cookies in silence, looking at each other with curiosity.

Emily asked the little creature, "You're a fairy, right? I'm Emily."

"You may call me Flee," the fairy said. "I once had a human who knew me by it."

"What happened?"

"It moved away," Flee said matter-of-factly. "I miss it greatly, but that was a long time ago."

"I see," Emily said slowly. "I once had a friend move away. I was very young, but I think sadness is bigger when you are small."

Flee looked at Emily thoughtfully, then nodded as though she had come to a decision. "You will be my human now."

Emily sputtered a laugh into her lemonade. But Flee looked very seriously at her.

"This is not a laughing matter."

"You can't be serious," Emily protested. "You can't *claim* people."

"Fairies most certainly *can*," insisted Flee. "Haven't you heard of Peter Pan? He was a very famous human who belonged to a fairy."

Emily's mouth opened and closed like a beached fish. "You mean Tinkerbell and Peter Pan were real?"

"*We* don't call her 'Tinkerbell,' of course, but I don't expect you'd be able to pronounce her real name."

The humidity of an oncoming storm sat heavily in the sun's heat. Emily's little cottage was vastly different from when she'd bought it three months ago.

The new roof darkly contrasted against the fresh coat of paint. The once-broken window had not a scratch in sight. Flowers and small bushes filled the garden bed surrounding the house. Emily no longer worried that Barroll would fall through the porch boards, though the new ones still creaked beneath his weight. The front door had a fresh coat of navy blue.

Barroll sat in the grass rolling himself in mindless circles. Flee watched him from beneath the shade of the porch.

Emily was just touching up the shutters with a matching navy, which were drying on cardboard in the lawn, when a large hare with a rack of antlers charged into the yard, yelling at the top of his lungs.

He barreled into Emily, who shrieked and sprawled onto her back. The jackalope landed atop her and began throttling her, at least, as much as a hare could throttle someone with those tiny paws.

Barroll rushed over, pushing at the jackalope to try to get him off. Flee fluttered over, batting and pulling at the jackalope's long ears.

"You said the smell'd go 'way when ya stopped paintin', but you ain't stopped paintin,'" bellowed the jackalope. "You kept paintin'. And paintin'. AND YOU'RE STILL PAINTIN'!"

"No!" Barroll cried. "Almost done! Done today!"

Flee spouted, "This is my human. How dare you attack my human."

Emily recovered some modicum of her senses to realize the jacka-lope didn't weigh so much, so she rolled him off and got up.

"Look," she said, "I'm sorry. When Barroll said 'rabbits,' I thought he was talking about *normal* rabbits. I didn't know I was offending you."

The jackalope marched up to her, his chest puffed in indignation. "See here! That is no excuse for—"

"AND," she interrupted, "I'm terribly sorry for taking so long. This is about the last of the painting I'll have for a long while. Would you like some lemonade? We were just about to take a break anyways."

"This Jack don't drink lemonade," the long-eared creature said, turning up his nose slightly.

"I think I have some carrots in the fridge somewhere," Emily offered. "They aren't the freshest but it's what I can offer you."

The outrage faded from the jackalope's face, and he stammered some incoherent protestations before grumbling, "That sounds mighty nice. Thank you, ma'am."

A late summer thunderstorm darkened the sky one evening after a long day of tilling a patch of soil for a winter garden. Jack had decided that he was the one to teach her the ways of home-grown food, and Barroll and Flee found it amusing to watch her mess around in dirt.

The four of them tromped into the house just as the first large drops of rain pelted the roof.

Emily kicked off her mud boots by the door and followed the creatures into the kitchen. She filled the kettle and set it on the stovetop, then poured lemonade into a plastic cup and a thimble. She pulled fresh farm-grown carrots out of the fridge and set them in front of Jack.

The kettle whistled and she steeped a teabag in her favorite mug, bringing it to the table where the others sat. Emily sipped her tea, peering through the steam at her friends. She smiled at the thought. She'd come here to be alone, but she found that this was much, much better.

Sneakers of Joy

GREGORY O'DONNELL

Kali Harper lugged her overstuffed duffle bag down the narrow dormitory hallway, her sneakers squeaking against the freshly waxed floors. Around her, voices echoed in a chaotic symphony—laughter, excited greetings, and the unmistakable sound of someone attempting to shove a mini fridge through a doorway.

She navigated around boxes and bags piled in the hallway and families in group hugs and selfies. She hugged the bag closer to her chest, feeling like an outsider crashing someone else's party.

When she finally reached her dorm room, there were little colorful cards taped to the door. One read, "Madison and Kali Roomies!" in colorful marker. Others were thoughtful welcoming notes from some of the floor resident advisors and counselors. The dorm door was already propped open, revealing a whirlwind of activity.

Inside, her new roommate sprawled on a bed, chatting animatedly on her phone under a newly strung set of fairy lights. Her dark curly hair was pulled back, and her tank top declared "Good Life" in bright, glittery letters. She was a freshman majoring in medicine.

Kali hesitated in the doorway. "Uh, hi. I'm Kali."

Madison glanced up and broke into a dazzling smile. "Oh my

gosh, you're here! Finally! I've been dying to meet you!" She hopped off the bed, practically bouncing. "Okay, so I'm Madison, obviously. I've already claimed this side, but you can have that one—it gets the morning sun. Do you like the smell of lavender? I got this diffuser thingy, but if you hate it, I can totally put it away."

Kali blinked. "Lavender's fine."

"Yay!" Madison clasped her hands together. "We're gonna have so much fun this year. I'm already planning an improv night for our floor. By the way, do you sing?"

"Not really," Kali mumbled, setting her bag on the empty bed. The idea of standing in front of a crowd made her stomach twist.

"Well, you'll have to try!" Madison chirped. "Oh, and there's a beach-themed party this weekend. Everyone's going. You have to come!"

Kali forced a polite smile. "Maybe."

In truth, the idea of a party made her want to hide under her home-made quilt and never come out. Back home, she'd spent Friday nights at youth group or curled up with her parents watching old movies. The bustling, extroverted energy of college life felt alien—and exhausting.

That night, Kali huddled under her blankets and started a Zoom call with her mom, keeping her voice low to avoid waking Madison, who had drifted off with earbuds in.

"Hey, Mom. How was the drive back? Eight hours is a long haul."

"It wasn't too bad. I stopped a couple of times—found a really neat craft store along the way and picked up a beautiful set of earrings. How was your first day settling in? How's campus life?"

Kali hesitated. "It's...different," she admitted. "Everyone here is so loud and confident. I feel like I don't belong."

Her mom's warm eyes softened through the screen. "Cutie, it's only your first week. Give yourself time. You'll find your place."

"What if I don't?" Kali's voice wavered. The quiet rhythm of home felt so far away, and she longed for one of her mom's hugs, the kind that made the world feel smaller and safer.

Her mom's voice was gentle but steady. "God's got you, Kali. He's walking with you every step of the way, even when it feels scary."

Kali nodded, trying to hold on to her mom's reassurance. But as the call ended and she stared at the unfamiliar ceiling, the homesickness settled deeper into her chest.

≈≈≈

The next morning, Madison cornered Kali in the dining hall as she poured cereal into a bowl. "Okay, you can't just mope around here all weekend. We're going to that party, and you need an outfit."

"I have clothes," Kali said, stirring milk into her cereal.

"Not beach clothes," Madison countered. "Come on, let's hit the thrift stores. They're, like, the best part of this town."

Kali hesitated but eventually relented. A small part of her was curious about the town beyond campus. After breakfast, the two set off. They wandered through a couple of secondhand shops, Madison chattering nonstop while Kali sifted through racks of clothes, feeling increasingly out of her depth.

As they turned a corner, Kali's attention snagged on a small shop tucked between a bakery and a bookstore. Its faded sign read, "Ruby's Curiosities" in whimsical, looping letters.

Something about it felt inviting. "Let's go in here," Kali said.

Madison wrinkled her nose. "It looks kinda dusty. But okay, your call."

Inside, the store was a delightful chaos of vintage knickknacks, mismatched furniture, and shelves crammed with everything from antique teapots to feathered hats. The air smelled faintly of scented candles and old books.

"Welcome!" a voice called. A woman emerged from behind the counter, her silver hair piled into a loose bun and her eyes sparkling with mischief. "I'm Ruby. Let me know if you need anything."

Kali nodded, feeling oddly comforted by Ruby's warm presence. She settled into a relaxed posture. She wandered deeper into the store, running her fingers over a rack of brightly colored scarves.

Then she saw them: a pair of neon-pink sneakers with glittery shoelaces. They were perched on a display stand like a prized artifact, catching the light in a way that seemed almost magical.

"Oh wow," Madison said, peering over Kali's shoulder. "Those are...something."

Kali reached out, hesitating before picking them up. They felt surprisingly light in her hands.

They were oddly colored with unusual stripes, but she couldn't deny they made her smile.

"Good eye," Ruby said, appearing at Kali's side. "Those are special, you know."

Kali raised an eyebrow. "Special how?"

Ruby's smile widened. "They've got a way of bringing out the best in people. But only if you're willing to take a leap of faith."

She looked for the size of the shoes and couldn't find one. So she tried them on. They were a perfect fit.

Kali glanced at Madison, who was now examining a sequined purse. Something about Ruby's words resonated. She took the sneakers off and turned them over, noting the faint scuffs on the soles. They weren't new, but they seemed well loved.

"How much?" Kali asked.

Ruby waved a hand. "For you, sweetheart, seven dollars."

Kali hesitated for only a moment before pulling some crumpled bills from her pocket.

Ruby handed her the receipt, leaned in, and whispered, "You'll see what I mean soon enough."

Walking out of the store, Kali peered down at the sneakers in the bottom of the brown paper bag she carried. They looked utterly absurd. But for the first time in days, she felt a flicker of excitement, as if something unexpected might be waiting just around the corner.

A week passed and Kali began to settle into her new campus-life routines. The improv night finally arrived. The resident advisors transformed the common room into a tropical paradise with paper palm trees, twinkling fairy lights, and inflatable beach balls bouncing between the clusters of students. The air buzzed with music, laughter, and the sugary scent of punch.

Kali lingered near the entrance, tugging at the hem of her sundress. She'd reluctantly slipped on the neon-pink sneakers, figuring no one would notice her feet in the dim lighting.

But she felt self-conscious nonetheless, as if they were a spotlight announcing her awkwardness.

Madison darted past, already swept into a group of friends. "Come on, Kali! Dance!"

Kali shook her head, offering a weak smile. She edged toward the snack table, hoping to blend into the background. The music was loud, the crowd overwhelming. She wished she were back in her dorm with a book.

As she reached for a cup of punch, something strange happened. Kali's feet tingled, and before she could process it, the sneakers tugged her forward. She stumbled into the open space at the center of the room, nearly colliding with a guy holding a soda can.

"Uh, sorry," she mumbled, but before she could retreat, her feet started moving. Not just moving, dancing.

Suddenly, her hands reached out and grabbed the bewildered boy. "You know how to swing dance?" Kali blurted, her voice tinged with both panic and excitement.

"Sort of?" he said, dropping his drink as she spun him onto the open floor.

To her amazement, her feet launched into a basic step, and she guided him into the rhythm. With an enthusiastic tug, she pulled him into a pretzel move, her arms weaving and twisting with a surprising level of coordination. The crowd gasped in delight as they untangled, her partner laughing along as if he'd forgotten he was being dragged.

From there, Kali dipped low into a playful mop move, her feet sweeping exaggeratedly across the floor. Her partner caught on quickly, mirroring her motions and adding a playful flourish. She couldn't stop grinning as they moved in sync, the music seeming to swell with every beat.

A hush fell over the room as they hit a particularly wild combination, Kali spinning out from her partner's arms in a whirl of controlled chaos. Her cheeks burned, and she froze for a moment. Everyone was staring.

But then, someone cheered. "Go, Kali!"

The crowd erupted into applause and laughter. One by one, they joined in, attempting to mimic her moves or simply clapping to the beat. What started as a simple beach-themed party turned into all-out swing dance extravaganza.

The sneakers guided her through another twirl, this time sending her partner into a dramatic dip that had the crowd roaring with approval. She caught sight of Madison grinning and clapping along.

Kali laughed, light and unrestrained; she let the music carry her. For the first time since arriving at college, she wasn't worrying about fitting in or saying the right thing. She was simply...joyful.

By Monday morning, Kali's quiet walk to her first class was interrupted multiple times.

News of the "dancing pink-sneakered girl" spread like wildfire across campus. Strangers waved, called out her name, or mimicked her now-famous moves.

Kali couldn't believe it. She'd spent her first week feeling invisible, and now, suddenly, people wanted to talk to her. Some approached to compliment her moves, others just wanted to know where she got the sneakers.

"They're magic," she'd reply with a smile and a mocking laugh.

Encouraged by the positivity, Kali decided to wear the sneakers more often. Each time, the result was the same: as soon as she slipped them on, the invisible music started, and she couldn't resist the urge to dance. It wasn't just her, either. The energy seemed contagious, drawing people in like moths to a flame.

In the quad, a group of students clapped along as she spun and twirled. In the library lobby, even the usually grumpy librarian cracked a smile as Kali broke into a graceful slide-step while holding her books. Each dance seemed to bring people together, creating moments of shared joy and laughter.

The first semester settled into the cooler days and cloudless blue skies of autumn. One afternoon, Kali sat on the grass near the student center, the sneakers resting beside her as she caught her breath. A girl with bright red hair approached, holding two cans of soda.

"Hey," the girl said, offering one. "I'm Zoe. Your moves are sick."

Kali laughed, accepting the soda. "Thanks. Honestly, it's not me, it's the sneakers."

Zoe raised an eyebrow but grinned. "Well, whatever it is, it's awesome. You've got the whole campus talking."

They fell into easy conversation and Kali learned Zoe was a graphic design major who also felt out of place at first. By the time they parted, Kali felt a warm glow. For the first time, she was making friends, real friends.

The crisp afternoon sun bathed the campus quad, where students gathered for the annual fall picnic. Brightly colored blankets sprawled across the grass and the aroma of barbecue mixed with the sound of upbeat music blasting from nearby speakers. Kali sat on the edge of a fountain, nervously sipping lemonade as her newfound friends, including Madison, chatted animatedly around her. She'd brought the sneakers, of course. They peeked out from her tote bag, the glittery laces catching the sunlight. A small, mischievous part of her hoped they wouldn't act up today, but a growing part of her couldn't wait for the magic to take hold again.

As Kali scanned the crowd, a group of sharply dressed students approached. They moved in unison, their coordinated outfits and confident strides screaming "dance crew." It was the Varsity Vibes. And at their head was Troy, a campus celebrity of sorts. His easy smile made Kali's stomach flip.

"Hey, you're the pink sneakers girl, right?" Troy asked, stopping in front of her. His voice carried a hint of mockery, but his smile seemed genuine enough.

Kali hesitated. "Uh... I guess?"

"Well, we've been hearing about your moves," Troy said, folding his arms. "Thought we'd see what the hype is all about."

Kali's cheeks burned. "It's really nothing special. Just for fun."

"Fun?" Troy raised an eyebrow. "How about a dance-off, then?

You and your magical sneakers against us."

Madison gasped. "Oh my gosh, Kali, you have to!"

Kali's heart raced. A dance-off? Against The Varsity Vibes? She barely knew how to dance without the sneakers, let alone with them. "I don't know..."

"You can totally do this!" Madison encouraged, grabbing her hands. "Besides, it's all about having fun, remember?"

The crowd, catching wind of the challenge, began to gather. Phones came out, and someone turned the music louder. Kali glanced at the growing audience, her anxiety bubbling up. But then she looked at Madison's eager face and the cheerful energy around her. The sneakers seemed to hum from inside the bag, as if urging her to take the leap. "Alright," Kali said, standing. "Let's do it."

The crowd cheered as Kali slipped on the sneakers. The moment her feet settled into the shoes, the now-familiar tingling sensation spread through her legs. She stepped into the center of the walkway, a makeshift dance floor, facing Troy and his crew, who were already stretching and warming up.

The music shifted to a fresh beat and Troy stepped forward with a confident grin. He started with a smooth Dougie, rolling his shoulders and gliding effortlessly across the floor, his head nodding in rhythm. The crowd clapped in sync as he transitioned into the Robot, his movements sharp and mechanical, his arms and legs hitting every beat with perfect isolation. Then, with a playful smirk, he slid into a flawless Dab, dropping his head into the crook of his arm as the crowd erupted in cheers. Troy finished with a spin, pointing to the crowd with a wink as if to say, "Top that."

The sneakers didn't wait. As the music shifted into a new beat, they took over, sending her into a whirlwind of ridiculous, uninhibited moves. She hopped, shimmied, and performed a wobbly pirouette that ended with her nearly toppling over. The crowd erupted into laughter, not out of cruelty but sheer delight.

Kali felt herself loosening up, leaning into the absurdity of it all. She pointed dramatically at Troy, then moonwalked backward in exaggerated slow motion. Someone in the crowd shouted, "Legendary!"

Troy smirked and joined in, stepping into the circle with an improvised routine. He mimicked Kali's moonwalk, only to trip over his own feet. The crowd roared as Kali burst into laughter, extending a hand to help him up. The moment shifted from competition to camaraderie, and soon, everyone was on their feet, dancing together.

The dance-off became a spontaneous celebration. Friends, strangers, even professors joined the fray, their movements uninhibited. Kali couldn't stop smiling as she twirled through the crowd, high-fiving and laughing with people she'd never met.

When the music finally ended, the quad erupted into cheers and applause. Troy clapped Kali on the back, laughing. "Okay, you win, pink sneakers girl. You've got moves."

Kali grinned, her heart swelling. For the first time, she felt completely at home. Not because she'd won, but because she'd shared something real with the people around her. The sneakers sparkled in the sunlight, and Kali couldn't help but feel a small, quiet gratitude for the ridiculous, magical shoes that had brought her here.

The once timid girl who avoided speaking up in class now strutted through campus like a queen, her steps always accompanied by the faint echo of cheerful beats.

One afternoon, Kali slid into a seat in the library. The usual chatter and rustling of pages were absent; only the soft hum of fluorescent lights and the occasional cough punctuated the air. She opened her laptop and took a deep breath, ready to tackle her essay.

Then it happened. The sneakers started tapping against the floor, creating a rhythm so infectious that Kali's legs moved of their own accord. Her feet kicked out, her hips swayed, and before she knew it, she was halfway into a Charleston, the chair toppling behind her.

"Shhh!" The librarian's sharp hiss cut through the room. Students glared over their books, and Kali's cheeks burned as she wrestled her rebellious feet back under the desk.

The sneakers weren't done. In her anthropology lecture the next morning, they struck again. As Professor Cardwell detailed burial rites of ancient civilizations, Kali's feet tapped a syncopated rhythm beneath the desk. Her sneakers yanked her upright and propelled her into the aisle, where she executed an unintentional samba.

"Miss Carter," the professor said, raising an eyebrow. "Unless this is a presentation on the dance rituals of the Olmec people, I suggest you return to your seat."

Laughter rippled through the lecture hall as Kali sank back into her chair, mortified. She could feel the amused stares, the whispers behind her back.

In the days that followed, the sneakers grew more insistent. At the grocery store, in line at Starbucks, even during a quiet walk in the park, they compelled her to dance.

Kali's frustration grew as she tripped over her own feet, spilled her latte, and earned disapproving looks from strangers.

"Why are you doing this to me?" she muttered one evening, glaring down at the sneakers as she kicked them off onto her bedroom floor. They lay there, still and silent, their bright colors mocking her.

For the first time in weeks, Kali slipped on her old sneakers the next morning. Without the sneakers, the world felt duller, quieter. But the thought of another public spectacle was unbearable. She skipped class, avoided her friends, and spent her evenings scrolling through social media, envying the curated perfection of other people's lives. Loneliness settled over her like a heavy blanket.

She caught her reflection in the mirror one night. Her once-bright eyes were rimmed with shadows, her shoulders slumped. The sneakers sat untouched in the corner, their vibrant pattern dulled in the dim light.

"Maybe it wasn't the sneakers," she whispered to herself, voice trembling. But the thought brought no comfort. All she knew was that her life, once infused with the music of possibility, now felt more silent than ever.

One night in the bleak dark days of early December, Kali stared at her laptop screen, waiting for the familiar chime of the Zoom call to connect.

Her reflection in the darkened monitor looked as tired as she felt. When her mother's face appeared, the family room fireplace behind her, Kali's chest tightened.

"Hi, sweetie," her mom said, her voice warm but tinged with concern. "You doing okay?"

"Not really," Kali admitted, her voice cracking despite her attempt to sound casual. She fiddled with the edge of her sweatshirt, avoiding the camera. "I feel like everything's falling apart, Mom. I thought those sneakers were making me happy, but now my life just feels...messier."

Her mom tilted her head slightly, listening intently. "Messier how?" she asked with a soft voice.

"I've been so caught up in chasing this magical feeling they gave me," Kali said, her words tumbling out. "But I've lost sight of everything else. My classes, my friends—it's like I've been running in circles, and I don't even know what I'm chasing anymore."

Her mom's eyes softened, and for a moment, she didn't say anything. Kali's throat tightened as tears threatened to spill.

"I've been praying about this, you know," her mom finally said. "Praying that you'd find some clarity and peace. Maybe it's time we pray together."

Kali blinked. "Now?"

Her mom smiled. "Yes, now. God's always listening, Kali. And sometimes, talking to him out loud—with someone who loves you—can help you feel less lost."

Kali hesitated, then nodded, wiping at her damp cheeks. Her mom bowed her head, and Kali mirrored her, closing her eyes as her mom began.

"Father God, we come to you tonight with heavy hearts but open hands," her mom said, her voice steady and calm. "You see Kali's struggles and her pain, even when she feels like she's wandering in the dark. Please remind her that her joy comes from you, not from things or circumstances. Give her the courage to trust in your plan, even when it's unclear. And let her know she is loved, by you and by those around her."

Kali's voice trembled as she added, "God, I don't know what I'm doing anymore. I need your guidance. Please help me find joy in the life I already have and trust that you're working in me."

When they finished, an unexpected peace settled over Kali. She opened her eyes and saw her mom looking at her with an encouraging smile.

"Thanks, Mom," Kali whispered.

"Anytime, sweetie," her mom said. "And remember, God's got you. Always." After she ended the Zoom call, Kali paused. As she sat in the stillness, a realization dawned on her: the sneakers had never been the source of her joy. They had only given her permission to be herself, to take risks and connect with others.

Kali took a deep breath and stood, her steps lighter than they'd been in weeks. As she left the room, the faint sound of her own sneakers against the linoleum floor felt like its own kind of music—soft, steady, and full of promise.

Kali woke the next morning with a sense of clarity. For weeks, she had been at odds with herself, but now she felt ready to take a step forward. She decided to organize a campus-wide event: a "Sneaker Swing Dance Party." It would be her way of thanking the people who had made her feel welcome and celebrating the joy she had discovered within herself.

Posters went up all over campus: "Bring your brightest sneakers and your best dance moves!" Kali's new friends rallied behind her, helping spread the word. Even the Varsity Vibes got involved, offering to perform a choreographed routine to kick off the party.

The night of the event, the student union was transformed into a vibrant dance floor. Strings of fairy lights crisscrossed the ceiling and colorful sneaker cutouts decorated the walls. A playlist of upbeat songs echoed through the space, drawing students in with its infectious energy.

When the clock struck eight, Kali stepped onto the center of the dance floor.

"Thank you all for coming!" she called, her voice steady and strong. "Tonight's not just about dancing—it's about celebrating the connections we've made and the joy we can share."

The crowd cheered as the music swelled. Kali took the first step, leading a simple dance that quickly grew into an exuberant routine. To her surprise, the sneakers didn't take control this time. They seemed to trust her, letting her lead with confidence and grace. Her friends joined in, and soon the entire floor was alive with movement.

The dance party became a night to remember.

People who had never spoken before danced side by side, their laughter blending with the music. Groups formed spontaneously, creating conga lines and circles where everyone took turns showing off their best moves.

Madison danced with Kali, the two of them spinning and twirling with carefree abandon. The skeptical Varsity Vibes amazed the crowd with their performance, and even Professor Cardwell made a brief appearance, nodding approvingly from the sidelines.

Kali stepped back for a moment, watching the scene unfold. It was everything she had hoped for and more. The joy in the room was tangible, radiating from every smile and every step.

In that moment, Kali realized something profound. The real magic was in the people around her.

The sunlight filtered through the glass windows of Ruby's small shop, casting kaleidoscopic patterns on the worn wooden floor. Kali pushed open the door, the familiar chime of the bell ringing above her. The shop still smelled of candles and old books, a comforting blend that felt like a warm hug.

Ruby looked up from behind the counter, her eyes twinkling as if she had been expecting Kali. "Good morning, sunshine," she said with a knowing smile. "What brings you here?"

Kali held up the sneakers, their vibrant colors as striking as ever.

"I came to thank you," she said, her voice steady. "For everything. These, they changed my life."

Ruby stepped around the counter and gently took the sneakers from Kali's hands. "Oh, my dear, it was never about the sneakers. It was about you finding your joy, your courage. These were just a nudge in the right direction."

Kali hesitated, her fingers brushing the edge of the counter. "I think I'm ready now. To start college, to meet new people, to just…be myself. I don't think I need them anymore."

Ruby nodded, her expression thoughtful. "That's the thing about these sneakers. They always know when their work is done. And when it's time, they'll find someone else who needs a little magic."

Kali tilted her head. "Someone else?"

Ruby's lips curled into a mysterious smile. "Joy is a journey, Kali. These sneakers have a knack for finding those who are just starting theirs."

Kali looked down at the sneakers one last time, feeling a pang of nostalgia mixed with gratitude. Then, with a deep breath, she turned toward the door. "Thank you, Ruby. For everything."

"Thank you, Kali," Ruby replied. "For believing."

As Kali stepped out into the bright summer morning, she felt lighter than she had in years.

She wore her own periwinkle blue sneakers and walked away from the shop, ready to embrace the future. Her heart was full, and her path felt clear.

In a cozy corner of Ruby's shop, the sneakers sat on a shelf, waiting. Their colors seemed to shimmer with anticipation. The next morning, a timid young man with glasses and a nervous smile wandered into the shop. He glanced around, his eyes landing on the vibrant sneakers.

Ruby appeared from behind the counter, her smile as warm as ever. "Looking for something special?" she asked.

The young man hesitated, then nodded. "Maybe."

Ruby gestured toward the sneakers. "Try these. They might be just what you need."

As the young man picked them up, a spark of curiosity lit up his eyes. Ruby watched with a knowing smile as he slipped them on.

Closed Doors

VELLA KARMAN

I'm in a standoff with the watercolor painting across the room.

It's a boy alone at a bus stop. He holds an umbrella the color of the sun.

A field frames the bleach-washed sunset billowing across the sky behind him. But you can see he's waiting for a ride. And when I watch him wait, the painting somehow tells me that the bus won't appear for a very long time.

I drop my gaze from the painting and shake the tiny purple balls of popping lavender boba in my drink before I take a sip. The menu called it the galaxy drink.

I wonder if they're watching me drink it right now.

You'd imagine that I could render a name more specific than "my pursuers" to the people chasing me. But that's what they are. Pursuers.

They wear floor-length black robes. They're not from my home, they're human, even though they hunt me like an animal, and I do not *think* either of them are witches.

The front wall of the boba shop is made completely of glass, allowing rays of sunshine to bounce against the art-covered walls and sleek modern floors. The glinting glass door, which I stand next to, overheats in the rays like a purring cat. It's the perfect summer afternoon.

Perfect. Aside from the fact that I'm trapped.

I haven't seen my pursuers at all today, but it doesn't matter if they're here or not because I'm still trapped.

I've only been cursed for six months now. Feels longer.

I've only been chased for six months now. Feels longer.

I've only been a castaway for six months now. Feels LONGER.

It haunts my every thought…I never used to walk through doors in my dreams. Red or otherwise.

No matter how much I wish it, I'm not home. I left my paradise and look what it got me. A curse.

A literal stinking curse (pardon my language).

I know that's not actually cursing. I grew up sheltered. Even though I'm fifteen, a curse word has never escaped my lips.

Another person approaches the door to the boba shop, a college girl with dyed purple hair and soft-looking jeans.

My muscles jerk taut.

The door swings wide with a wave of humidity.

I try to slip through the doorway while the college girl holds it open for herself. Unfortunately, I bump into the invisible wall. And her.

Curses. Now they know where I am.

So far, I'd managed not to alert them to my presence in this city. I drop my head into my palm.

Maybe it's time to give up. To stop the cat and mouse game and join the cats. Instead of finding a new door, maybe they can drag me through the old one.

Or maybe they'll boil me alive in a vat of magic potions.

Who knows what they want…they've never tried to negotiate. In fact, they've never tried to talk to me.

The girl with purple hair is staring. "You didn't even leave." She wrinkles her nose and turns away. That's when I remember that I haven't showered in days.

Bacteria must be building up in my armpits at this point.

I return to my seat at a small window-side white table.

My problem with showering is the limited number of hotels in this town. You see, after I've walked in the front door of a hotel, I can't walk out again. That's my curse. If a door closes behind me, I can never go back through it.

So to use a shower again, I need to find a hotel I've never been to before. Because if I've been there before, I can't walk through the front door. And it's typically looked down upon to enter a hotel through the window.

If I did, they wouldn't give me a room and I wouldn't be able to shower.

Another thing: bathrooms usually only have one door.

That means if I walk in and close the door, I can never walk out. Don't ask me how I'm taking care of the necessities.

One time, I forgot.

It's not so bad after I'm in a hotel room. I leave the bathroom door open because there's no one else around, and it's all great.

My method is efficient. Only, in order to leave the bathroom door open, I have to close the door joining my room to the hallway. So I enter and exit the hotel room through the windows.

It took me at least two weeks to realize I could use windows. It's a pain, because I always need a first-floor room, but it's better than sneaking through back exits and setting off fire alarms trying to reach the dining room for breakfast.

Either way, one time I forgot the curse entirely. I took a half-asleep shower.

I only really woke up when my head jolted upright under the stream of hot water and my brain exploded with the realization that I had no way of getting out.

It was an upright shower, with a glass door and a metal loop for a handle. I'd closed it completely.

The manufacturers had produced the glass with wavy patterns in it. Through the wavy patterns, I saw the door to the bathroom—also completely closed. Curses.

My panicked glance went from item to item in the shower with me. The drain would not allow me passage, it was only three inches wide. The door handle, the hot water, the wavy glass, none of that could be used as a tool for my escape. I felt so alone.

And yeah, I have been alone for the past few months. Away from my family. Cursed. Separate from every other human on the planet.

But I could still ask for help sometimes. The first time I locked myself in the bathroom by accident, I called the front desk and the hotel manager sent the maintenance guy to help me.

He removed the hinges from the doorframe and pulled the door free, which worked.

The curse is weird. I'm unable to walk through if a door shuts behind me, but if the door disappears (thanks to some confused handyman), the doorway is fine.

I couldn't ask some confused handyman to remove the hinges of the shower door though. I was showering! And anyways, I didn't have my phone.

I sat on the floor of the shower and cried. I wasn't even decisive enough to finish showering or just turn off the water.

Every option felt wrong.

Eventually, I realized my phone was probably in the bathroom with me. I shoved my wet face against the glass. It lay there, on the counter. If I could only escape the shower and dress, I could call the front office.

That's another reason I can't stay at one hotel very long. By the second time I've called the front desk for maintenance, specifically door-related maintenance, they watch me with darting eyes.

And I haven't even broken down any doors myself.

I don't think I can. Not that I ever tried to beat down a door before the curse, but I imagine it's easier without a curse. Whenever I try pounding against a door, I feel something pounding back. Every touch of my fist to the surface of the door stings my hand.

After a long time of crying on the shower floor, the air became steamy. I still hadn't turned off the water.

Shivering, I examined the ceiling to see if I would suffocate or if there were enough cracks to breathe.

That's when I noticed the shower door didn't extend all the way to the ceiling. A section of maybe one and a half feet was open at the top of the door.

I'm sure you've never climbed over a shower door without any clothes on, but there's no way of avoiding the fact that it's uncomfortable. Extremely uncomfortable.

Trains are great. Planes are not. (Think about it for a minute. I'm sure you'll understand.)

I slurp up another pearl from my boba drink. Now that I've hit the invisible wall trying to go through the door, I probably only have a few hours before my pursuers show up. It's like they have a radar for it.

The witch told me I need to transport through a red door that looks like home in a city named Persimmon (it's a witchy fruit). Believe it or not, there are four cities in the world named Persimmon.

I already inspected three of them from gutter to mountaintop.

It has to be here, in the last Persimmon. If I find it, the red door will act as a sort of teleportation device. And I will be home and the curse will be gone. Lifted, done with me.

This city echoes home, even the boba shop, with its star-themed menu and glass walls. It's sickening. If I'd started here, instead of the Persimmon in India, I'd have known it was the place.

All week I have scoured the streets of this town, looking. But I've not found many red doors, or even many colored ones. What if the witch was lying?

I stare at the door of the boba shop.

How can I walk through another door? How can I commit again and again to this life of misery?

I jerk my cup in circles across the slick surface of the table and the boba pearls inside roil like a pot of boiling water.

Even if it exists, I doubt I'll ever find it. My pursuers will be here in a matter of hours. Avoiding them will take everything I have.

You know why the witch decided to curse me? Some acquaintances shoved me through the door of her cottage. After glimpsing the witch, I'd flattened myself onto the floor.

The witch had been humming, bent over a desk, hair matted, mist rising from the potions she was mixing in glass tubes.

I'd stayed on the floor of the cottage, the wooden planks roughening my cheek. There was a multicolored rug about five inches from my nose, and on the rug lay a purple stone. A shining, glimmering, glittering stone.

It was a stupid dare.

First to follow them out of paradise, then the whispered taunts as they shoved me into the cottage to "bring back something witchy" because they knew I was "too scared."

They weren't allowed to be right about me.

I'd broken the cobwebbing fear which held me in place, reached out my hand, and clenched the stone in my fist.

But I couldn't decide what to do next.

The witch found me there, still clinging to the floor like a ladybug. "Oh, sssnake sssnuck in, did ssshe?" Her jaw jutted away from her rosy cheeks like she'd eaten one too many toads.

I'd shaken my head, opened my mouth to speak, and no words released themselves from my lips.

The witch had raised her (thankfully empty) hands in pronouncement. "There are sssome doors you don't want to see behind, girlie." And she had cackled. "Once you walk through a door, there'sss no going back...*now.*"

After she pronounced the curse, she'd magicked me away. What she didn't know is that I still had the stone clenched in my hand, like a pearl tucked away inside a clam.

I didn't mean to take it, Witch. Seriously. I'm sorry. Please don't kill me.

I sigh. I don't even know if that's what my pursuers mean to do.

I force myself to stop staring at the last remaining pearls of my galaxy boba drink and scan the room again.

There is the front door and the entrance to the back room. It's covered with a rainbow-colored flag hanging from a curtain rod over the doorway.

This is why I typically avoid restaurants.

Every once in a while, I've found a restaurant with two doors—one marked exit and one marked entrance. I wonder then if anyone else has been cursed like me. Why else would an architect do that?

I've survived because most big grocery stores are built with at least two doors. For example, both Walmart and Target have multiple entrances and exits.

So, how did I end up inside of a boba shop with only one door? On this afternoon, the perfect summer afternoon, I had grown tired of pacing the streets alone. Sweat stuck to my armpits. Giggling groups of girls my age were crowding the sidewalks.

When I saw the boba shop, I stood and stared for fifteen minutes, debating going inside. Even when I opened the glass and metal door, I debated slamming it shut before I passed the threshold.

Now, here I am. No way out, a mostly empty cup of boba in my hand. I've memorized the artwork and floors and tables of the shop.

I pour the last of the popping boba balls in my mouth and the cup is finally empty.

I've never told anyone. It's not like I signed a contract or anything, but nowhere in the curse contract of the witch's doomed predictions did she mention the inability to tell anyone. I just haven't, not even the confused handymen.

I stand and drop my empty boba cup in the silver trash can standing beside the door.

Pretending to appreciate the artwork, I move closer to the back doorway one step at a time. I'm not sure I'll leave. It's one more door I can't walk back through. Why not save my pursuers the trouble?

The interior decorator of this space hung a painting only three feet away from the entrance to the back room. I linger.

Apparently, I linger too close, because someone behind me yells.

"Hey!" The college girl with the dyed-purple hair and the soft-looking jeans stands behind the counter.

"Where are you going?" she says.

I shrug. "What's it matter to you?"

"It looked like you were trying to sneak into the back room."

I lower my eyebrows. "What if I need to use the back door?" I ask. Not that it matters.

The girl with purple hair nods at the front door. "Use *that* door like everybody else."

"What if I can't walk through that door?"

She rolls her eyes and opens her hand to the customer in front of the counter. "Eight dollars and fifty cents."

I've stopped walking, so I guess she assumes I've given up.

I mosey through the slats of rainbow fabric and into the back room. It's dim in the space, storage boxes arrayed along the walls.

I scan my surroundings for an exit to the building.

A hand squeezes the upmost part of my arm. I guess it's over. The fish caught the plankton. At least until the sharks arrive.

The girl with purple hair stands behind me, the rainbow drapes falling across her shoulders. "One sec," she throws at the customer in front of the counter. Then she turns to me, the corners of her lips towards the ground and her eyes fierce. "Look, I need to mix that guy's drink and you're making this hard."

I clench my fists. "I'm. Not. Trying. To."

Those words escape my mouth angry. I guess I do care.

Her eyebrow twitches upward, her jaw tight. In the dim hallway her hair appears black instead of purple.

"I need out," I say in a small voice. "Please."

"Then go out the *door*." She backs into the shop, clearing the curtain from my path with her shoulder as she drags me by the bicep. Her free hand sweeps towards the front door I've already walked through, her hand snapping into position to point at it.

The sensation of drowning creeps upward from the base of my skull.

I've spent two hours in this shop already. Am I really deciding that it's the last place I'll be free?

"I'm cursed!" I yell, my face red in blotchy patches.

I stalk across the shop and to the front door. I wrench it open, using all my weight because of the force of the curse. I am panting now.

I attempt to step through the door, wincing a moment before I feel the burning heat repelling me from the entrance.

My pursuers probably felt that. Heck, it's not like I care if they catch me.

The girl with purple hair follows me. "You're just faking," she says. She shoves me between the shoulder blades. I collide with the invisible wall.

I slide backward, protecting my face with my arms.

Her mouth drops open. After a glance over her shoulder at the counter, she grabs my hand.

This time she walks through the door herself, the arm holding my hand trailing behind her.

When my wrist touches the barrier, her motion stops. It's like a dog reaching the end of its rope, being yanked backward.

She pulls, but I still can't traverse the doorway. The tiny invisible hairs on my arm singe against the white-hot barrier, and I pull my wrist free.

The girl stands on the other side of the door and stares. A summer breeze ruffles her long purple hair. "You weren't kidding."

I intake air, breath hissing between my teeth as I rub my arm. "It hurts." I raise my eyes, and then I see them.

My pursuers are across the street and down the block.

The prolonged attempts to cross the barrier must have drawn them straight to me. The expression on my face doesn't change. My mouth is fixed in a straight line.

The girl with purple hair returns to my side of the doorway, walking as if she has a tail tucked between her legs.

Her voice lowers. "I'll show you the way out."

She leads me through the shop, every customer in the place staring at us, particularly one middle-aged man with a long beard and a scowl. I guess he's the one waiting for his drink.

I stop beside the counter. "You can make his drink first if you want." My heart beats double in my chest.

My pursuers are nearly here and I'm not running.

The purple-haired girl twists around. "Oh yeah. Forgot about that." I can tell that her decision is made before the words emerge from her mouth, butterflies swooping to avoid the outstretched net.

She'll make the bearded man's boba.

Maybe my pursuers will barge in before she's done.

The purple-haired girl gives me puppy eyes and I fix my gaze on the floor. Her sympathy weighs as much as a brick. It could break windows.

"If you would just say 'I'm sorry, that sucks' and move on with your life, that would be greatly appreciated." I grind my teeth.

The girl with purple hair turns her head a few degrees to the side. "I'm sorry, that sucks," she repeats. Then she extends her hand. "My name is Jess."

I shake her hand. "Brooke." She could be the last person to know my name.

I don't know what I'll do. I still don't know what I'll do.

Is this crazy? Is this where I might die?

They're crossing the street now. I see two men in loose black robes. Invisible wind spreads their cloaks in ripples of black velvet like anime villains running twenty-five miles an hour.

My pursuers look like they chase cursed beings for a living, which they do.

Jess has gathered materials from machines and coolers and iceboxes until her plastic shaker is filled to the brim.

She pours the concoction into a cup and hands it over with a large black straw. The grizzled man pounds the straw through the lid, slurps, and turns away.

One of my pursuers pauses on the sidewalk in front of the building.

His eyes flicker like fire.

He surges forward.

I grab at Jess's shoulder with both hands. "Get me out of here. Now!" The tone of my voice varies along with the hitching breath in my lungs.

Her eyes widen. We run.

The rainbow cover blocking the way to the back room slides over my shoulder and we race through dark passageways.

"I'm being chased." I toss in her direction. "By those men. And

I-I don't know where I'll go next, but—" I pant for a moment. "I don't want it to be with them. Not right now."

I follow her hair like a beacon through the maze of boxes in the back room. A dusty haze rises as we bump into boxes, the dust coating each of my breaths like ashes thrown from a burning building by the wind.

At the end, she gestures to a uniformly gray door with a silver handle. "I'll stop them!" she cries, turning. She stomps, planting her foot on the concrete floor. It's as if she's a brick wall. A crash of metal echoes down the maze to where we stand. Jess waves me away with one hand.

I'm staring at the door handle, twisting it, opening the door to release a doorframe of light into the dim backroom. Fresh air washes over me. I pause at the threshold.

For the last six months, I haven't chosen anything in a split second.

In this second, I am the first domino to fall. This unbroken chain of upright tiles, balanced in a chaotic chain, will turn into a toppling cascade of color.

I pull the purple stone from the pocket of my skinny jeans, kneel behind Jess, and place the stone against the side of her left shoe. The polished rock shimmers cold against the foam of her white sneaker.

I stand, pat her on the shoulder, turn to the doorway… .

And I take my next step.

Circus of the Moon

JULI OCEAN

I carefully settled down on my bed. Too much movement made the springs bang and the frame squeak and earned me demerit points from my stepmother, Flavia. Too many demerit points earned me an earlier bedtime—a whole hour earlier, when it was still daylight and the other boys in my neighborhood were playing street ball. In summer, that was the worst punishment, to tuck into bed when the sun hadn't yet shone gold on all the houses.

Kids were still outside playing tag and calling, "Ollie-ollie-ox-en-free!" They were being called to dinner and plating up freshly grilled burgers and Nathan's Famous Franks with ketchup and sweet pickle relish. They were lighting sparklers in the twilight, the sweet and acrid smell of sulfur drifting in the air. They whooped with delight when their parents granted extra time to play after supper.

The air was wild with the approaching night, and bedtime as far off as the coming shadows. Dew-cooled blades of grass licked the palms of their bare feet while they ran, carrying glass mayonnaise jars with holes drilled in the lids, chasing after blinking fireflies.

I didn't usually lie down when Flavia sent me to bed early. I couldn't. There was too much going on out there. I had learned to creep to the window to spy on the fun below, staying out of sight behind thin curtains. The neighbor kids had already stopped ringing our doorbell after dinner, asking if I could come out to play.

Though drop-dead gorgeous, after marrying my dad a year ago, Flavia had developed a super sensitivity to all things noisy, or maybe it was a sensitivity to all things boys. Anytime I made a sound or spoke "too loudly," she put a hand to her head and winced. The neighbor kids said I was unlucky because I had a sick mother. I didn't bother to correct them. My real mom had been buried a long time by then.

This summer night had looked promising. The day had begun hot and sticky, with melted ice cream bars after a lunch of sweet pickle and cold American cheese sandwiches on Wonder Bread.

I had run around the yard with the neighbor kids, pretending to be an airplane. Then I wanted to "fly" past our house on my bike, to feel the wind rocket past my ears and my hair stream straight back. The other kids scattered to grab their bikes and follow.

I started down Big Drop Hill screaming with excitement. I pedaled as though trying to outrun an eighteen-wheeler. None of the other kids were even close behind me. I had already turned around and was halfway up the hill to my house when I heard Dad calling my name.

My yelling had triggered yet another migraine in Flavia. She was presently in bed but had instructed my father that I would be going to bed straight after dinner.

At 4:45 p.m., I said goodbye to my friends, meticulously washed up and sat in my place at the table by five.

"Nolan, do you know why you're going to bed early?"

"Flavia has another headache. She says it's my fault."

While my father quietly cranked open a can of soup, he allowed me to butter bread for cheese toasties.

Dad frowned. I knew that once I went to bed, he would sit in a lawn chair on his rooftop garden. Hidden behind trellises of leafy squash plants, walled in by potted sunflowers, he would put on his headphones and crank up his music as loud as he could stand it. Then he'd secretly smoke funny-smelling cigarettes. Later, he'd sleep on the couch.

"I didn't mean to, Dad. I was outside, half a block away."

"I know, Son."

"No one at Justin's house gets headaches and he's way louder than me."

His voice crouched, like it was keeping its head low to escape notice. "It isn't easy having a stepmom."

"I wish we had a dog instead."

This father-son conversation was supposed to make me feel better, but it didn't. I wished I could send Flavia back to wherever she came from. Almost from the day she moved in, she seemed miserable.

She'd been the only child of a single mother, never had brothers, never had any children of her own. She slept much of the time. When she was awake, she complained about only one thing: noisy me.

I dawdled over my soup and sandwich, happy to be hanging out with my dad, even though we only whispered. I managed to stretch dinner to a quarter past six. I ate the last bite of my sandwich and Dad softly picked up our dishes.

"Go take your shower and I'll be up to say good night."

I climbed the stairs two at a time, mouse-like. Our bathroom had a door that opened onto the roof to a sort of balcony. It ran the length of the house and went past my bedroom window. I wasn't allowed out there unless Dad was with me. After Flavia moved in, he said it was his favorite spot in the house. Dad grew lots of plants: sunflowers, moonflowers, vines, and bushy green plants.

I sat in his spot once. It was almost like being in the woods. Three surrounding walls hid his chair and opened to the starry sky. From his chair he could see Mr. Canetti's front walk, Big Drop Hill, and a deep gorge in the backyard.

When Dad thought no one was looking, he'd sit out there in his little slingback beach chair, hidden in his self-made fort. From my window, I'd see a flickering light and smell something sweet burning. When I asked him about it once, he said it was a meditative incense, our little secret. I liked having a secret with my dad that Flavia didn't know about.

Dad and Flavia's room stood directly across the hall from mine. Their door remained closed even when they weren't in it. It seemed like all Flavia did was sleep and that she wanted everyone else to do the same. Sometimes she would emerge to use the toilet. On those summer nights, she closed and locked the door from the bathroom to the balcony. Later, Dad would come back in through my window. Then he'd go sleep on the couch downstairs.

When I finished my shower, I tiptoed back to my room to dress in clean underclothes. Dad tapped lightly on my door and came in. After prayers, he tussled my hair. After a proper tucking in, he left. Before long, the door creaked in the bathroom and Dad stepped out onto the balcony and got into his chair. I heard the crack of a can opening, then the scrape and spark of his lighter. If I concentrated, I could almost smell incense. I crept quietly out of bed and peered through the window screen. Dad was barely visible sitting amid the moonflowers. I saw the wispy trail of smoke, the backward hiss of inhalation and a stifled cough, then a fog drifted through the plants like tendrils and rejoined in a low-flying cloud that drifted toward my window.

My bed was positioned in the corner between two windows. The cloud rode a slight breeze out the other window and I followed it with my eyes. I sat on the trunk at the end of my bed, watching and listening to the kids in the neighborhood. I even read a Spider-Man comic book while sitting there, until the waning sunlight disappeared completely. I tucked the comic book carefully under the foot of my mattress.

I could still hear my dad on the roof, making the same *ffffffffffft* sound every now and again, followed by a little cloud of burning sweetness that sailed lazily through one window and out the other. I guess he was enjoying his garden as best he could. I wondered if he ever missed playing ball in the park or riding bikes when it was just the two of us. I wondered if he missed Mom as much as I did, even though I was really little when she died.

I shuffled back toward my bed and tripped. I belly slammed the floor so loudly it rattled the windows in my room. Any moment Flavia would burst in telling me how many demerits she would attribute to my latest disregard for complete and utter silence.

She didn't come.

In the dim light, I looked for the cause of my fall and noticed bear paw slippers. Why were they sitting out? I only wore them in winter. It was July. I tried shoving them under the bed with my foot, but they were heavy. In the hazy dark, I crawled to my nightstand and fumbled around searching for the flashlight. When I found it, I shined the light on the floor. Two orangey brown fur feet slippers pointed out from under the bed. I reached down with my hand to push one under the bed and it pulled away.

Odd.

I reached for the other one and when I touched it, it felt warmer than I expected, like someone had recently worn it. Then it moved. *What the…?*

"That tickles."

Where did that voice come from? I looked behind me. No one. Back at the window, Dad lounged in his beach chair, his long monkey feet sticking out beyond the tuberose pots, tapping in time to some beat audible only to him. No one else was out there.

I went back to the remaining slipper, wondering where all my strength had gone, why a slipper suddenly seemed to weigh eighty pounds. When I held it with both hands, a giggle erupted from somewhere. It sounded like it had come from under the bed. I slowly knelt, flashlight pointed forward, and ever so slowly I leaned down and looked under the bed.

And that's when I saw him.

As an underweight ten-year-old, I could fit into a normal-sized vertical locker at school (and behind the pillows of my bed when I wanted to hide from Flavia). I know how uncomfortable it can be for any grown person to be wedged under a bed. I saw two big green eyes, stripey fur and a very long tail. Not the dust bunnies I expected to find.

"Who are you?" I asked.

"I'm Griff. You must be Nolan."

I wondered how he knew my name and how he got under my bed. *When* did he get under my bed? My mind felt like a fireworks display, each spark a question, and now was the grand finale.

"How long have you been under there?"

"Oh…I don't know. I heard you taking a shower." While lying on his side, Griff yawned. His mouth was big enough to stick my whole head in, and his two rows of enormous pointy teeth were gleaming white.

"Are you going to come out and eat me while I'm asleep?"

"No. Little boys don't taste that great, showered or not, unless you have a lot of dragon sauce. I notice dragons are very hard to come by these days. I was just taking a nap before my next mission." Griff stretched out his front paws, which looked very similar to my hands, only twice as big and covered in orange fur.

"I didn't know you were there," I said.

"I'm very good at keeping quiet."

"Maybe you could teach me." I lay down on the floor where I could see Griff better. "I'm always getting into trouble for being too loud."

"When are you too loud?" Griff asked.

Just then I heard Flavia's feet on the hardwood floor.

"Shhh!" I motioned to Griff to stop talking and barely had time to snap off the flashlight and close my eyes before my door burst open.

"What in the world! What's going on in here?"

I looked up at her sleepily from the floor.

"I guess I fell out of bed."

"Well don't just lie there. Get up and get back in it! Some people are trying to sleep and you're disturbing the peace!"

I got up slowly from the floor, sliding under the sheets carefully, worried about squishing Griff. I pulled the sheet over myself and waited for her to leave.

"That will be two demerit points."

"Two?"

"I was sound asleep and you woke me. If you argue I can add one more."

"It was an accident," I mumbled.

"Should I get your father?" She folded her arms across her chest. I shook my head. "That's what I thought. What's that smell?"

"I think I have gas from dinner," I lied. I hoped by some small miracle Dad would notice my light was on. I knew where her next stop would be. Her bladder had awakened her, not me.

"Please be quiet in here, you understand me?"

"Yes."

"Yes, what?"

"Yes, *ma'am*."

She looked around like she expected to find something, then turned off the light and closed the door with a sharp little bang.

She'd say the wind caught it.

Things like that were never her fault. In the next moment, I heard the interior bathroom door close, then the bang of the balcony door slamming shut and being locked. After a time, water ran, the towel bar rattled and squeaked, then she padded across the hallway and back into her room. If I could hand out demerit points, she'd get them for always slamming doors.

I hung my head over the bed, looking at Griff upside down.

"Am I squishing you?"

"Not at all. Who was that?"

"Wait just another minute. Something else is getting ready to happen."

I lay back down in bed just in time to hear my dad fold up his chair and lean it against the house. I heard the door handle rattle from outside and Dad mumbled something under his breath. A moment later, the screen in my window slid up.

"Nolan, you up?"

"Dad?"

"I'm coming through. She locked the door again."

"Okay."

"Just go back to sleep, don't mind me." He climbed in the window and closed the screen quietly. Then he silently opened my door and gingerly shut it behind him. Next, I heard the squeak of their bedroom door. I hung my head over the side of the bed again.

"The first was Flavia, my dad's wife. The second person was my dad."

"She doesn't seem very nice," he said quietly.

"She isn't. By the way, it's safe to come out now."

"Pull my paw." He stuck his orange fur mitt forward and I got out of bed and pulled with all my strength. Eventually, he freed himself from the tight space. When he unfurled himself and stood tall, he was bigger than my dad. He brushed off dust bunnies and ran his enormous paw the length of his tail. He had the head of a lion and the body of a bear. He had leopard spots on his front and stripes on his back and arms. And two giant wings. I gestured for him to sit on my bed.

"What are these demerit points about?"

"It's her way of making me go to bed early every night."

"Bed early? I'm just now waking up."

"Do you sleep all day?"

"Usually. This is my favorite time to go out."

"After dark?"

"Definitely. After dinner and after dark. Oh, it's fun!"

He made the ache in my heart more pronounced. At least the neighbor kids tried to downplay how much fun they had when I couldn't be out with them.

"My dad was going to let me go out after dinner this year since I'm not a little kid anymore. But so far, with Flavia, I haven't been able to."

"But it's summertime!" His eyes shone in the evening glow.

"I know." My smile slipped, my shoulders sagged, and a very long sigh escaped my lips. I stared at the floor.

"I can get you out. That's why I've been sent here."

"Really?"

"I'm not just some super morphing dust bunny. I have special powers. One of them is that I am so quiet no one can hear me."

"I don't believe you."

"Ask me to do something and I'll prove it to you."

Because of my demerits, I'd missed out on dessert for the last week. Flavia made delicious desserts with berries and bananas with pudding, and today she'd made peach cobbler—my all-time favorite.

"Okay… There's peach cobbler in the fridge. I'd like some of that with ice cream. While you're at it, get yourself a bowl too, if you like."

"*Pshhh.* Easy peasy. Wait here."

I couldn't believe my ears. He gave me a big, bird-eating grin and then left through my door. I strained my ears listening for a single sound. Before long, my bedroom door pushed open again and there was Griff. In each hand, he held a bowl of peach cobbler with a glob of vanilla ice cream melting over it.

I quickly pulled him into my room and quietly closed the door behind him. He held out two plastic spoons with his tail. Plucking one, I dipped quietly into the bowl. The cobbler was still warm.

"Plastic spoons?"

"Super stealth eating. Very quiet."

After we finished dessert, Griff stood by the window.

"Now that we're all fueled up, are you ready?"

"Ready for what?"

"Your first big summer night adventure, of course!"

"Outside?"

"Nolan, I thought you were a big boy, ready to go outside."

I looked out the window, wondering what exactly was out there. Now that I had my big chance, fear felt like lead shoes on my feet. The great big unknown was just beyond the ledge of my bedroom window.

"I am a big boy," I said without much conviction.

Griff came over to me and slung his arm around my shoulder.

"The first adventure is the toughest one. I know. I was ten once, too. Tell ya what…" He padded quietly over to the window and slipped the screen open. "Let's just stand on the balcony in your dad's garden. Let's look at the sky."

A smile spread across my face and I nodded eagerly.

"Okay!" I said, starting toward him.

"You might want to put on a little more…" He pointed at me, and I saw what he meant. I was still dressed in just my skivvies. I pulled on a pair of surfing Jams and a T-shirt and held my arms out at my sides.

"How's this?"

He gave me the thumbs-up and then motioned me toward the window. I had never actually seen Dad go out through the window, just come in. It seemed a little tricky. I sat on the ledge and stuck both of my bare feet out onto the roof. The sweet, heady scent of tuberose was heavy in the air, along with butterfly ginger, jasmine, and tiny purple four-o'clocks in earthen pots. I waited on the roof while Griff maneuvered his way out of the window. He was incredibly quiet. He made not a sound.

Everything looked different in moonlight, slightly silvery, softly glowing. It seemed like being awake in a dream. The air was warm and the night seemed to have its own song. Griff stood behind me, hand on my shoulder, while I drank in this otherworldly scene. It felt as though every nerve in my skin was on hyperalert. I waited for Flavia to come rushing out and yank me back inside as though I was some kind of stringed puppet.

Just then, Griff leaned down to my face, so quiet I didn't hear him move, but I felt his whiskers on my cheek.

"Can you hear it yet?" he asked.

"Hear what?"

He looked out of the corner of his eyes and put a finger to his lips. Then he closed his eyes.

"Close your eyes, take a breath as deep as you can…" He pulled in a long, deep breath. I sucked in the night air along with him. It felt magical, full of possibility. A shout now would be heard for miles, it was so still. The birds had quieted and only crickets crooned.

"Hold it for ten seconds and let it out through your nose, slowly… Close your eyes and listen again…and tell me what you hear."

Even after following his directions, I didn't hear anything. I took one more deep breath, held it for ten seconds…let it slowly escape…I heard something. I listened harder.

"Music?" I asked, looking at Griff. A smile wandered over his face and he nodded.

"Where is it coming from?" he asked.

"I don't know, I—"

Griff put his paws up as if to say, *slow down.*

"Just listen."

I closed my eyes again and concentrated with all my energy. I breathed slowly and felt myself calming. Then I heard the music again and it was easy to pinpoint. I opened my eyes.

"It's carnival music and it's coming from over there." I pointed west. The skyline looked brighter there, just over a stand of maple trees. If I tried extra hard, I could almost make out a Ferris wheel through the fluttering leaves.

"That's right! Good." Griff looked toward the western sky then turned to me.

"Is it the county fair?"

"No, it's the Circus of the Moon. It's only open after the sun goes down. Would you like to go?"

"Can I?"

"Of course," he said, shrugging one shoulder.

"How far away is it?"

"A mile, maybe two."

"That sounds far," I said. My shoulders were already giving up on the idea.

Griff chuckled. "You really need to get out more," he said. "If you want to go, we're going."

"How are we going to get there?"

"*Pshhh.* That's the easy part. Wanna go for a ride?"

The light glittered in his eyes and I felt my heart wake up.

Instead of standing tall like my dad, Griff stood on all four paws and lowered his chest to the roof. "Grab my mane and pull yourself up."

The ground looked even farther away when I peered over the edge of the roof. I shuddered and wound my fingers in his hair. Griff looked back at me, teeth glinting in the light of the rising moon.

"You have a tight grip?"

I nodded, and my eyes felt big as pies.

Griff hunkered down and shifted his feet a few times as if finding his perfect stance. I breathed in the night, feeling like a spring coiling up, screwing together tighter and tighter. Then Griff leapt like a giant cat. I felt the cool night air rushing past my ears and my hair plastered flat against my forehead, the rest of it whipping my neck. We were going faster than any bike down Big Drop Hill.

When we didn't immediately land, I opened one eye.

We were flying high above the treetops and heading toward a brightly lit area with a Ferris wheel and a giant wave swing. The lines for the rides were short, I guess because it was late. Most kids would be home getting ready for bed.

Not me!

For the first time this summer, I was out late. No one noticed as we flew nearer to the circus and landed by a string of concession stands. No one gave Griff so much as a lingering look.

"What do you want to do first?" he asked.

"Can we ride the roller coaster?"

"Of course!"

I ran to the line with Griff right behind me. I was taller than the stick they use to measure kids and the operator let me pass. I got in a car near the tail end and Griff got in next to me.

"If you feel like screaming, it's alright. Some people do it just because it's fun. It's practically expected."

"Really? And I won't get in trouble?"

"Flavia will never hear you."

The car lurched forward and began chugging up the track. My

hands clenched the safety harness across my chest as we inched ever upward on the silvery track. By the time we got to the peak, I could see past my house, for a hundred miles in every direction. It lasted only a second. The people in the cars that had gone over the top were already screaming. The car whipped over the top and then I felt like I was looking at Earth from the moon.

I screamed until I was hoarse. Griff rolled his head back and laughed. The cars careened through several curves, one loop de loop and then cruised to a controlled stop where more people waited to board.

"Can we do the wave swing?" I asked.

"Yes!"

Griff seemed ready to ride anything; he was entirely fearless and had a big happy grin on his face. We rode every single ride until my legs felt wobbly.

"I feel like I'm spinning even when I'm standing still," I said.

He stuck out his furry mitt and I held it. When I weaved away from him, he pulled me back. Griff won at Ring Toss and asked me to help pick out a prize.

Aside from the usual stuffed cartoon animals, they had stuffed comic book characters. The Hulk, Captain America, and my favorite: Spider-Man.

I pointed. Spider-Man had Velcro tabs on his hands and I pressed them together so he hung off my back.

Griff led the way to one of the food trucks.

"Ever had an elephant ear?"

"That sounds disgusting!"

"It's all part of the adventure. Everyone will ask if you got one. You really don't want to miss out."

I must have looked unconvinced. He ordered one for himself and began happily chewing. He waved it under my nose and offered me a pinch. It smelled sweet and warm and like cinnamon. It tasted even better.

"Why didn't you tell me they weren't real ears?"

He snickered and ordered one for me. We walked awhile longer, watching other kids running with sparklers and couples holding hands. I noticed people floating above us in swinging ski-lift-type seats. My mouth was full, so instead of speaking (Flavia says it's rude to talk with your mouth full), I pointed.

"Yeah?" Griff asked. "I think it's up ahead."

We got in line to ride the lift. Soon they clicked us into our seats and we were sky bound—like riding in the palm of a giant. We looked down on the sparkling lights lining booth awnings and strung between carnival games, listening to music grow louder and fade away as we passed high above. Somewhere fireworks were shooting off and the sky intermittently brightened with rainbows of bursting light.

"You having a good time?" Griff asked.

"The best ever."

By the time we were getting close to the other end of the park, we had finished our elephant ears.

"I have to get you back soon, Nolan. But there's one place we should go before we leave."

"What is it?"

"A Wish Come True."

"What is that?"

"It's Katu the Invisible. You go into a tiny room and wait. You have to be very, very quiet. If you are quiet enough, a being will appear. If you see him, he has to grant you one wish."

"I thought it was three wishes."

"That's the genie in a lamp. This is different. Only one wish granted in a lifetime. And Katu only comes out if it's absolutely silent."

"I don't know if I can do that. I suck at being quiet."

"You don't. You're really great at it. I think Flavia exaggerates."

As we exited the ski lift, Griff pointed out a banner that said "Katu the Invisible" over a bright blue tent a few yards away. Holding my shoulder, he crouched down to look me in the eyes.

"Trust me, Nolan. You can do this."

It wasn't so much a room as a tent inside a tent. The music and sound of the crowd seemed to disappear as the tent flap fell into place behind me. A string of lights ran in a circle around the top of the big tent, illuminating a sort of mini stage.

On it in the center ring was a trampoline, a small cannon, a lion tamer's chair, and half a dozen tiny bales of hay. Outside of the ring were two more very small tents. I guessed that Katu was in one of them. The room held eight metal folding chairs, fairly close to the little stage. I decided to stand and wait. I breathed so slowly, I doubt my breath would have steamed a mirror.

I thought about my wish. I could wish for a dog, but I felt sure that it would bark and Flavia would be harder on me than ever before. I could wish that I was a much quieter boy, or that my mouth was permanently closed somehow. Maybe I needed to live somewhere else. Maybe Flavia needed to live somewhere else. How could I ask for one thing and get all the things I really wanted? What did I really want?

I wanted to be able to go outside and play and have fun without worrying about Flavia's headaches. I wanted to play catch with my dad and go to the park and go fishing. I wanted to be able to watch movies after my homework was finished during the school year and have my friends come over. I wanted the neighborhood kids to be able to ring the doorbell and ask me to come out and play. And I really wanted a dog.

I thought about all of this while staring at the impossibly small stage. I don't know how long I stood there, but suddenly, I heard a little tiny noise. Someone coughed, then kept coughing. A flap of one of the little tents flew open and a tiny man came out with his back to me, still coughing and hacking. I leaned forward, eyes wide.

He stood about four inches tall and wore a tattered vest with a rumpled shirt and curl-toed leather shoes. He wore no tie or jewelry and his white hair stuck out at odd angles all over his head. In one hand, he held a miniature cigarette. Unaware of me, he bent over nearly double, a long wheeze following each cough until he finally caught his breath. Then he stood tall, breathing in deeply. He put the cigarette to his mouth and turned. When he noticed me, he jumped. His hand immediately covered his heart.

"You scared me. I didn't know anyone was in here!" he said.

I smiled.

"What are you, about ten?"

I nodded.

"Have you been there long?"

I nodded again. I had been taught by Flavia not to speak unless spoken to. I wondered if I would still get my wish if I said anything? He looked at the lit cigarette in his hand and dropped it quickly behind his feet where he stepped on it.

"You didn't see that, did you?" He stifled another cough.

I nodded.

"Aren't you going to say anything?"

"You're Katu the Invisible?"

"Yes." He looked at me and puffed out his chest. "Yes, I am! Who wants to know?"

"I'm Nolan the Silent." I waited to see what he would do next. He looked at me as if he were doing the same.

"So you're really not invisible."

"I'm invisible when there's too much noise. You're the quietest boy I have ever met."

"Thank you. You're the most visible invisible person I've ever seen."

"So I suppose you want me to grant a wish."

"Yes."

"This is a very important decision, Nolan. I can only grant one wish to you for your entire life. You understand?"

"Yes."

"Did they tell you once I grant this, it's irreversible. That means…"

"You can't undo it."

"Good. So you do understand."

"Yes."

Katu stepped inside the other tent and brought out a long thin strip of paper and a little pen.

"Take your time and write it down on this magic paper. Be sure to sign your name. What is your wish, Nolan?"

I took the paper and the pen. I laid it on the stage. Suddenly, the very wish I needed seemed to crystallize into thought and the thoughts became words. After I wrote them, I stared at them on the paper.

I wish my life with my dad would go back to the way it was before he met Flavia.

I handed the paper and pen back to Katu. He read it and nodded once, wound the strip of paper into a tiny little scroll and set it in center stage. He took out his lighter and touched the edge with the flame. In a flash, the paper disappeared.

"You cannot tell anyone your wish until after it happens. Understand?"

I nodded.

"Good luck in your life, Nolan."

"The same to you, Katu."

I waited until he disappeared into his tent and then I exited through the tent flap. Griff was talking to the ticket taker, a very pretty woman with long black hair and catlike features. He straightened up when he saw me, eyes bright.

"How did it go?"

"I got to make a wish!"

"I told you you could do it, didn't I? Tell me everything that happened." As we walked away from the tent I explained every detail of my conversation with Katu, everything except what my wish had been.

We neared the gate where we had entered the circus and he paused.

"Well, Nolan. How was your first summer night of adventure?"

"It was a lot of fun. I had a great time. And you were right."

"About?"

"Katu said I was the quietest boy he had ever met."

He patted me on the head and grinned.

"It's getting pretty late. I think we better be heading back."

I nodded reluctantly. I didn't really want to go back, but I knew my dad would miss me. Eventually, I would miss him too. As I climbed onto Griff's back, I thought about my wish. I wondered how this would all turn out.

"Unfasten Spider-Man's hands and put them in my paws." Griff reached back for them. I placed one in each mitt and Spiderman's arms somehow stretched until they reached around me and Griff like a belt. I splayed my fingers into his great mane and held on. I felt him shuffle a few times and then hunker down and leap.

The stars were bright overhead. I thought I saw the moon smiling as we flew through the starry skies. I hoped that my dad hadn't come back into my room after we'd left. I didn't want to make him worry.

I thought about the days when Dad showed me how to hook a worm and throw it into the lake. I remembered how proud he was of me when I caught my very first fish. He showed me how to clean them and then we cooked them on a campfire near our tent in the woods.

I remembered how close he had been to getting me a dog. We'd looked at some Boston terriers and there were only a few of them left. We couldn't agree on a name that day and we'd gone to a dog park for more ideas.

When Griff and I were over the tops of trees, I felt my eyes getting heavier and heavier. It was the happiest I had felt since my mom died. Even though I tried to stay awake, before we reached home, I'd fallen asleep.

The next morning, I woke up in my very rumpled bed still wearing my clothes. Rain poured outside my window. Lying there, listening to the strength of the storm, I felt content. I woke up slowly, with a pervasive feeling of good fortune. I had traveled somewhere... At first the memories were evasive, foggy and without form. But I kept pulling at them, trying to unravel a jumble of barely defined images. There were stars, a swing, Spider-Man...

Then it came back to me: Griff, sneaking out my window, Circus of the Moon, carnival rides, midway barkers and ring toss, a big, stuffed Spiderman doll. I remembered elephant ears and the lift across the entire circus grounds. Then I remembered Katu the Invisible. It had been a magical night.

I looked under my bed, but Griff wasn't there. He'd said he had been in my room on a mission.

It had been real, hadn't it?

My dad knocked quietly on the door and came in. He noticed the rain puddling on the floor like our collective sadness. He strode to each window and closed them. Then he sat on my bed, hands on his thighs.

"How'd you sleep last night, Nolan?"

"Fine, I guess."

"We didn't keep you up, did we?" he asked, furrowing his brow.

"Keep me up?" I sat up in the bed and scooched next to him.

"Flavia and I had another big fight." Dad closed his eyes and sighed.

"I was probably still out," I said, rubbing my eyes.

"You mean asleep?"

"No, out with Griff."

"Who's Griff?"

I proceeded to tell him about finding Griff and our talk and riding his back to Circus of the Moon, and how he'd won a big Spiderman doll at the ring toss and all that we had done.

"There's no circus in town, Nolan. The county fair is still two months away." He put his arm around me and gave me a sad look.

"Dad, I promise, I was at a circus. I even saw Katu the Invisible!"

"How could you see him if he's invisible?" Dad asked, side-eyeing me.

"He isn't *really* invisible. You just have to be very, very quiet, and then he comes out of his little tent. If you're not quiet, he doesn't come out. Everyone knows that, Dad."

My dad sat there a long time looking at me. He glanced toward the window by my bed, tapping his thigh.

"Was the smoke from my incense blowing in here last night?"

I shrugged my shoulders, pretending I didn't know.

"Nolan?"

"Maybe."

"Son, I know I haven't been a great dad since I hooked up with Flavia. And I took up some stupid habits that I see now were also affecting you. For what it's worth, I'm giving those up." I thought I understood what he meant. "I see now that I was doing things to avoid her, like escaping into my garden, the incense, and some other grown-up things. So maybe what happened last night is all for the best."

"What happened last night?"

"She was yelling and banging doors and stomping through the house…" He paused to look at me, his eyebrows up in the middle of his forehead. "You really didn't hear any of this?"

"Nope. I told you. I was out with Griff."

He looked at me sympathetically for a moment and ruffled my hair.

"Well, anyway, Flavia moved out. She won't be coming back. It just wasn't working for either one of us."

Then I remembered Katu the Invisible and the wish.

"You say Flavia is gone?"

"Yup."

"For good?"

"Yup. She isn't welcome here anymore."

"So it's just me and you like it used to be?"

He nodded. "We can go back to the park and play catch if you're not too grown up to be seen with your old man."

"We can go fishing?"

"Yes."

Just then, the doorbell rang.

"I'll get it!" I bolted down the stairs, hoping it was Griff, here to make introductions so he could hear about how the wish turned out. When I got to the door, I could see it was a woman. I opened the door wide and there stood Flavia. She tried the screen door but it was locked.

"Good morning, Nolan." Flavia said in a tone as brittle as ice.

"Good morning, Flavia. How can I help you?"

"I forgot something, if you could just let me in…"

I checked to make sure the screen door was latched, then crossed my arms. She tried the door again and her face darkened. I shook my head and grinned at her. Her eyes turned to slits.

"I don't think so," I smiled. "Dad said you aren't welcome anymore."

"Now, Nolan…"

"I can get my dad if you like."

"Yes, please do that."

I sucked in the biggest breath I could and then called my dad.

"DAD! IT'S FLAVIA!" I yelled at the top of my lungs. I slammed the door shut in her face and ran up the stairs.

I found my dad still sitting on my bed. His brow was furrowed and the corner of his mouth turned up into a curious smirk as he examined a stuffed Spider-Man doll in his hands.

"She said she forgot something."

"I'll talk to her," he sighed. Then he stood and handed me the doll with a wink. "Make your bed. We're going out for breakfast and then to the park."

I don't think I've ever smiled bigger.

After my bed was made, I started down the stairs. The rain had stopped and I could hear their voices on the front porch. Making my way toward the door, I saw them talking to each other. My dad looked over her head, like he didn't care what she was saying. He shook his head several times, then held out his hand. She took a ring from her hand and stormed off in a huff. She got into her little car and drove away, nearly hitting our neighbor's mailbox.

After she'd gone, he came inside.

"You hungry?"

Dad didn't talk about Flavia again. At the restaurant, he let me order anything I wanted off the menu. The sun came out as we finished our breakfasts, and a little wind kicked up. We drove to the park to play catch and saw how soggy the green areas were. Flavia would never have permitted me to play in a field so drenched and muddy.

"Can we still play, Dad?" I asked.

"I don't care if we have mud up to our knees. We're manly men."

I giggled. "But what if we get mud past our knees?"

"That's what washing machines and laundry soap are for."

We had the whole field to ourselves. After a dozen rounds of catch, mostly spent running after the ball, Dad pitched one just beyond my reach. I leaped to catch it and slipped. I landed on my back, soaking my clothes in the wet mud.

"You okay?" Dad asked, heading toward me. Suddenly he tripped and fell face-first. Dad raised himself up and I stifled a laugh. Muddy water ran down the whole front of his body. Dad looked at me and started laughing.

We were both laughing as he pulled me to my feet and we walked to the car. He spread a tarp from the trunk on the front seats.

As I sat next to him in the front seat, Dad put his arm around my shoulders.

"I missed this," he said.

I just nodded.

Then, slapping my muddy thigh, he said, "We're gonna have the best summer ever." He started the car. We rolled down the windows and drove home with the wind blasting past our ears.

Confessions of a Mermaid Outcast

THIRZAH

It's easy to tell when you're unwanted. Usually, there'll be subtle hints. If you're talking to someone who doesn't like you, they may look to the left, right, up, down—anywhere but your face. They may speak in a tired or bored tone with you, but immediately light up when speaking with anyone else.

They may invite you to parties, or other fun events, as an after-thought—or they may not invite you anywhere at all.

But of course, the easiest way to tell if you're unwanted is when someone tells you so—directly to your face.

I was sitting on my favorite rock, sunning myself, when I heard a splash. When I opened my eyes, my older sister, Pearl, sat next to me. She shook her mane of curly raven hair, spraying me with water.

"Pearl!" I held up my hands in front of my face to block the drop-lets. "Do you really have to do that?"

Pearl laughed. "Perhaps not… But this will probably be the last time I'll ever be able to."

I frowned, lowering my hands. "What are you talking about?"

Pearl tilted her head to the side as her silver eyes met mine. It was one of the only features we shared, passed onto us by a mother who I barely remembered.

"I just spoke with the elders. They've finally decided to expel you from the colony."

The waves crashed against the rocks, over and over again. Seagulls called from overhead, and the sun glinted off the water, and yet somehow it felt like the world around me had halted. My heart felt like it had just been stabbed by the spine of a sea urchin.

"Oh…"

Pearl raised an eyebrow. "That's a far calmer response than I was expecting."

I swallowed hard, blinking back the tears that threatened to sneak into my eyes. "Did they…give a reason?"

"You're simply too much of a hazard to the colony," Pearl said as she combed through her hair with her fingers. "Between your hair and tail, you can't do anything or go anywhere without attracting predators. It's inconvenient for the colony to spend so much time and energy protecting the colony from the beasts that you draw toward us each day."

I slowly nodded. "So…they want me to fend for myself from now on?"

Pearl smiled. "Exactly. You're a fast swimmer, so maybe you'll be able to survive long enough to find a safe place to live."

"And if I can't?"

Pearl eyed me. "What sort of question is that?"

I looked away. "Am I allowed to say goodbye to the others first?"

"Do you really need to?"

"I suppose not…"

Pearl hummed. "Then I suppose that this will be the last time we see each other, dear sister."

Before I could respond, Pearl shifted her position and used her tail to launch herself off the rock and into the air, diving back into the water below. I stared at the spot where Pearl had disappeared, her features etching themselves into my mind. Her black hair, her tail covered in beautiful blue scales.

If I looked even a little bit more like her, would I have been forced to leave? Or perhaps if I was just a bit more useful, had just a few more talents and skills, would the colony believe that I was worth protecting?

I would never know. They had made their decision, and now it was up to me to make mine. I was safe as long as I remained above water, but the moment I dove beneath the blue, I'd face dangers on all sides. The obnoxious whirring of a motorboat interrupted my thoughts and echoed across the waves. I dropped down, laying as close to the rock as possible before peeking up. The motorboat jumped over the waves, following the horizon line to an unknown destination. Two humans were on board, unaware of all the dangers lurking below the waves they traversed.

Stupid, ignorant humans. Swimming, sailing, and playing in the ocean for *fun*. If they had to live the lives merpeople lived, would they still find the water nearly as entertaining?

The motorboat continued to skip across the horizon, getting smaller and smaller. But as the boat slowly moved beyond my line of sight, a thought entered my mind. A thought so wild—so absurd and foolish—that it might actually work.

Getting captured by the humans was far more difficult than expected. Which, knowing humans and what they called "marine technology," made perfect sense. Their sonars and submarines were practically *useless*. Even a mermaid who didn't quite have a pearl in her oyster could easily evade the humans' attention. In fact, I practically had to swim into their nets in order to finally get caught.

But from there, it was smooth swimming. The humans took me ashore to a structure called a "Marine Research Facility."

At first, I was placed into a small tank. Different humans entered the room to examine me.

Was the subject injured?

No.

Was the subject in good health?

They weren't certain, but it appeared to be.

Could the subject understand human speech?

No…but it appeared that the subject had the ability to learn.

I had decided ahead of time to keep my knowledge of the different human languages a secret. It was better if the humans saw me as nothing but a helpless, scared creature who couldn't survive without their help—which was, unfortunately, the truth.

Even the humans seemed to notice.

"The coloring of her hair and tail would make her a target for most marine predators," a man said as he examined my snow-white hair and pearlescent scales. "She and her kind must have very good defense mechanisms to survive in open waters."

"Or perhaps they don't, and their species is going extinct because of it," a blonde-haired woman replied.

The man nodded. "We'll have to do some more research—and send some people to search the area where she was found. Perhaps there are more of them out there."

If the humans knew I could speak, and that I understood everything they said, they probably wouldn't be nearly as open with me as they were now. But that's exactly what I wanted. It was in my best interest that these silly, ignorant humans underestimated me. I'd let them think that I was like any other "marine rescue case." That's how I could keep myself safe.

It was the only option available.

There were seven humans in charge of Project First Intelligent Sea Human—or F.I.S.H. as they called it. The name itself lacked creativity, but I could admire the effort.

All seven of the humans were tasked with seeing to my care, entertainment, or protection. It took a while for me to familiarize myself with all of them, but soon enough, I knew all their names and occupations.

First, there was the "Principal Investigator" otherwise known as Mina Vaughn. From what I understood, she oversaw the entire project. She was in charge of things like "ethics" and "finances." Stuff that was apparently important for project F.I.S.H. to succeed. She was also supposed to make sure that the other members of the project stayed in line and followed the rules—which means that she spent most of her time yelling at the other humans. Especially Gary.

I personally liked Gary.

Or at least, I liked *messing* with Gary. As a "Behavioral Neuroscientist," part of his task was to figure out how I was adapting to my new environment and how I communicated. Why they needed to make a simple task like that into an entire job was beyond my understanding...

Anything with eyes could tell whether or not I liked the aquarium pool that they had placed me in. And did they really need a scientist to figure out that my mouth isn't merely for decoration? Obviously I could vocalize. In fact, I could sing for hours, or have a nice, long conversation with any one of the humans studying me if I wanted to.

But why would I want to? I didn't need their company or attention. All I needed was their protection. There was no need to complicate things.

I ignored all of Gary's efforts to engage with me. Sometimes I just turned my back toward him when he was trying to get my attention. Other times I'd swim around in circles or hide out in one of the fake caves they placed in my aquarium. Apparently, my actions "ruined the integrity of his data"—and is probably why Mina would yell at him so much.

Out of all the humans in the project, I found Finn McAllen the most tolerable. They called him an "Animal Husbandry Expert" but to put it in simple terms, he was the one in charge of everything that had to do with my food—choosing it, preparing it, and even deciding how much of it to give me. Since he controlled my food, it was in my best interest to give Finn as much positive attention as possible—even if it meant swallowing my pride as a mermaid and swimming up to and smiling at him every time he walked by, or performing some sort of underwater maneuver, like a somersault. It must have worked, because Finn started including something called "smoked salmon" with my meals, and it was far better than regular salmon could ever be.

Since arriving at the facility, I had spent most of my time around Cora Johnson and Oliver Vaughn. They were the ones who first examined me. Cora was a "Research Trainer," and Oliver was an "Animal Care Specialist." Both of them were in charge of making sure I was happy and had plenty of things to keep me occupied.

At first I was insulted by their patronizing methods of tossing red and blue spheres into my tank and encouraging me to play with them like I was a child, or placing hoops in the water for me to swim through. But when I spurned their "toys" they adjusted their attempts.

Oliver stuck two vertical lines on the outside wall of my aquarium, then placed two horizontal lines over them, making an open, grid-like pattern. Then he grabbed two "dry-erase markers" and made a circle in the center of the grid. Cora encouraged me to point to one of the open grid slots, and when I did, Oliver handed her one of the markers and she drew an "x" in it. The process continued until Oliver managed to draw three circles in a row on the grid, winning the game that I didn't know we had been playing.

It seemed rather unfair to me—playing a game without explaining the rules. But Oliver used the bottom of his shirt to wipe off the marks on the grid, and we played again. This time, *I* got three Xs in a row, and won. So all was well with the world.

Eventually I learned that the name of the game was tic-tac-toe, and it became one of our regular activities.

The last two members of the team were Lina Errins and Todd Barnett. Lina was a "Marine Veterinary Technician" and Todd was a "Doctor." Lina was used to taking care of sick animals, while Todd took care of sick humans. Apparently they weren't sure who would be better to take care of me, since in their minds I was half human and half fish, so they had simply hired both human and animal healers.

Nobody who was part of project F.I.S.H. had any idea how to treat me—more like a human, or more like a creature of the sea. But since almost everyone on the team had worked with dolphins before joining the team, they used a lot of their previous knowledge to engage with me.

In fact, being the shallow-minded and ignorant beings that they were, the humans seemed to think that I shared a *lot* of similarities to those cunning creatures. I would never admit it out loud, but if I was being honest, I could understand why. After all, I was *far* more intelligent than a fish, *and* I also had a tail. But unlike dolphins, my tail was covered in pearl-like white scales that shone blindingly bright under direct light. I also had a human-like torso and features—nose, eyes in the front of my head (instead of the side), hair, and ears. Though, my hair was long and white, which seemed to be as rare of a color among humans as merpeople.

And my ears, while they were on the side of my head like the humans' were, had a fin-like appearance, and were the same pearlescent color and sheen as my tail. And unlike dolphins, I didn't communicate with clicks and whistles. I couldn't use echolocation, and I certainly wouldn't die just from being out of the water for a couple hours.

But since the humans had no other creatures to compare me to (I wasn't even going to acknowledge the manatee remarks), it was difficult to fault them for their ignorance.

After moving me from the small examination tank, they had placed me in a huge dolphinarium within the marine research facility.

As the name would suggest, the dolphinarium was a large aquarium ordinarily used to house dolphins, but they had quickly adapted it to suit me. It was two decks high and oval in shape. The top of the aquarium was open, and on that floor, there was a ramp, similar to the ones used for boats at docks. My meals would be served by the ramp, and I would eat while sitting on it. It wasn't quite the same as sitting on my favorite rock, but it was still nice. There was also an underwater gate leading to the outside portion of the aquarium—though it was locked.

The part of my aquarium located on the first floor was far different from the second. The bottom of the oval tank was filled with sand, pebbles, and shells. They had placed fake coral and rocky cave-like structures at the far end of the aquarium, against the wall. There was also plenty of seaweed growing.

The aquarium faced an "observation room"—a long and somewhat narrow space with a couple desks and workstations. The room was open, only broken up by the three equally-spaced rectangular pillars that supported the second floor. The middle pillar had a big, black rectangle mounted to it. On either side of the observation room were doors. The door to the right of my aquarium led to the "offices," while the door to the left of my tank led to the "laboratory."

All in all, my first few days among the humans weren't horrible. I had plenty of food that I didn't have to hunt for, places to hide and rest—away from the humans and their prying eyes, I didn't have to constantly be on the lookout for predators, and nobody blamed me for putting others in danger simply for existing.

While my situation still wasn't ideal, it was far better than fending for myself in the ocean or enduring the stares and snarky comments of my fellow merpeople.

No, compared to all that, lowering myself to live at the mercy of the humans was preferable. And while the humans were performing all their tests and examinations on me, I was doing my own tests and experiments…on *them.*

Besides messing with Gary, I had plenty of other ways to test the humans running project F.I.S.H.

All I had to do was try things out and see how they reacted. With Oliver and Cora, I'd be enthusiastic about their games and plans one day, then act shy or disinterested the next.

But to my surprise, this experiment yielded bizarre results. When it became clear that I didn't intend to participate in their games, Oliver and Cora began to talk to one another while I studied the pearly-white scales on my tail and pretended to ignore them.

"Maybe she's bored of tic-tac-toe?" Cora suggested. "We've probably played it with her well over a hundred times by now…"

Oliver stuck his hands in his pockets, glancing in my direction. "True… We should try something else while we wait for the packages to arrive."

"Why don't we try playing her some music, or turning on the

TV?" Cora pointed up at the large black rectangle mounted to the pillar across from my tank. "I'd like to see her reaction to technology, and it's possible that the more exposure she gets to our language, the more she'll want to try using it for herself."

Oliver tapped his foot against the blue floor of the observation room. "True..." he admitted. "I've worked with some dolphins in the past who appeared to really enjoy watching television or listening to the radio. But I suppose the real question is, do we really want to get a mermaid hooked on soap operas or rock music? Since she shares more human traits, I don't want to risk exposing her to the wrong media..."

"Why don't we start with nature documentaries," Cora said. "Or we could have her listen to some classical music."

Oliver nodded. "Exposing her to educational content might help us break through the communication barrier... At the very least, I suppose it's worth a try... All right." He straightened. "I'm going to ask Mina if we can borrow her CD player and her Vivaldi and Mussorgsky collection. Can you find the remote and look for a good documentary?"

Cora blinked. "Your sister has an entire collection? I'm not sure what type of music I assumed she'd listen to, but—"

"Oh, she *loves* classical music," Oliver said. "We used to go to a lot of concerts and ballets with our parents when we were younger. It brings back fond memories."

As Oliver finished speaking, the door leading to the laboratory opened, and Mina entered. "What's going on here? Is there a problem?" Her hard-soled tennis shoes tapped against the shiny blue floor as she walked toward the small group.

Oliver smiled. "Oh, we were just discussing some alternate ways to keep our guest occupied until our new supplies arrive."

Mina raised an eyebrow. "All right, what have you come up with so far?"

"We were thinking it might be nice to introduce her to some nature documentaries or some classical music," Cora explained, glancing at Oliver.

Mina hummed. She turned to face my aquarium. I lay on my back in the water, flicking my tail up and down, propelling my body back and forth along with it.

Mina turned back to the others. "Fine. Just be sure to document everything and let Gary know. I've just spoken to maintenance, and they said that the outdoor section of the aquarium will be ready for use within the next week."

"Really? That's great! The water toys we ordered should have arrived by then," Cora said, smiling. "If our mermaid friend is feeling more comfortable around us by then, then perhaps we can make a pool party of it."

Mina raised an eyebrow. "A pool party?"

Cora nodded. "Why not? It might be a great way for all of us to bond with her."

Mina sighed. "Plan your party, just don't go overboard." She stole another glance at me, then turned back to the others. "I have some phone calls to make. Don't forget to document everything." She started walking toward the other end of the room without waiting for a response.

As the door leading to the offices shut behind her, Cora turned to Oliver. "I'm surprised she didn't shut that idea down immediately."

Oliver blinked. "Oh, you mean about the pool party? Well it's a genuinely good idea. We've all been cooped up inside this facility for days now. I think it'll be good for both our guest and ourselves if we can get some sun."

I knew what music was. I had heard plenty of motorboats and yachts blasting the stuff out across the open ocean. Some of it was tolerable, but a lot of it simply didn't appeal to me. I wasn't familiar with the "TV" but it sounded interesting—and from what I could tell, it was probably similar to the smaller devices that humans carried around. The "laptop computer" and the "smart phone." I would have liked to examine both devices for myself, but apparently they don't operate in water very well—just like books.

But if a "TV" could be enjoyed from within my tank, then perhaps I really *would* like it.

As for the "pool party" that the scientists discussed, it sounded…bizarre. Did humans usually host parties around pools of water? Was it some sort of ancient tradition? I knew they enjoyed spending time at the beach—laughter was a common sound to hear if one was swimming anywhere near a populated area during warmer weather—but parties?

I was familiar with parties. My fellow merpeople often hosted at least one celebration per moon cycle. Sometimes it was to celebrate the birth of a new member of the colony, other times it was to honor someone's heroics. Those parties were open for the entire colony to attend.

My sister and her friends would often host their own private parties, but I was almost never invited to them. The one time I was allowed to attend, it was because my sister was hosting the party, and I begged her to let me.

I shouldn't have bothered. Nobody actually wanted me there. Even my sister.

No, I didn't have any fond memories of parties. "Pool" related or not. But if the humans were so excited to host one, then maybe there'd be something good about it. I just needed to be careful and not get my hopes up too high.

They had been dashed against the rocks like ships during a storm, time and time again as it was.

~·~·~

Perhaps I was a bit too hasty with my degrading remarks about human technology. Yes, their "sonars" and "submarines" were sub-par and unimpressive, but after nearly an entire week of watching the "TV" I had to admit that not all human inventions were useless.

The TV expanded my entire world, making it seemingly endless. One moment I was watching kangaroos hopping around the Australian outback, the next I was watching enormous snakes slithering around the Amazon rainforest or watching a desert scorpion strike at its prey.

Land was far more beautiful than I could have ever imagined. Canyons, rivers, valleys, snowy mountains, and forests… Some of the colors I saw were as vibrant as the coral reefs I grew up admiring.

The planet I lived on was bigger than I thought. There was so much I didn't know—so much that I wanted to learn.

I always thought that humans were ignorant because of how little they knew of the sea. But after witnessing for myself just how little *I* knew of the land, it no longer seemed appropriate.When I wasn't watching TV, I found myself interacting more and more with the scientists. Cora and Finn brought in different animals to introduce me to—a cat, a dog, a bearded dragon, a parrot, and a chinchilla. They could all only breathe air, so I didn't get to swim with them, but I got to hold or pet some of them while sitting on the ramp on the upper deck of my aquarium.

I had never felt anything as soft as the chinchilla's fur. And while the cat did unnerve me when it started licking my tail (I had seen on TV that cats like to eat fish), I felt far more at ease when it laid purring in my arms.

Later on in the week, I shocked Gary by humming a song. He was so surprised that he nearly forgot to document my "vocalization." But luckily he remembered, and for once, Mina didn't yell at him.

Under the supervision and support of Dr. Todd and Lina, Finn opened up my meal options to some of the foods that regular humans eat.

If I thought that smoked salmon would be the best food I ever tried in my entire life, then I was dead wrong.

The most delicious, most flavorful, most wonderful food I've ever eaten (so far) is the mango fruit.

I had never tasted anything so sweet and juicy until the moment Finn offered me the small, orangey-yellow cubes to try.

Out of all the scientists, I spent the least amount of time with Mina—though I saw her often enough, coming and going, on or off the phone. But every time she passed by, she'd glance over at my tank, looking to see where I was.

So I was surprised when, the night before the "pool party" was supposed to take place, Mina came in and sat down in a metal folding chair Oliver and Cora had left sitting in front of my tank in the observation room.

I swam over, resting my tail against the sand at the bottom of the tank to balance myself.

Mina looked at me and smiled. It wasn't her usual grimace, or one of the tight-lipped smirks she usually gave people, it was a genuine, bright, and open smile.

"Hi there," she said, her voice quiet. "I know I haven't spent a lot of time around you, but there's a reason for that… Do you want to know what it is?"

I almost nodded, but stopped myself just in time, staring at her blankly instead.

Mina glanced around, then leaned closer toward the glass. "I want to be your friend."

I blinked. Of all the people in the research facility, Mina was the last person I would have expected to hear anything like that from.

"But the thing is, it's unprofessional—and slightly unethical to befriend the subject of ones' research," Mina continued. "I've seen it ruin studies in the past, so I've always tried to be as careful as possible. But in your case, I'm a little lost. There are protocols for dealing with animal subjects, and even more protocols for dealing with human research participants, but there aren't any protocols for dealing with mermaids. I've been doing my best to keep my distance, and ensure that no boundaries are crossed, but I'm not sure that I'm making the right decisions." Mina studied me. "From both the data collected, and from my own observations, I've come to the conclusion that…you've been lonely."

I continued staring at Mina, reaching up to move my flowing hair behind me.

"I…know how that feels," Mina admitted, her voice quiet. "I've been lonely too—even with my brother around. My work takes up the majority of my life, and I've never felt right about befriending my coworkers, so…it's just been me. But maybe that will change one day. Maybe I'll be able to figure out some sort of work-life balance that includes friendship. And maybe…we can be friends. At least until you can find yourself some more." She tilted her head to the side, her green eyes meeting mine. "How does that sound?"

I slowly reached my hand out, laying it against the glass of my tank.

Mina's eyes widened, then her expression melted into another smile. She extended her arm, placing her hand on the other side of the glass, over mine.

"Very well then," she whispered. "Friends it is."

After Mina finally left, I swam back into the cave I preferred to sleep in, but sleep itself eluded me.

The scientists often referred to me as their "mermaid friend," though I had never taken their words seriously. But now, I *officially* had a friend.

Now what? What was I supposed to do with that fact? And what exactly were friends supposed to do?

My sister and her friends would spend a lot of time together—hunting, exploring, or just hanging out with each other. Hunting was unnecessary for me since all my meals were provided by Finn, and though my aquarium was rather large, there wasn't a lot to explore (and even if there was, Mina could only breathe air). As for hanging out, sitting in front of my aquarium and talking to me probably wasn't the most interesting activity in the world.

My sister and her friends would talk and laugh with each other, or sing together. But I had chosen to keep my knowledge and use of the human language a secret. So what was I supposed to do? Could I really be Mina's friend if I didn't do any of the things that friends would normally do with each other?

I fell asleep without an answer to any of the questions swirling around in my mind. I was so caught up in my thoughts that I completely forgot about the planned "pool party" until the gate dividing the inside of my aquarium pool from the outside opened and Oliver, Cora, and Gary encouraged me to go explore. As I swam out into the sunshine, the rays of light glinted off my scales and warmed every inch of my body—inside and out.

The outside part of my aquarium pool was a large, gourd-shaped area surrounded on all sides by white concrete. There were four blue pool chairs on either side of the long part of the pool.

A white table with a blue umbrella sat between each pair of chairs—meant to provide humans with shade and a place to put their snacks and beverages.

Unlike the indoor part of my aquarium, the outdoor area had no sand, rocks, or plants. Instead, the entire area was a vivid blue color. The only decoration was a rocky structure in the center of the pool, similar to the one I used to sun myself on back when I lived in the ocean. I immediately swam over and pulled myself up onto the structure.

The entire pool area was surrounded by a tall fence that was impossible to see over. Seeing as my existence was supposed to be kept a secret from the outside world, the sturdy fence made sense. Though it would have been nice to see more of the outside world above the waves. But even with the fence blocking my view, I could tell we were close to the sea. The scent of salt lingered on the breeze, seagulls squawked—a few even flew overhead, and the distant chorus of waves washing up against the beach filled my ears. If I closed my eyes, I could almost picture that I was back in the ocean.

The thought made my chest tighten. Not from longing, or regret—but dread.

"Do you think she likes it?"

I opened my eyes. Gary and Cora stood at the edge of the pool, watching me. Both of them wore black and blue wet suits.

Cora smiled and waved at me. "Yeah, I think so," she said, glancing at Gary. "She probably just needs to get used to being back outside. It seems Oliver was right about the sunning hypothesis. Seems some of the mermaid myths really are based in truth."

Before Gary could respond, the back door to the facility flew open and Mina appeared, carrying a platter of smoked salmon and a bowl full of fruit—including mango. She stuck her foot out to catch the door before it could slam back into her, and then Oliver appeared behind her, reaching out to keep the door open as Mina walked toward the nearest table.

Gary grinned. "Is that for us, or our mermaid friend?"

"I'll give you three guesses," Mina said, placing the dishes down on the table.

"Finn really went all out today," Cora said as she examined the food.

Oliver smiled. "Well, it *is* a party. Speaking of which, I believe Todd and Lina are working on getting *our* food prepared. I'm going to go grab the water toys."

"I'll join you," Cora said as the two of them headed for the door.

"Hurry back!" Gary called after them. "It's about time that we get this party started!"

Twenty minutes later, I understood why Cora was so excited about the idea of having a pool party.

Oliver had brought out the water toys he had talked about. There was a large blue, yellow, red, and white sphere called a "beach ball," and for a while we played with it—hitting the lightweight beach ball around in a circle, faster and faster until someone inevitably dropped it. After that I enjoyed my meal of salmon and fruit. Then, Oliver offered me something called a "water gun" and from that moment on, *no one* was safe from me.

With everyone scrambling to get out of range of my water gun, Mina's warnings of "no running in the pool area!" fell upon deaf ears, but once I hit her square in the face with a blast of water, I knew I had made a mistake.

Next thing I knew, *I* was under attack. Mina caved in pretty quickly for someone who was strict about "ethics" and "professionalism."

She had two extremely large water guns, spraying me at full blast in the blink of an eye. I finally had to dive back into the pool just to escape her wrath.

When I resurfaced, everyone was laughing, and Mina's face was completely red.

"I'm so sorry," she said to me. "I didn't scare you, did I?"

"*I* was scared and I wasn't even the one who you were shooting at," Gary said with a wide grin on his face.

Mina glared at him. "Would you like me to change that?"

Gary threw up his hands in surrender. "Nope! I know better than to start a war that I can't win."

I ducked my face back beneath the water to hide my laughter. My...*laughter?*

When was the last time that I had laughed?

I rose back up, watching the different members of project F.I.S.H. interact with one another. No one looked awkward or out of place. No one looked like they'd rather be anywhere else. Even Gary seemed to enjoy himself—Nobody here was alone or unwanted. Not even me.

When I lived in the ocean, even when I was surrounded by my family and the others in my colony, I still felt alone. I was either barely tolerated, ignored, or scorned. I deserved their treatment of me. Or at least, I thought I did. If I couldn't be useful to the people in my colony, then what right did I have to be treated like a valuable member?

And yet, here I was among the humans. The beings who I had always thought of as ignorant, obnoxious, and selfish.

Somehow, they were far more welcoming and accepting of me than my own kind. From the beginning I had set out to deceive them, and to this day, they still believed me to be a helpless, mute mermaid. What did they really have to gain by treating me so well? Why did they care so much about earning my trust? If research was all they wanted, they could keep me in a small tank and feed me nothing but sardines.

But Mina, Oliver, Cora, and the rest of the group decided I was worth more than the bare minimum.

While my own sister thought of me as a useless hazard, these humans saw me as someone who deserved care and respect. They saw me as a potential friend.

Despite living in a tank, somehow I was more free now than I had ever been in my entire life beneath the vast sea.

Even if I had the opportunity—even if I woke up one day and my scales and hair were more like the rest of the colony's, I wouldn't want to go back.

The marine research facility was home, and each member of Project F.I.S.H. had begun to feel like a friend to me as well—even Gary.

But if I was going to stay here, if I was going to accept these humans as my new colony—my new *family*—I couldn't keep hiding the truth.

I swam up to the side of the pool and pulled myself up so that I sat on the concrete. Everyone's conversations stopped, and all eyes turned to look at me. I glanced around at the seven members of Project F.I.S.H., took a deep breath, and smiled despite feeling like an entire school of fish was swimming around inside my stomach. "Hi…" I said, as everyone's faces filled with shock. "My name is Shell, and there's something you should know about me…"

Gravitational Issues

VANNAH LEBLANC

A phenomenal weight crashed against my chest as I woke up.

Cracking my eyes took a phenomenal effort. Not in the usual way that eyes want to lead the body back to sleep on early mornings. No, it was as if my eyelids themselves were coated with lead.

Like my whole body was.

What is…?

I stretched under the covers and they felt odd against my skin. The mattress pressed into me; or did I press into it? I pinched myself, but when it turned out that this was not a dream, I forced myself to get up. I had to push my body up and off the bed and when my feet hit the ground and I tried to rise, I found myself on the floor, as if it pulled me down. *Pinned* me down.

…What in the world? My thoughts themselves seemed thick, as if stuck deep in molasses.

I looked around me. My heart pounded, but the rest of my room around me seemed normal: my bed hovered a couple of inches over the ground, as did the clothing I had left lying around my room. My dresser sat tethered to the floor by its usual binds, and my phone drifted around its charging cable. As usual, all the objects that interacted with us human beings or animals, floated just a little off the ground. The ground itself, of course, was not included in the floating part, unless you counted our planet floating in space. Natural Levitation, some called this phenomenon. To me, it was simply life—until now.

I stretched my arm to take hold of my cell phone, but the floor pulled at my arm too. I let out a breath, forcing my fingers around the device anyway and finally taking hold of it. Thank goodness it turned on normally, the scratched screen lighting up to its usual lock screen picture, depicting my best friend's tiny dog, Molly, running above the long grass in a neighboring field. In the photo, Leila and I both hopped after the dog, laughing. That morning had been so much fun.

The first thing I did with my phone, of course, was call my mom.

It was early; the morning sun barely poked through my blinds. Mom picked up, I sighed in relief, and the sigh itself felt like it was dragged toward the floor. What was happening to me? My heart beat faster and that cleared my head just enough to remember to speak.

"Mom?"

"What is it, Cassava?" her sleepy voice asked.

"Mom, there is…there are like…*tendrils of force* pulling me to the ground. It's as if…as if I was bound to it!"

I heard movement in my parents' room as weighted blankets were pushed back. I heard a fluttering over the hardwood floors coming down the hall. Finally, a knock at my door. By that time, tears had flooded my eyes and were dripping *down* from my cheeks.

"Come in?" my voice shook, and the more I tried to move, the weirder I felt. In a desperate attempt, I managed to pull myself to my feet by leaning on my desk chair as the door creaked open. My mom paused there, her fluffy slippers barely touching the floorboards. She combed a couple fingers through her staticky hair and let out a quiet yawn.

"What's the matter?"

I let go of the chair, took a step or two, and tumbled back to the floor just like a clumsy toddler. Hadn't I learned to walk ages ago?

"Oh, honey." My mom's voice echoed against the hardwood floor I had just faceplanted onto. She walked over to pull me back to my feet and her own were brought forcefully against the ground as she helped me up.

"This happens to some of us," she explained. Concern creased her eyebrows, but her features did not reflect any of the confusion that I felt. "It's called gravity."

Well, at that moment, the whole gravity of the situation—no pun intended, as those are of extremely bad taste, according to Leila—dawned on me. I felt even heavier as I understood the full scope of what was happening to me. Gravity? What a dreadful thing! It wasn't supposed to affect us humans. At least, very little. It did not affect our pets, either, or our homes, or our entire *lives*! Things floated; that was how it was meant to be, wasn't it?

Wasn't it?

"What…what do I do?" I asked. My thoughts crashed in a jumble, one over the other in a tangled mess. Mom looked at me, and it was compassion that pulled at her smile lines. Was this truly the right time to smile?

"Unfortunately, there isn't much to do, my love." This time, I didn't even roll my eyes at being called her 'love.' My mother went on, "I suggest you just go about your day. Things should return to normal on their own."

So I did. I dragged myself over to my dresser, where I pulled the first pair of shorts that floated up from the drawer: formerly grass-stained jeans that Leila and I had DIYed into shorts by cutting them just above the knees. Then I pulled a mostly clean T-shirt over my head. This wasn't how it was supposed to be. This wasn't—

The doorbell rang and I knew I was behind schedule. As Mom

opened the door downstairs, I heard Leila's voice asking for me. It was the last day of school and we were going to walk together, grabbing a slushy or something to celebrate along the way.

Huffing, I hurriedly pinned my hair into a bun and strands fell out—falling downwards. When I took hold of my backpack, it somehow crashed against me, adding to the already dizzying weight.

"Cassavaaaaa!" Leila's voice chimed with a tonality similar to that of the doorbell.

Tumbling down the stairs hurt more than I would have imagined. It seemed like there, gravity grew even fiercer, able to pull me lower toward the ground, and it revelled in that cruel deed. I practically *crashed* in front of Leila, then offered a wan smile. Still, I responded with the same tone. "Leilaaaaaaaa!"

The sarcasm almost didn't show in my voice—almost.

"Well, we won't have time to grab slushies if we don't leave now," Leila said. Then she took a step back and looked at me as I pushed myself up from the floor with both my hands. "What is wrong with you?"

"Slushies?" my mom interrupted, eyebrows raised.

"Oh, it's just our way to celebrate, Mrs. Armstrong!" Leila chimed.

My mom still scowled, but let it slide. "Make sure to at least eat something healthy before school, I don't want you to have all that sugar sitting on an empty stomach!"

And we were off. About a whole five steps onto the street, I had to stop to catch my breath and the straps of my backpack dug into my shoulders like knives. I laid it down and it floated beside me.

"You could just try pulling it," Leila suggested, her eyebrows still raised at weird angles in an expression I couldn't quite pinpoint.

But as soon as my fingers touched the bag, gravity caught hold of it again, and it crashed to the ground.

Leila rolled her eyes and swung my backpack to her other shoulder, carrying both our bags—weightless to her as her slightest tug pulled them along by the straps. They hovered behind her, as if mocking me. My friend, too, had a smirk on her lips. "Well, aren't you an interesting creature."

Leila called everyone and everything creatures—still, at the moment, the remark stung. Wasn't it enough that I had to carry myself? I proceeded to show my annoyance by being much less chatty than usual. Not that I could have been very talkative even if I wanted to. Breath came with difficulty, and words were all but out of reach.

By the time we reached the end of the street, sweat dampened my T-shirt. And by the time we reached the corner store to buy our frozen drinks, I was downright panting, worse than Molly after a whole hour of floating around in the field. Still, everything else around me hovered slightly over the ground, nearly unaffected by the Earth's pulling force. Why was it targeting me? What had I done? I really didn't like this experience. I really—

As if the day couldn't get any worse, I managed to make a mess in the corner store.

As Leila finished paying, she tucked the extra change into her pocket and zipped it so the money wouldn't float out. Then she handed me my slushy: a big, shiny, plastic cup with beads of water condensing along its edges. My own throat was parched and I tipped the cup eagerly.

Usually drinks, when tipped, would bubble out into the air and the droplets would be easy to catch with my mouth. That's how people *normally* drink. But when I did that, the bright blue goo fell straight onto my T-shirt and, as if moved by a life of its own, slid down the fabric until it crashed at my feet with a very sad *plop*.

"Well, ain't *this* gonna make a grand entrance in school," Leila said hesitantly, looking at my now-spotted shirt. Her chirpy demeanor had toned down a bit, thank *goodness*. I could not have kept up with it.

She put an arm around me—a light, weightless arm. But when I tried to lean on her, she stumbled and almost fell to the ground with me and the remaining drink.

She frowned. "Let's make it to school, shall we? Maybe…someone there will know how to help you?"

The hope was feeble, but worth a try. Not that this try was easy. With each step, it felt as if I was carrying the weight of the whole world on my shoulders.

And maybe I was.

In class, my feet hurt, the vertebrae of my spine compressed on themselves, and sweat soaked my T-shirt. As my teacher asked me to stand to answer a question, my knees buckled under my weight and, next thing I knew, I was on the floor again. My classmates, too full of energy on this last day, were laughing, and sweat poured down my back. I bit my lip.

So that's how the summer started.

Even though Mom had said that things would likely go back to normal on their own, they didn't. Even the specialist my parents took me to a good week and a half after the end of school couldn't do much. He told me to stay active if I could as I waited for things to return to normal. Assuming that they would. Even for this, there was no guarantee. I wanted to cry right there in his office. I squeezed my eyes shut in a long blink and tasted tears.

I learned to live with the weight. Every morning, the strength of our planet dragged me down as I tried to clamber out of bed. And every morning I would rise anyway, the weight settling on my shoulders like a flood after a tidal wave. I stood in front of my mirror, combing the tangles out of my stubborn locks. My clothing hung on me like dried-up rags on a clothesline, and my hair didn't catch in every gust of air like other people's. And when I found myself a summer job selling hot dogs on the beach in a little stand held down with old ropes, the heat seemed to tire me out even faster than it did other people, as they floated along the coastline and I had to walk.

I spent the best days of summer sitting alone in the thin shade of the stand's roof, my boss off wandering somewhere, supposedly trying to attract customers. Whatever technique he used, it didn't work. I had loads of time between customers. Alone, my thoughts ached as much as my feet.

And then, one scorching day, I met Martin and he made me laugh.

Martin was about my age, maybe a year or two older. He had large, blue eyes and ears that he could wiggle on demand. Despite his casual air, the first thing I noticed about him was the way that he leaned against the lifeguard's ladder, strong and frail at the same time. Both his feet were firmly planted in the sand.

As the boys of the group he was half part of skipped in the sand, tossing volleyballs and jumping over waves like a skipping rope, Martin watched, slumping more and more against the wooden ladder, his feet digging grooves into the sand. Clearly, he wished he could join, but something kept him from it.

After awhile he walked over to my stand, where I sat, not having sold a single hot dog that morning. He asked for fries. I had chips. He nodded in compromise.

We shared a bag under the stand's sunshade, both bored enough to ignore the fact that it was totally awkward to share one small, half-filled-with-air bag of potato chips with a total stranger in the shade of a totally isolated and decrepit food stand on an otherwise totally sunny and crowded beach.

"You know, I often see you here, selling hot dogs," Martin said once the chips were gone and an awkward silence had settled instead of the crunching. At least he was nice enough to say "selling hot dogs" and not "pathetically awaiting the far-off day where this stand actually fulfilled its one purpose."

"What else do you do in the summer?" He started scrunching up the empty chip bag in his hands, looking at me as if what I might say was much more interesting than any chips or fries.

The words "I love sports" raced to my mouth, but I choked them back before they came out. I *used* to like sports. Now I burdened any team I tried to join, with both my feet planted and my reflexes stiff from the heaviness that coated every movement. I was useless. Even Leila, who had tried including me regardless, had eventually given up. It's not like I had particularly encouraged her efforts, but still.

"I like to sit and watch," I said finally, my voice as flat as the food stand's bank account must be. It was a wonder the thing was still running.

"Then you're right in your element!"

"I suppose I am," I said. A gust of wind blew across my hair, and I lifted my chin just a little higher.

A smile lit up Martin's blue eyes. He was a strange-looking lad, like my dad would say, so tall he looked like he might fall over when he stood, and with many, many dimples when he smiled. He almost seemed cartoonish, but in the cutest way.

From that day on, Martin and I spent our free time together. He would come by the hot dog stand and help me sell snacks or pass the time, and I would accompany him on long walks by the water, boats floating in the waves on one side and cars above the gravel road on the other. With him, I always felt like part of the weight resting on me volatilized, and like I was just a little closer to floating again. Just a little bit.

Soon, August came around the bend, chillier, more nostalgic. The weather itself seemed heavy with unfallen rain and clouds that loomed but never broke.

Martin and I were on one of our usual walks in late afternoon. I had been in quite a mood that day. It was my day off, which was even worse than working. My parents were visiting old friends in a neighboring town, so I had spent all day on the couch, picking at a loose thread on one of the blue cushions.

But now we walked on the beach, hand in hand. I refused to let my glum mood ruin our time together. But it was as if Martin had caught the same mood. He lagged behind me, dragging at my arm.

"How about the big rocks over there?" I asked. We had never explored the collection of small cliffs by the beach. Martin shrugged his shoulders.

"Come on," I insisted. I took a deep breath of salty air and, without warning, let go of his hand and started running, kicking off my sandals.

This section of the beach was quieter; most people stuck to the smooth sand and clear water sectors, congregating in those places. Here, it was more rocky and the waves were larger. I realized, with a glance at the sky, that sunset was approaching and the rising tide burbled over the rocks. Martin ran beside me and the wind tossed around his mop of sun-bleached hair, half blinding him as he ran. My own hair, for once, felt free, but only because of the strong wind.

We stopped as we approached the cliffs, which shadowed the sand and the water in a premature dusk.

"Ah…it's…something else to run when there's gravity, eh?" Martin was bent over, one hand holding the sandals I had kicked off, the other on his knee. Panting hard. His usual smile was not there, which was even more unsettling than the stubborn clouds hanging above.

"Maybe we should head back soon," he said when he finally managed to catch his breath.

I planted my fists on my hips and cocked my head. Had he always looked so thin, so tired? "No," I announced. "Not before this good ocean air has given you back your usual colors. Come!"

I grabbed his hand and dragged him along, approaching the looming rocks. A cold current of air seemed to emanate from them.

"Ouch!" I gasped. Something sharp had pricked my foot. It was *not* nice having the full weight of my body mass when stepping barefoot on sharp objects. But did I put my shoes back on? Absolutely not.

I needed adventure. Maybe if I could find that...maybe if Martin could find it too...but as I thought this, the heavy weight seemed to settle over me again. Was exploring really the thing to do right now? Would it really change the shadow looming over my mind like the cliffs loomed over us?

Small pointy seashells dotted this section of the beach. My thoughts drifted to Leila, and to the seashell necklaces she used to make for us, and every other kid on our street. We hadn't seen one another that much lately.

The more Martin and I kept walking, the taller the cliffs grew. And that's when I realized what was truly odd about this place. Apparently, Martin did too.

"Cas, have you noticed that nothing here floats? Like, not even the small seashells on the ground?"

He was right, of course. For some reason, we were not the only ones affected by gravity here. It should have been comforting, should have made us feel less out of place; it really didn't. I guess there hadn't been humans around here for a while.

"Should we...go back?" he asked. The eeriness of the place did not escape him either.

I looked at my friend and chose to ignore the way his head hung so low it might as well have been attached to a ball and chain. There was something on this beach. There *had* to be. And this something called me onward. "Soon," I said, not really meaning it. "Look, there are caves up ahead. Wanna check those out?"

Without waiting for a response, I pulled him along.

Yeah, why *hadn't* I seen much of Leila lately? Was it because of the gravity? Was it really so hard to be around me?

The "cave" we were nearing was really more of a slit in the cliff. It was wide enough for two people to walk in, but still too narrow to be a real pathway, and after a few feet, it grew dark. I lit the flashlight on my cell phone, motioning Martin onward. Was it me, or was he sickly pale? I decided it was probably just the lighting.

My family also hadn't been the kindest. Mom and Dad had gotten into arguments about me and my "condition," and my older brother, gone for college, had decided not to come back for the summer. He was "too busy," apparently. I missed him.

Dad hadn't cleaned the pool this summer, perhaps because he was afraid I would just sink. I probably would have. I pushed down the annoyance at not having had the choice for myself though, stepping deeper into the cave.

My thoughts continued to tumble. They were not stuck in molasses anymore; they were in a stew. A really thick and gross one.

Shadows danced with each step we took. Small droplets of water lined the cave's walls. Something shone up ahead; I motioned Martin onward.

And work? Yeah, the rare people who came to buy hot dogs and chips always looked at me with just a glimmer of suspicion in their eyes. I could see it. I was different; they knew it. They pretended not to notice, but they knew.

And they did nothing to help.

The shining glimmer soon revealed itself as only a puddle, the still surface of which shimmered when my flashlight pointed at it. In fact, water ran along the whole length of the cave, heading inward.

My thoughts continued to spiral, turning to Martin. He had been so nice at first, but something had seemed off with him lately. He...he—

He dragged behind, almost tripping with every step. I caught his eye and smiled, although I couldn't quite keep the annoyance from my face.

"Cas...Cassava." His voice was barely stronger than a breath. Oh, what was wrong with him? Wasn't the fact that we both suffered from constant gravity enough?

At that moment, he tripped.

I waited for him to rise again, but he didn't. "Come on, Martin. Just get up. We're almost there."

I walked back.

Why was he like this? Why was he so...

I searched for the word. Annoying? Unpleasant?

I forced a compassionate tone out of my mouth anyway, if only to avoid an argument.

"Martin?"

He hadn't gotten hurt, had he?

I plodded through the puddle that separated us, kneeling by his side. "Martin, are you alright?"

He barely lifted his head and his lips formed words, but they were drowned by the constant splashing along the cave walls. Part of me wanted to chide him, tell him that surely we were almost at the end of the cave. His lips moved again and I leaned in to hear what he was saying.

"I'm...I'm sorry I'm such a burden."

Something snapped inside of me at that very moment.

The weight was dragging my friend down. I saw it now in his eyes. And I felt it inside of me too, stronger than ever: the pressure I had been trying to ignore was pressing against my ribcage.

My thoughts started grinding louder than the cave's *drip*-dripping. And Martin wasn't usually exhausted like this; nor did he like to complain for attention or try to play the victim. This... this wasn't his fault.

Nor was it mine that gravity had started affecting me on the first day of summer.

And the Martin I knew? The one who helped me sell snacks at the beach just because he was kind, the one who made me laugh and walked around the town or along the beach with me for hours—*he needed help*.

I took back my sandals from his hand and put them on. I helped him roll onto his back and pulled his head into my lap, out of the wet sand. He could barely keep his eyes open. Poor Martin. My heart started pounding, like on that first day when gravity had started affecting me. Where were other people when I needed them?

"Martin, we have to get out." My voice echoed on the cave's walls.

It was around that moment that I realized that the small stream coming into the cave was not merely passing through. It was the tide, and it was rising. If we didn't get out soon, we would be trapped.

Or worse.

I tried to pull my friend to his feet, but he was too weak to stand. So I forced my aching limbs to drag him, groaning under the effort of our combined weight.

I missed Leila. I wasn't mad at her—I simply *missed* her.

With Martin's arm around my shoulders, my light in the other hand, I started pulling us both toward the exit. *Out.* The word resonated in my head, louder with each step, the water inside the cave creeping higher and higher and my own feet growing heavier and heavier. Would we even make it out on time? Would I get to see Leila again? And my brother? And spend time with my parents?

Oh, if only Martin and I had no gravity. If we could simply float out. This would make things so much easier! The water almost reached my waist, Martin's head barely above the surface.

I stumbled and Martin took a plunge in the dark water, dragging us both down. I dropped my phone with its flashlight.

"Oh, shoot—"

I stumbled again and fell under, Martin slipping from my grasp completely.

The water swirled with dark shadows.

I felt all around with both my hands and feet. My eyes caught sight of a weak light, much deeper in the water. My cell phone. Its flashlight was still on, outlining an underwater landscape of blacks and greys. I saw a form, half-floating in the death-coloured water.

I dove toward Martin.

There. My arms wrapped around him and my legs pushed us both toward the surface. The weight of Martin's inert body broke all our momentum. A groan escaped my lips, turning into a flock of reflective bubbles.

Our heads finally broke the surface of the water. There, only a short distance away, I could see the entrance of the cavern, and the dark-blue skies beyond, framed with rock.

Almost. Almost there.

The water still rose and our heads nearly scraped the cave's ceiling. *Almost.* I gave it all that I had left, rushing us toward the dying light of day.

We finally broke out of the rocky tunnel and stumbled onto the beach. Water kept on rising against the cliffs, though. *We still needed to get to higher ground.*

Emotions twirled and bumped inside my brain, pounding against my skull. Martin slumped beside me. I took hold of him again, right as the sky above burst into rain. It poured down on us, washing away the stale water from the cave.

Something felt different. Something—

My feet weren't touching anything. That's when I realized it. I held Martin against me and, as the tide rose, we rose above it. I wiggled my feet in the air. No, I wasn't imagining it all.

I was floating.

And Martin was floating with me.

I let the light breeze drift us along the beach, back toward where we had come from. In the distance, boats still floated just above the water, cars still drove a few inches off the roads. Houses were held down by solid binds, and in the distance, mansions in the wealthier part of town floated, long staircases leading up to them. The sun set in a fiery glory, painting the whole sky in its wake and turning the rain into a pink haze all around us.

"Martin, can you see that?" My voice came out as a whisper, but my heart pounded again.

Martin's eyes fluttered open. All he did was smile, with his many dimples and blue eyes.

"Watch us fly," he whispered, in the cheesiest tone I had ever heard.

Then his smile spread, and all of the weight I carried lifted out of my reach, all the way to the clouds ablaze in color. And the ground called to the millions of water droplets, pulling them down, down— but this time, without dragging us along.

Summer Miracles

KANN

The earliest memory I have...is quite strange. Peculiar. I wouldn't have believed it was anything but a dream if it hadn't changed the way I saw my whole world.

I was about four years old, and my father had taken me outside to look at the stars. It was a clear night, so clear that you could see the Milky Way twinkling across the sky like a smooth, foggy belt.

"See those stars up there?" My father knelt at my level, his strong arms wrapped around my waist. "Each one is full of immense knowledge."

"They're just little dots in the sky," I insisted. My four-year-old brain comprehended things far more than most toddlers my age, and yet, I still couldn't see stars for what they were.

"They're so much more than that." He picked me up and held me against his hip with his left hand. He stretched his right hand up toward the sky, palm open.

I watched, wide-eyed, as one of the twinkling lights sailed straight toward his hand, landing softly on it. It was the brightest light I had ever seen, far brighter than the moon, brighter even than the sun shining on the hottest summer day. It didn't twinkle; it burned. But it wasn't a hot kind of burn—it was more of a piercing. My father looked at me, smiled, and promptly swallowed the star.

I kneel in my window seat, looking out past the neighborhood houses blocking the starry night sky. I don't know what I'm looking for, exactly, but I am looking for something. Anything that might point to where my father is.

Gone. Gone. Gone. For four years, as of today. No one knows where he went, or if he is even alive.

"Franny, honey, dinner is ready," Grandma calls from the kitchen.

I ease up, stretching as my bones creak. I am seventeen years old today, and my bones are creaking. It figures.

I should never have let my father teach me how to swallow stars. There is power in them, yes, but a celestial, supernatural power that brings the kind of knowledge that only God himself is meant to have.

So much knowledge in one star, enough knowledge for several lifetimes. But swallowing as many stars as my father did…it would be enough to drive anyone mad.

I hurry to my mirror and run a brush through my brunette hair. Wouldn't do to have a rat's nest at dinner. Grandma wouldn't stand for it.

"Franny, dinner is getting cold!"

I set my hairbrush down. "Coming!" Grabbing my claw clip, I pull my hair into a ponytail and then hurry to the kitchen.

"It smells delicious," I say as the honey aroma meets my nose.

Grandma smiles, her eyes crinkling.

I sit at the table, and Grandma and I enjoy sweet-and-sour chicken. It's hard to enjoy something like this when all I can think of is my father's disappearance.

I wish…I wish he were here. Celebrating. With me.

"What's on your mind, honey?"

I glance up, and Grandma has that look about her face where she is reading me like a book. Her dark blue eyes zero in on my lighter ones. "Just lost in thought, I guess. Summer dreams, you know?"

Grandma cocks her head. "You know I don't believe in those." She clucks her tongue and then stands up, heading over to the freezer. "Dreams are useless unless you do something with them." She pulls the freezer open, rummages around, and pulls out a container of strawberry ice cream. My favorite. "But summer miracles?" She clanks two bowls together as she fills them with ice cream. "Those are something to believe in, as the Lord himself performed miracles."

"There's no such thing as miracles," I mutter under my breath. I know that wishes can come true, but only if you think about your wish in the last moments before you fall asleep on the night of your birthday. It doesn't happen often, but it does happen. Not miracles, though.

Grandma sets one bowl down in front of me. "Happy birthday, honey."

"Thanks, Grandma." I dip my spoon in the ice cream and then take a big bite, prepared for the brain freeze that is sure to come.

I lay in my bed, staring at my canopy stretching above me. Ruffles hang down the side. When I was a little girl, I felt like a princess in this bed.

Now, I feel like a prisoner.

Summer miracles, indeed. I squeeze my eyes shut and cover my head with my quilt, trying to block out the memories.

My father disappeared four summers ago, on my thirteenth birthday. What was once a summer dream became a nightmare. My life, gone.

Sleep is impossible. I throw my covers aside and step over my clothes littering the floor to reach my bookshelf. I pull out a silver photo album, then sit down on the ground, leaning back against the bookshelf.

I flip open to the first page. There is my mother, her baby bump on display. Every month while she was pregnant with me, she took a photo, her shirt pulled up so that her tummy could be seen. Each of those photos is documented in the first page of the photo album.

I turn the page. There are both my parents, their arms wrapped around each other as they hold me. My mother is looking at me adoringly, her smiling face pressed against my cheek, and my father is kissing my mother's head.

A tear drips down my cheek. I hastily brush it away as I turn the page.

To the last page of photos where my mother is present.

It's my first birthday party, and my entire family is gathered around me and smiling. My grandma is there, of course, as are many of my parents' extended family and friends. I don't know their names, not anymore. I suppose I could ask my grandma, but I don't want to end up crying in front of her.

I touch the page, my finger tracing the line of my mother's cheek, and I can't keep the tears from falling now.

My mother died that night. My father was loading me into the car while my mother carried the decorations and presents and loaded them into the back of the car. The car being parked right by a main road, vehicles drove past them all the time.

No one expected the drunk driver to be driving eighty in a thirty zone. She was hit and gone instantly.

I lean my head back against the bookshelf and close my eyes. My mother, gone on my birthday. My father, gone on my birthday. Both in the summer.

Neither would be gone if summer miracles existed.

I slam the photo album shut and slide it back onto the bookshelf, my hands shaking.

I've got to get out of here. I've got to get away. I can't just lay in my bed right now, trying to sleep. I need to find something, anything that might offer some semblance of relief.

I grab my phone from the dresser, slide on my slippers, and pull a hoodie over my pajama shirt, then quietly open the door. I listen. No sound comes from the living room or the kitchen, so Grandma has gone to bed. She'll have her white noise on, so she won't hear me, but I'm still going to be quiet anyway. Closing my door behind me, I tiptoe softly down the hall, grabbing my keys and wallet from the side table beside the front door. I unlock the door and pull it open. It makes that sucking sound when the door pushes against the squishy stuff at the top, and I wince. But I hear nothing at all coming from Grandma's room. With the tips of my fingers, I push the screen door away from me as I close the front door behind me. Turning, I support the screen with one hand while locking the front door with the other.

I hurry to my car, stepping across the dew-covered grass. I should've grabbed some real shoes before heading out…oh, well. I'll just be gone for a couple hours.

I hop in my car and put the key in the ignition. I glance over my phone screen, going into my settings app. I type in 'Life360' and then set it to 'never.' I don't want Grandma looking for me right now. I'll be sure to turn the tracking back on when I get back.

I put the car in drive and pull out onto the main road. I'm not sure where I'm going yet; I just need to get away.

I fight to keep my mind blank as I drive, mind-numb. I turn on the right turn signal, check my side mirrors, and then turn. I keep driving, just going through the motions. Stopping at stop lights, turn signal on, turn signal off, cruise consistent. All monotonous. All boring. All empty.

Just like June 21 always is.

I end up parked beside a field of wildflowers. My head rests on the steering wheel, and I feel like crying. Turning off the ignition, I get out of the car and climb onto the hood, leaning back against the windshield. I pull out my phone and open Instagram. I go to my profile and search the people I am following. Alex Harmon. My father.

I scroll through his profile. His brunette hair is the exact same shade as mine, except his hair is curly and mine is stick straight, like my mother's was. I smile a little as I see the photos he used to post of him and me.

A photo of him holding six-year-old me on his shoulder.

A photo of me reaching up for the sky, as if for a star.

A photo of him holding my hand and walking down a dirt path.

I wish he would come back.

I turn off my phone and lean back against the windshield, tears dripping down my cheeks. Closing my eyes, I struggle not to cry as I drift off to sleep.

"Franny!" Someone shakes me. "Franny, wake up."

I turn my head away from the sound. "Go away," I mumble. I reach down to grab my blanket and pull it over my head. I crack open one of my eyes, and harsh sunlight pierces my vision. My back hurts. Where am I?

"Franny, it's me."

Carefully, I sit up, the blanket sliding to my feet. I rub my eyes, then shade them so the light doesn't blind me. The hazy form of a man forms in front of me, and I rub my eyes again. And I meet his eyes.

They're blue. Just like Grandma's.

Just like mine.

"Daddy?" I whisper. Tears fill my eyes, and I cover my mouth with my hand as I struggle not to scream. I'm not sure if it's an angry scream or an excited scream, and I'm not really sure I want to find out. My wish. My wish came true.

He climbs up onto the vehicle and sits beside me, his arms wrapped tight around my shoulders. "I've missed you so much, my dear girl," he says. He kisses my head.

I want to hug him back, but I don't know that I can. I shake myself out of his arms, sliding off the car and turning to face him. I cross my arms, narrowing my eyes at him. My chest is tight. "Where were you?"

He doesn't answer. Instead, he slides off the car and comes to stand directly in front of me. He moves as if to hug me again, but I step away.

"Where were you?" My fists clench. "You've been gone four years."

His eyes seem sad. And that's when I notice how…different he looks. His skin has taken on an almost shiny quality, as though he is coated in fairy dust. His hair is no longer the dusty brown it used to be—it is a strange silver color, as though it is made from metallic strands. And his face is thinner, more drawn than it used to be.

My fists slowly relax. "What happened to you?"

He smiles a little, looking at the sky. "Nothing."

I glance at the sky, then back at him as realization dawns on me. "You didn't…you didn't swallow more stars, did you?"

He just looks at me, his eyes boring into my own. "Franny, honey, I think you know the answer to that."

I slap my hand to my mouth before I can say the words threatening to pour forth from my lips. I want to yell at him, scream that stars aren't meant for humans, that the knowledge in them is imparted by God for God, not for humans, and certainly not humans who have attempted to find the knowledge and make themselves like God. It didn't work at the Tower of Babel, and it most assuredly won't work here.

But I don't say all that. "What do you want from me?"

He places a hand on my arm. I nearly pull it away. "I need you to help me."

"Help you how?"

His eyes seem to be crazed, frantically searching my own. "You have the ability to touch the stars as well, now that you're seventeen. I need you to take them down for me."

This time I really do pull my arm away, stepping back and staring at him in shock. "You need me to...steal stars for you?"

"Not steal, *per se*." He cocks his head as he stares up into the sky. "I think of it more as...intentional borrowing. I can't borrow them anymore. They've rejected my touch. I need someone they'll respect."

"But the stars won't be returned. Because they'll be gone." I brush past him, back to the hood of my car, grabbing the blanket and folding it. My hands shake, but this simple act makes me feel as though I am more in control of the situation. "I can't do it. I won't." I open my car door and toss the blanket inside. "And if I do it, you'll continue to feed yourself something that is too much for a human mind." I slam the door shut and turn to him, my hair flying behind my back as my hands land on my hips. "And you think you're strong enough to withstand the knowledge? Look at you!" I gesture at his figure.

My father looks down at himself. "What are you talking about? This is the new and improved Alex Harmon." He runs his fingers through his silver hair. "I'm a better man than I was four years ago. I'm a better man than I was ten years ago. I'm a better man than I ever was before because of the stars."

I don't really know what to say. So, instead of speaking, I just nod. "Uh-huh."

He isn't finished. "And this is a dream of mine, Franny. Can't you understand that?"

I can understand that. But still, I don't believe it. "There's no such thing as dreams."

"There are." He takes another step toward me. "And I can show you how to make your dreams come true—this summer."

I hesitate. I don't agree with his decisions, but he has the knowledge of the stars inside him. And I *did* wish that my father would return. "Alright. I'll help you."

In a world like the one we live in, you would think people would stare at the man beside me who seems to twinkle in the starlight and has hair the color of the Milky Way. But no one takes any notice of us as we make our way through security and board the plane.

I have a window seat, and my father sits next to me, in a middle seat. The flight attendant says something at the front of the plane, but I don't know what it is. I'm just staring out the window up past the setting sun and towards the stars twinkling faintly in the distance.

It's so easy, really, to do what he wants me to do. While of course airplane windows can't be opened naturally, my father has already made a plan.

And he's whispering it to me now.

"I have a window seal cutter in my phone case behind my phone," he whispers. His breath is hot against my ears. I don't look at him, just press myself further into the window. "You're going to cut the seal off the window, and the window should pop out. Just reach up and take one, then hand it to me."

Yeah, this isn't going to go poorly at all. But I don't say that. I feel claustrophobic, like this whole plane is going to collapse in on me. The pressure from the altitude coupled with the dull roar emanating from the passengers is wearing on me, and I know that the oxygen is going to get sucked out of the plane as soon as the window opens.

And people will know the truth, and I'll be forced into some sort of science lab to be experimented on to figure out how I can do what I do, if I don't die first.

He slips the cutter into my hand. I finally look down at it. The sharp blade lays flat against my hand, cold and almost feeling the way bitterness would if it were a tangible thing.

I kind of want to squeeze it, let the blood drip down my hand. Maybe physical pain will take away this emptiness I am feeling inside.

But, of course, I don't.

I turn the blade to the window and proceed to saw through the seal. It's easy; this blade is sharp. In no time at all, the seal splits open, and I push the window.

And it plummets out of the plane, falling, falling, falling.

Perhaps it would be better at this point if I fell, too. Then I wouldn't be trapped here.

Suddenly, emergency sirens begin blaring as oxygen masks drop from the ceiling. The flight attendant calls over the PA, "Stay calm! Your oxygen masks have disengaged from the ceiling and are available for your use. We are turning around and will make it back to the original airport shortly. Please stay calm, and expect some turbulence."

I just keep staring down, down, down, and my father shakes my arm. "Take a star!" he hisses.

A tear trickles down my cheek. This isn't the father I remember, and I don't know what else to do. Choking back a sob, I reach up and pick a single star out of the sky as the airplane begins to turn around.

The sirens are still blaring. What I thought was a dream has turned into a nightmare.

The star shines in my hand, an ethereal sort of vision. I don't want to hand it over to him, give him something that's going to destroy him even more.

"Give it to me," he says, leaning closer. My hand is still out the window, the star out of his reach.

I stare at the star longer as it begins to burn my hand.

"Give it to me!" My father is screaming now, clawing at my arm and pulling me away from the window.

I can't. I can't do it. But I've got to get away. I've got to.

I let go of the star. It flies back up into the sky.

Then I push myself out the window. My father, still holding onto my arm, isn't expecting this, and suddenly, we're both falling, falling, falling through the air.

This is the end. But perhaps this isn't the worst way to die. A star was saved, and its knowledge is safe from both my father and me.

I don't scream, resigning myself to my fate. It doesn't make sense to spend my last moments screaming.

My father isn't screaming either. He's still got ahold of my arm, but slowly, slowly his silver hair is…fading?

He wraps his arms tight around me. Wind whistles past my ears, but somehow I can still hear these words coming from him: "I've got you, Franny. Don't let go. I've got you."

I don't question if I hear him right or not. My mind is whistling just as loud as the wind.

But slowly, slowly, the wind somehow begins to diminish, almost as if we're not falling so fast, so far.

The ground is getting close, but it's not at an alarming speed. My father's arms feel so tight it's as if he's suffocating me, and that's when I see it.

A sheer veil surrounding us, pulsing exactly the way a star does.

His arms grip me tighter. And the tighter he grips me, the brighter the veil gets.

We're slowing down, slower and slower. My brain is beginning to comprehend this as I see my father begin flickering in and out, his body fading and solidifying, fading and solidifying.

The ground is only a few hundred feet away now, and we've slowed to a crawl. We hit the ground gently, both our feet flat on the ground. The veil disappears, and I fall to my knees, leaning forward and panting. Now this, if it were a fantasy novel, would be the best time to scream. But I'm not in a fantasy novel, and instead I just feel like I'm going to be sick.

My father reaches down and grasps my hands, helping me stand. He gazes at me, tenderness in his eyes. He looks like his old self now—he no longer twinkles like the stars, nor is his hair silver. But... he's still fading, slowly becoming lighter and lighter. And that's when I realize.

He just used...the stars he had inside of him...to save not just his own life, but mine.

I meet his eyes, my mouth falling open. "Y-you gave up the thing y-you wanted so desperately...for me?"

He touches my face. "I was so wrong, Franny." He takes my hands and squeezes them tight. "My eyes were opened when...when I saw you pushing yourself out of the plane."

"But...you..." I don't know what else I'm going to say. There's so much I want to say, to yell at him for the pain he has caused me over the last day, to cry because he gave up the stars for me, to freeze and not say anything at all. But I do none of these things. Instead, I wrap my arms around his waist. I can feel that he is hesitating. "I forgive you, Daddy."

He slowly brings his arms up to my back, drawing me close. He tightens his grip, and it's not strong enough, not like it should be.

But still, my father embraces me, his arms wrapped around me as tight as they can be. "I'm so sorry," he whispers into my hair, "so sorry."

His arms aren't strong; they are light, literally. Slowly, slowly, his body twinkles and fades, sparkles soaring up into the night sky.

I hug him close, crying. I don't bother wiping away the snot dripping onto his clothes. I just hug him as though my life depends on it. Or, perhaps, his life.

"I love you, Franny," he says softly, a crinkle in his voice.

"I love you too," I whisper.

Suddenly, my arms collapse in on themselves, and I fall to my knees. All there is in front of me is a faded shadow of a figure growing more and more translucent as more of his life is sucked into the sky.

I think I might have seen a hint of a smile, but his entire figure is gone before I can tell for sure.

Gone.

For good this time.

Summer dreams aren't real. I know that now. Summer dreams aren't meant to be believed in because dreams are one of those things you aren't meant to grasp, much like the stars in the sky.

But maybe, just maybe, I can believe in summer miracles.

Turn to Face the Wind

FAITH TEVY

On a beach crowded with people, I sit alone. I watch the surf come in and out, such brilliant white froth battering the dark, gleaming sand.

Rising on the horizon line, a long belt of ominous clouds is coming to hide the sun, but for the moment, the sun's determined rays pierce the sky. The crashing of thunder sounds in my ears every time the waves smash into each other, and I have been sitting here so long that the tide is beginning to encroach upon my space. Yet I sit, and I watch.

All around me, people are together. A group of teenagers is playing a game using a small trampoline-like device set on the ground, spiking a palm-sized yellow ball onto the black net and hooting when it ricochets into the air. Small children scamper along the seashore, collecting shells, digging holes, and squealing with glee when they uncover a sand crab. Adults engage in an intense game of volleyball, flinging themselves into the air and onto the ground for the sheer sake of earning their team a point.

However, they are not the ones I watch. I look for the walkers, those who come and go on this beach. Women, chatting as they plow through the vast stretch of sand in their bright, floral activewear.

Men, bobbing in puffer jackets that protect them from the cool ocean breeze. I enjoy observing the teens that tumble by, chortling, joking, and jostling each other as they talk and tease and figure out how society works. Out of them all, my favorites to watch are the older couples. Aged lovers, hair gray from time, glide up the sunbaked sand hand in hand. They gaze at their surroundings, turning to each other from time to time to share what they see. They don't walk with a mission or greater purpose other than to simply be together. They are the only ones here who have been around long enough to know how precious and fragile life really is, and they understand the importance of simply *being.*

So I sit. And I watch. And I try to figure out what it is everybody seems to know but me.

Spread behind me is an expansive picnic blanket. A wide cooler sits right in the center of the multicolored fabric, filled to the brim with salty preserved meats, creamy cheeses, crisp crackers, and bright, tart fruit fresh from the farmers market.

Several bottles of sparkling apple cider sit next to the closed cooler, unopened and sweating in the sun. Plates lie untouched, and the seagulls have long since stolen the bright pink napkins.

Books are stacked in a neat pile next to the cooler—my favorites, ready to be shared and discussed. Several bright blue beach chairs huddle next to the blanket, folded up neatly. There's a party waiting to happen on that blanket. Food to be shared. Laughter to ring through the air. Friends to love one another. It's waiting.

The breeze becomes a strong wind buffeting my face, and the storm clouds begin to encroach on the sun, sending a firm chill through the air. From my perch in my bright blue beach chair, I don't even bother to check the time. They're not coming. I know they're not coming.

Folding my bare, cold arms over my stomach, I stretch my legs out in front of me. I got here hours ago and prepared a space for my four best friends. It took me three trips on my bicycle just to get everything down to this beach, and I knew I'd have to do it all over again just to get home, but I didn't mind. I stopped waiting three hours ago, and since then, have sat here alone, watching people move around me. I tell myself that I don't care. My friends are entitled to do whatever they want. Why would I need them, anyway? I can talk to myself.

Giving myself a firm nod, I attempt to solidify the walls in my heart. However, within moments, they begin to crumble, leaving me exposed yet again. Despite those forced, stubborn thoughts, the sting behind my eyes tells me that somewhere inside of me, I *do* care. I care very much.

I stare down at my hands. Cracked, dry, over-washed hands that are suffering from my constant obsession with cleanliness. Over and over, I have tried to make amends with the compulsive actions, but as I bend my fingers and watch the skin around my knuckles crack, I know that, even here, I am struggling. Especially here.

I lean my head back on my chair and stop watching the world around me.

In all of my best daydreams, this afternoon was beautiful. I laid out all that I had to offer, and invited those I thought would want it. I was more than ready to offer my heart and share my struggles with some of the people that I trusted most, but no.

I would have at least thought the girl that I'd grown up with since birth would show up.

As I sit here alone, I finally let myself admit what I've known for months. That friendship has been broken for awhile now. It was only a matter of time before it shattered.

Part of me honestly hoped that somehow, someone would want to sit here with me. Out of all the hundreds of people walking by, I had longed for at least one to stop and chat with me. To see me. A fragile, foolish hope, rebuked every time someone walked right by without so much as a second glance. Now, the storm clouds have overtaken the sun and almost completely fill the sky, pushing away the sunbathers, game players, and casual walkers. Even the surfers begin to leave the beach as the waves become sharp and unpredictable.

Shaking my head at my own naivety, I push myself out of my chair and stand, brushing dry hands over the goosebumps bristling up my arms and legs. After shaking the sand from my shorts, I fold up the chair, a shiver running down my spine. Hauling the suddenly heavy chair back to the blanket, I throw it on top of the other chairs and grab the sparkling apple cider, ready to clean up.

The tears that I had tried to convince myself were not there batter against my eyelids, and my throat burns and tightens like I have swallowed hot coals. I take a deep breath, unwilling to cry in public.

However, when I lift my head, I see that there's no need for such precautions. The beach, now grey and dreary, is completely and totally empty. I am alone.

I can't help but pause and spin around in a complete circle, taking in the complete and utter emptiness surrounding me. Tears fall fast down my face and a small sob breaks free from my chest. Turning back to my task, I scoop up the large stack of books and attempt to shove them all into my bag, sorrow and rage churning in my chest so fiercely that I can scarcely breathe.

Of course, only on a day like today would I drop all of my books. And that is exactly what happens. My books burst out of my grip, seeming to explode into the air, and I yelp, jumping back as every single one of them drops into the sand.

For a moment, all I can do is stare at them, stunned. Some of my most precious friends, laying in the dirt like discarded trash. My eyes land on the one I care about the most and I gasp, dropping to my knees.

With all the caution and tenderness of a mother holding her newborn child for the first time, I extract my Message Bible from the sand.

More tears fall down my face as I find the well-loved pages full of grit and I shake my head, guilt wracking my body as I smooth out the wrinkled corners and run my thumb over new scratches in the smooth faux leather.

As I set to blowing the sand out of all the grooves, careful not to displace any of the flowers pressed in between the pages, the wind grows even stronger, and a soft rain begins to patter against the sand.

I ignore it.

I am so engrossed in getting the sand out that I almost miss the dog-ear on one of the pages. Thankfully I see it, and I sigh, shaking my head as I flip to the spot.

I reach out to pluck the page back into order, but before my fingers touch it, my entire body stills. Everything on the pages spread before me is clean and unmarked. Everything, that is, except for a single verse that stands out from within a frame of pink ink. The words held within those simple marks capture my entire mind, heart, body, and soul. I cock my head as my heart skips a beat, and I take a shuddering breath.

Psalms, chapter seventy-seven, verse one reads: "I yell out to my God, I yell with all my might, I yell at the top of my lungs. He listens."

My breath catches in my lungs, and I let my eyes rove over the verse again, absorbing the last two words. "He listens."

Looking up, I stare at the disjointed, disgruntled, dismantled picnic that I had intended for such beauty. I remember all that I had wanted to share with my friends, the things that I had been holding so close to me for so long, and that had kept me quiet for months. Both the beautiful and the hard. I was ready for someone to listen.

I drop my eyes back down to the Bible, and my chest tightens. The tears on my face have dried in the harsh wind, but my eyes water and the words before me have more meaning than ever before. Out of nowhere, a wild idea pops into my head and I blink a few times, stunned by the boldness of it. Carefully, I peer up and down the shoreline and double-check the windows of the expensive homes lining the beach.

Not a single soul is out in this weather.

Slowly, I get to my feet, and my heart begins to race as a small part of me wonders if I'm crazy, but I don't listen. I rip open the lid to my cooler. All of the food that I worked two weeks to pay for gazes up at me, completely untouched. I recall countless hours spent cleaning windows, walking dogs, and scrubbing floors for the money to finally purchase these groceries. In the moments where my feet hurt, my back ached, and I wanted to be doing anything else, I reminded myself that it would all be worth it. Shows what I know.

I kick the cooler over and dump all of the food and ice into the sand. Once the cooler is empty, I wipe it out with my towel and line it with the picnic blanket. I toss my phone, wallet, house keys, and headphones inside before adding the truly irreplaceable things: my books. I gently stack them, careful not to bend any pages, and I read the verse again before I stick my Bible right on top. With a nod, I seal the lid, draping my towel over it just to make sure all the cracks are covered.

Finally, satisfied that my valuables are considerably weatherproof, I snag my dark-blue hoodie from my bag and tug it over my head as I walk down to the ocean.

The storm has absolutely taken over.

It's hard to believe that the moody, raging, cloud-covered sky above me was ever blue. The waves smash into each other with fury, raging in a competition to see which one of them is the biggest, loudest, and most dangerous. A swell that could easily be as big as my house starts to form far out from shore, and for the first time, apprehension flickers through me. My feet temporarily slow, but I shake my head and continue forward.

The wind grabs at my hoodie, flinging the hood off of my head and unleashing my hair, the long strands whipping through the air and smacking me in the face like wet tentacles. More drops of rain whiz through the air, snapping against my face. I sputter and blink. When I reach the water, the choppy spray splashes up my legs, soaking me and I gasp. The icy water seems to pierce through my skin and stab at my bones, as if it's trying to torture me, and when I finally stop, I'm only calf deep. With every wave that tumbles in, the water rises well past my knees, soaking my shorts. The push and pull of the tide tries to drag me farther into the darkness. The water is so murky that I cannot even see my own feet, but I dig my toes into the sand.

I look up and feel like I am meeting the gaze of the tempest, daring it to knock me down. For several long minutes I stare into the storm, and I remember the verse.

"I yell out to my God, I yell with all my might, I yell at the top of my lungs. He listens."

Pulling my hands out of my sweatshirt pocket, I trace the cracks, the angry, overbleached redness, and see my own struggle so clearly painted before me. As I stare at the pale, unearthly pallor of my dry skin, something inside of me finally snaps.

Before I can think one more second about it, I inhale a sharp breath, ball my hands into fists, and scream into the ocean. Scream into the wind and rain. Scream into the thundering waves and sizzling foam. Scream into the storm before me and the storm inside of me. Scream out to my God, who is surely watching me right now.

For a brief moment, I am the sound of my yelling. I am the pain and the loneliness and the yearning to be well again. I am the storm, and in this moment, I don't realize anything has changed. When I finally run out of breath and the scream is forced to stop, I pause to inhale, tears streaming down my face. And I feel it.

The wind.

What was once a raging, impenetrable force blowing against me and kicking up trouble in the waves has somehow completely changed

directions and is now blowing from *behind* me. When the wind rough-
ly pushes against my back, I take a step forward into the water that is
now barely lapping around my ankles.

Stunned, my mouth drops open as I look up and realize all of the
waves that once roared toward me with vengeful fury have turned
their backs to me and are now crashing *into* the ocean.

My mind stumbles and stammers. Before I can think about it, the
wind whistles around me and a huge gust rushes at me. It actually feels
like someone shoves me from behind and I stumble forward a few
steps. A strange noise fills the wind. It's a murmuring, jumping sort of
noise, high and ringing. If my head weren't full of common sense, I
would say that the wind is laughing.

Another sharp thrust forces me forward even more, and this time,
I could have sworn that I felt hands on my shoulders. Turning against
the wind, I manage to catch a snip of the landscape behind me, and I
see no one.

The high, joyful noise flows all around as the wind grabs at me, trying
to pull me forward. I resist, completely and totally muddled and confused.

Laughter sings yet again and the wind seems to take my hands,
lifting them into the air and drawing me forward. With the pushing and
the pulling, I don't have any choice but to let the wind lead me into the
dark, uncertain ocean.

I take several more steps, and the water rises to only just above
my ankles. The waves have calmed a bit without the beach to crash
against, but are still churning and changing.

The wind continues pulling me forward, but as the water starts to
get deeper, I feel hesitation grasp me and I pause, resisting the pull
of the wind.

Suddenly, my entire world as I know it is forever changed.

The wind ceases what I now know was a gentle leading, and it
laughs. Hands seem to lift up my body, plucking me out of the ocean

and carrying me into the sky with the ease of a child picking a daisy. I am spun around a few times, and before I know what is really happening, I am being carried over the ocean, the water skimming under my bare toes.

For a moment, all of the breath leaves my body as I feel myself entirely suspended in the air. When I catch my breath again, reality sets in, and I scream for a bit to nobody in particular, completely terrified.

The wind pulses against my closed eyes, and when I open them, the frightened yell dies in my throat. All around me, there is nothing but ocean, storm, and wind. The waves are pounding in the same direction that I am being carried, and for the first time, I realize that the choppy waves are not dangerous—they're wild.

My tears are completely dry, and I tentatively stretch my arms out, feeling the wind fly through my outstretched fingers like satin ribbons. A giggle wells up inside of me and escapes into the wind.

The sound is captured and thrown through the air, chasing me as I fly. Looking down, I stretch my toes out and let them graze the top of the ocean. Straining my neck, I try to see behind me, and the wind flips me onto my back, giving me a perfect view of the ocean stretching far behind. A slightly hysterical, disbelieving laugh escapes me and is immediately echoed by the wind.

My mind tries to remind me that I am being carried over who knows how many miles of deep ocean, and somewhere, fear attempts to hamper the unbridled delight exploding in my chest. But all of the worries and anxieties blow away in the wind before they can even so much as try to speak.

Flipping back around, I face the horizon, my body completely relaxed and my arms outstretched. The wind is freezing, biting cold, and my nose, ears, fingers and toes ache, but I really don't care. Rain is hitting my face and I grin, my heart bursting as I taste freedom. All around and before me is the ocean and the storm, and it is beautiful. The clouds are a vibrant mixture of charcoal patches layered with light swatches that look like they are leaking sunlight. The waves are absolutely mammoth, larger than anything I've ever seen or imagined. Liquid silver spires reach into the wind and break against each other, shimmering like fish scales, sea-foam trailing through the brilliance like a fine white lace. There's a deep, thrumming navy blue underneath it all, adding a startling contrast to both the waves and sky, so strong that it is more of a presence than a color.

My heart is singing. It almost feels like the wind is cradling me in its arms or cupping me in its hands, and I feel completely safe in its embrace. I soon discover that if I tilt to the left or to the right, I will drift in that direction, and if I lean too far to the right, I will spin circles through the air. Naturally, I twirl over the ocean until my spinning head demands a rest, but I laugh all the while.

Suddenly, from the depths of my memory I hear a voice reminding me of a verse in Isaiah, chapter forty: *"...those who wait upon God get fresh strength. They spread their wings and soar like eagles, they run and don't get tired, they walk and don't lag behind."*

My breath catches, and I whisper, in awe, "They spread their wings and soar like eagles…"

Almost in response, the wind lifts me higher, and I laugh.

Feeling the freedom of these words for the first time in awhile, I lean into the wind and yell, "They run and don't get tired!"

The wind bumps me up again, and I squeal.

"They walk and don't lag behind!"

Higher and higher I go until I am closer to the clouds than I am to the ocean. Even though I should be freaking out, I can't. I'm having too much fun!

"Those who wait upon God get fresh strength!" I scream into the expanse before me, feeling the words bursting from the core of my very being. "They spread their wings and soar like eagles, they run and don't get tired, they walk and don't lag behind!"

The wind, the words, the freedom—it all becomes a part of me. Rising through me, filling me, spilling out and spreading everywhere as I howl the words to the wind and believe every single one.

Like a chorus of a hundred crashing thunderstorms or a thousand roaring lions, the wind fills my ears and shoves me up into the clouds, leaving the ocean far behind.

I'm shocked into silence as I am submerged in the thick, heavy wetness of a cloud. Before I need to take a breath, the wind speeds me through the all-encompassing gray fog, and I gasp with shock and awe. Spread before me is what can only be described as the calm after the storm. The wind has carried me through the storm, and I find myself staring at the most beautiful sight I have ever laid my eyes on in my entire life.

I am completely and totally surrounded by thick, yet airy, mounds of clouds. Like a wonderland or a vast plain, the clouds stretch all around me in a never-ending array of stacks, shapes, and styles. This must be where the setting sun goes to rest.

A radiant ball of molten rose gold shimmers at the edge of the clouds, tame enough to stare at but still strong enough to make me squint. The sun casts golden, pink, and purple rays over and through all of the mounds, and the clouds are lit up with every imaginable color of the sunset. Neon orange is backed with a rim of shining gold, and gentle, rose pinks are shaded by dusky lavender hues. Vibrant rays of sun light up mounds of peach clouds and wispy, floaty stirs of feathering spin through the air in electric fuchsia patterns. Platinum white bands are stirred through it all, making the colors stand out even more.

The sky is the backdrop, colored a soft, barely discernible blush at the edges. The pink softly fades up into the palest of blue, shifting in shade and intensity until my head is tilted back all the way and I am staring up into a pool of deep indigo. A single star winks at me from the darkest part, and I smile.

The force of the wind eases, and I'm not so much flying as I am floating through the clouds. It's much warmer here, drying my wet hair and clothes in minutes, and I feel like I could wrap up in one of these clouds and stay forever.

Reaching down, I brush my fingers through the top of a cloud and watch the lavender vapors twirl and dance at my touch. Small strands drift away from the cloud, lighting up with their own bronze glow and tickling my fingertips.

Another murmur goes through my soul, and I feel a verse from Matthew chapter eleven rise up from my memories: *"Come to me, all you who are weary and burdened, and I will give you rest. Take my yoke upon you and learn from me, for I am gentle and humble in heart, and you will find rest for your souls."*

A gentle smile stretches over my face, and I whisper the words into the wind and clouds, feeling somehow that in this place, my whisper will carry farther than a shout would.

The wind seems to pause, and it changes shape. Settling me into the clouds, but not so close that they chill my skin, the wind tucks me into the sunset, and I rest in it, trusting that I'm not going to fall.

The colors change and I watch, feeling as if I am sitting inside of a mood ring. Slowly, the deepest of indigo above me welcomes more stars, and I stretch my fingers toward them, feeling like I could touch them if I stretched far enough.

The clouds encircle me, moving and changing like a watercolor painting and completely filling my vision. I sigh, totally at rest.

A touch startles me, and I look down at my hands. They're cold and aching from the wind, cracked and bleeding a bit, but I hadn't noticed them until now. I blink several times, stunned as it suddenly feels like someone is holding my hands. Warmth spreads through the dry bite that normally consumes them, and even though my mind can't figure out how, I see the barest outline of the wind taking on a form of its own. Silver strands adorn the hands holding mine, and I see small flickers of the strong, soft hands caressing my own cracked and tortured ones. My breath stutters as I inhale, and a tear runs down my face. The hands hold mine, and for some reason, I feel like they are holding so much more than just my hardened hands.

On a beach completely bereft of people, I stand before the ocean. The wind has long since returned me to solid land, and I watch as the surf turns back around to crash against the shore once again. The waves seem to fall differently, though. No longer fighting and competing, but moving together with a common goal, booming with merriment when they collide and send a pealing shout through the air. I look up and behold the sky as the quilt of mottled soot and cream-colored clouds starts to break apart. The setting sun is beginning to reveal the bright pink clouds that I know are hiding up there, and as the storm breaks into innocent puffs of cotton balls dipped into gray ink, the pale yet brilliant baby blue sky peeks through.

The sun finally pours past the clouds and its soft fingers reach out to touch my face. In response, I lift my chin and spread my arms. I close my eyes for a moment, soaking up the feeling of the rose-colored sun, and remember how it felt to be right next to it, hidden in the myriad of colors in the clouds. The only sounds in the air are the sizzling of the waves and the soft chirrup of sandpipers as they tiptoe up and down the beach. Somewhere, seagulls scream and the calls echo through the air.

Opening my eyes, I gaze at the ocean, watching as the sun leaks some of its color onto the surface of the water, turning it a bright, velvety burnt umber accented by silver ribbons of light. I remember the elderly couples that I saw walking on the beach earlier, and I smile. Looking all around me, I take in the ocean, the sunset, and the sand, then I turn to face the wind again, letting it rush over the waves and pour onto my face.

The wind curls over my face, giving my hair a quick toss, and I tuck my warm hands into my sweatshirt, breathing easily as I face God and speak, my voice trembling with emotion. "You heard me. You heard…and you listened."

Here I stand before my God and all of his magnificent creation. I rest in the God who is always right here to listen. I hold onto the hands that held me in the beauty of a living sunset. And I am not alone.

Leaving Lake June

LUCY GRECU

At Lake June, there's nothing quite like an August sunrise. The gray-glass water shimmers like glitter and the plain old sky lights up with shades of blue. Soft orange light floods over the colorful rocking chairs sitting in a line on the enclosed porch of our cabin and coats the tire swing hanging from the big maple beside it. The grass gets greener; the leaves light up like stained glass. And it's so quiet—the rest of the world is still fast asleep.

It was one of those early mornings near the end of August, on the final day of our annual family vacation. I was thirteen, and I watched the sunrise from the stand-alone hammock out in the grass. My hair was cut pixie short back then; a fluffy little mop of onyx, out of which squinted two olive eyes. I also had one of those clip-on hair feathers; it was pink and teal and about three inches longer than my real hair. It matched the rubber bands on my braces, which alternated pink and teal with each tooth.

And I'm pretty sure you could smell me from a mile away—I was wearing mosquito repellent like it was an eau de parfum. I was also dressed like the chair you throw all of your dirty clothes on—clad entirely in hand-me-downs from my cousins, from the worn-out graphic tee to the pink and white Twinkle Toes sneakers.

I stared up at the budding colors in the sky as my iPod blasted show tunes through my one working earbud. I tapped out the beat with my fingers while the birds chattered at each other. A blue jay bounced along the grass to my left, picking at the rocks and acorns with its shiny black beak.

Beside the hammock, glinting in the grass, was my granddad's watch, which I had only been given a few weeks back. The metal was tarnished and the watch itself was stone-dead—plus the straps, sticky with lemonade, were so stretched out that the thing didn't even fit on my little wrist. But I liked it anyway—it had character—so I dragged it around like Linus with his blanket.

The blue jay hopped over to the watch. It pecked. Then pecked again. In one quick motion, it bit the watch strap and flapped away. The hammock wobbled treacherously as I bolted upright.

"Hey!" I shouted, a little too late. "Excuse me—that's mine!" I tumbled out of the net, tossing my iPod into the grass. I darted after the jay, the rhinestones on the tips of my shoes blinking with every slap of my feet. All I could think was: *oh my gosh oh my gosh I can't lose that watch or Mom and Dad will kill me.*

I ran until I lost sight of any of the cabins, then things went downhill—literally. I tripped over my own dang foot and tumbled down an increasingly steep hill. I managed to cover my head, but I slammed my knee into some half-buried rocks. I rolled until the ground flattened out, then I sprawled on my back like a cartoon character that'd just been hit with a comically large mallet.

I ran my tongue across my teeth—no loose teeth and no loose brackets. *Good.* I sat up and brushed the leaves from my hair. I did a quick roll call of my bones. They all seemed to still be inside my skin at the very least, but there was a big scrape on my right knee.

I took a deep breath. The air was thick with the smell of wet leaves and dirt. I could hear the sloshing of the lake very faintly, but I couldn't see it. All I could see was trees, and those all looked the same as each other. I climbed to my feet and started brushing off the seat of my shorts.

Then I caught sight of what was right in front of me—a little ways away was the wide mouth of a cave. Roots and vines dangled across the maw like floss caught between crooked teeth. When I looked into the darkness, it seemed to look back.

Well, I thought. *That's just great.*

There was a shuffling of leaves, and my brain went *tiger!* before remembering that tigers don't really live in the woods of Maine. Then the mouth of the cave started to hum. I'm pretty sure it was the piña colada song.

The creature came out of the cave on all fours, but then it stood up and stretched. I blinked, rubbed my eyes, and stared. The thing was about eight feet tall, almost entirely covered in white fur. Its face, hands, and feet were a steely blue—its nose was a soft baby pink. Large gray eyes frowned out from under a thick monobrow of white.

I tilted my head, brow furrowing and eyes narrowing as my brain registered the fact that the creature was wearing a pair of beige cargo shorts and an unbuttoned Hawaiian shirt covered in pink pineapples. A large pair of aviator sunglasses sat on its forehead and its furry pointed ears were pierced with silver studs.

It leaned down and brushed some twigs and leaves aside, revealing a hole in the ground out of which it pulled a big red cooler. It popped off the lid and pulled out a human-sized bottle of beer, which looked funny in its massive hand.

That's when it caught me staring. Its already huge eyes widened, and it scrunched up its shoulders and bent its knees like it was trying to shrink down and disappear.

I raised my hand. "Um—"

The thing narrowed its eyes. "Wherever did *you* come from," it shouted, voice low like the rumble of an airplane during turbulence, "and whatever do you *want?*" Its accent was aggressively posh and surprisingly British—like James Bond or something—with breathy "r"s and booming "o"s.

I kept my hand up, blinking slowly as I tried to think of a suitable question. It just stared at me, holding its beer close to its chest as if it were afraid I would come over and steal it.

So I said: "I don't want your beer."

It raised one side of its brow. "That, Small One, is what they *all* say."

"Um," I looked to the left, then back at the creature. "Well, I can't have alcohol."

"Ah-h-h-h…" It looked me up and down. "In that case, I'm sorry for your loss."

I put my hand down. "That's not what I meant."

It pulled a ring of keys from one of its cargo pockets, using the bottle opener on it to crack open its beer.

I squinted again. "What are you?"

"Dear me—" It raised its eyebrow. "That's quite rude, now, isn't it?"

I rolled my eyes. "So what are you?"

It sighed. "You're quite the chatterbox, aren't you…"

"My name's Lilah."

"I truly don't believe I asked."

I crossed my arms. "You still didn't answer my—"

"I'm a *yeti*, alright?" He slipped the key ring around his thick wrist by the stretchy fabric strap. "Yeti—y-e-t-i. Are you quite done now?" He took a sip of his drink, suddenly taking great interest in the fingernails of his free hand.

I scrunched up my nose, the corners of my mouth pulling down like a sea bass. "Aren't you supposed to be in some kind of snowy mountain place?"

He rolled his eyes. "I'm on *vacation*." He struck a pose, gesturing to the Hawaiian shirt with his free hand. "Ever heard of a vacation, Small One? Don't answer that," he added with a sigh, "I'm being rhetorical…"

I started picking more leaves off of my T-shirt. "Look, I'm sorry to bother you, Mr., uh, Yeti," I said. "It's just—I fell down the hill." I nodded behind me.

The yeti tilted his head, monobrow pinching down. "All the way down?"

I nodded.

"What—all the way down, from the top?"

I nodded again.

"Honestly…" He shook his head. "Don't small ones like you usually have some sort of…parental outfit tailing you about?"

I shrugged. "They're sleeping, I think."

He put his free hand on his hip and glared at me. "And I suppose you had a terribly *brilliant* reason for trotting about the woods all by yourself…"

I let out a long sigh. "I was chasing a blue jay." After he didn't say anything, I added: "It deserved it—it stole my watch."

His glare deepened and he set his beer down on top of his cooler. "What a terrible idea," he muttered. With three long strides, he was at my side, shining his flashlight keychain into my eyes.

"Hey!" I squeaked, but he grabbed onto my shoulder with a hulkish grip before I could wiggle away. After a few seconds he turned the light off, but I kept seeing stars every time I blinked.

"Well, by some *miracle* you don't appear to have a concussion in that tiny little head of yours." He slipped the keys back into his pocket, then produced a large Band-Aid and a tube of Neosporin. He wiped the dirt from my knee with the fur on his wrist, which felt as soft as jumbo marshmallows, then squeezed a little ointment onto my scrape. With surprisingly agile fingers, he peeled the backing off the Band-Aid and stuck it on my knee, smoothing it down with his pointer fingers. "You shouldn't go chasing after birds," he grumbled. "You could've *broken* yourself in some way or another." He turned to leave.

"What's your name?" I shouted at him.

He sighed and turned around. "Barry."

I frowned. "Really?"

"What's wrong with that?"

I shrugged. "Nothing, I guess." I crossed my arms, adrenaline-fueled gears starting to spin wildly in my thankfully-non-concussed head. "You wouldn't be able to help me find my watch…would you?"

Barry raised the left side of his brow. "Why?"

I gestured at him with both my arms. "Have you seen yourself? You're much taller than I am."

"I'm on *vacation*—did you miss that part?"

"Listen—if I've lost that watch…" I raked my hands down my face as my doom became apparent. "Oh-h-h my gosh—my parents are going to kill me…"

Barry's grumpy demeanor wavered as his eyes widened. "Oh—my!" he gasped. "That doesn't seem right…"

I shook my head. "No no—not, like, *kill* me kill me. Not really."

"What an odd expression…"

"So will you help me?" I looked up at him with my well-practiced Puss in Boots eyes. "Please?"

His eyes narrowed into two thin slits, but finally he straightened his posture and sighed. "Fine," he muttered. "But don't kick me by mistake. Or on purpose." He scooped me up with his big gorilla arms and set me on his shoulders. He put his sunglasses on properly and I rested my chin on the top of his fuzzy head, then he started off into the woods past his cave.

"Jays have a very distinct smell," he said. "And this watch of yours—metal, was it? With a genuine leather strap?"

"Yep. And I spilled my lemonade on it yesterday."

I felt him sigh beneath me. "Very distinct smell, indeed..." He trundled along, sniffing the air every few paces. I sniffed the air too, but all I could smell was Barry's fur, which had an aura of pine and peppermint about it.

I rested my left elbow on his head, my chin propped up on my palm. "It's not like they even really care about that watch," I muttered. *But they* do *care about you being responsible*, I thought. "Dang it—they're not gonna trust me with anything ever again."

I felt Barry sigh again. "Humans do worry a lot, don't they..."

"Don't lump us all into one category—that's rude." My shoulders sagged. "But, yeah..."

Barry scratched behind his left ear. "Why's the watch important, then?"

I stared intently at my right thumb as I picked at my cuticle. "It was a present, of sorts."

"Was it an expensive gift?"

I shrugged. "I don't know. But it has character." I paused, then added: "It's all I've got left of someone, that's all."

Barry stayed quiet for a few seconds; there was just the *thump-thump-thump* of his massive footsteps against the forest floor. I started to wonder if he'd even heard me.

Then, at last, he put his hands on his hips and clicked his tongue. "See, I've never quite understood that one..."

I frowned. "What do you mean?"

"If it's a true thing, then I don't exactly see what the point is in friendship and all that."

"That's an odd thing to say."

"No odder than yours." Barry shrugged his big shoulders, causing me to bob up and down like one of those buoys on the lake. "If all you have left of someone is a silly old object, then you didn't know them very well, did you?"

That's weird, I thought.

But then I thought about it some more.

Eventually Barry tapped the tip of my left shoe with his big right thumb. "Are you still up there?" he bellowed.

I tilted my head. "More or less." I sat up straight and stretched my arms. "I just like that watch. I look at it and it makes me think of him."

"Nothing wrong with that, I suppose... But I still don't see why you hang on to it if you don't even like it that much."

"It doesn't fit me, either," I added. "And it doesn't tick."

Barry chuckled lightly. "You're an odd little thing."

∼∼∼

Soon enough, we found ourselves standing on the edge of the forest, at the base of a tall oak tree a few feet from the edge of the lake. Barry and I both craned our heads up, trying to see something in the boughs. He said the nest was up there somewhere.

Gingerly, I stood up on his shoulders, wobbling like a cup of Jell-O. I shielded my eyes from the morning sun with one hand, holding onto Barry's hand with the other.

"I don't see anything," I said. I looked down at Barry. "Can't *you* climb up there?"

His eyes rolled like breaking surf. "Don't be absurd...I'm far too heavy."

I extended my left foot towards the lowest bough I could see and pushed down on it with my toes. Seemed sturdy enough...

My ascent was slow at first. The bark was coarse against my palms—it was like swimming upstream in a sea of asphalt.

Between my panting breaths, my thoughts yapped at me. *Geez Louise...Mom and Dad are so totally going to never trust you with something ever again. What are you going to tell them? That you irresponsibly left the thing lying around? They'll take away your iPod for sure...* I then realized that I'd left my iPod in the grass, and I fought the impulse to thwack my head against the bark.

I caught sight of a bundle of twigs and fluff a few branches above me. I climbed higher. It was a nest, in the middle of which sat the blue jay, its feathers shimmering in the dappled sunlight just like Lake June—and there was a brown leather strap just barely peeking out from underneath the creature's body.

The jay looked me in the eye with its black, beady gaze. I hissed at it. Holding tight to the tree branch with my right hand, I shooed the jay with my left. It screeched at me, voice shrill and rough, and tried to bite my finger.

"Hey—!" I yanked my hand back, narrowly dodging the creature's beak. "Rude!" I shook my hand at it again, more violently this time. The jay stood, continuing to bark at me like a creaky cabinet door, and I took that as a window of opportunity. I grabbed the leather strap and yanked it back, but not fast enough—the blue jay bit down on the top of my hand. I yelped, recoiling backwards, my footing slipping from the branch.

I tumbled with no grace whatsoever—the tree was a Plinko Board and I was the little ball. My fingers locked onto the watch, as if holding onto it was my biggest problem in that moment. I flailed about with my free hand, eyes half shut, smacking into branches and grabbing hold of none of them. Leaves slapped against my cheeks; twigs raked themselves against my arms and hands. Wind whistled in my ears. My heart thumped in my chest like arrhythmic bongos. *I'm so dead,* I thought. *So, so, so dead—if I die here, Mom and Dad will totally kill me.*

Instead of pain and the hard dirt ground, I got a face full of white fur—a mouthful, too, and let me be the first to say that yeti hair tastes exactly like dog hair, if that dog had rolled around in a pound of granulated sugar. I sputtered and spit as I tried to find which way was up. I was met with Barry's big face looking down at me—his eyes obscured by his darkly tinted aviators, but I could tell he was frowning.

"You're very good at falling, I'll give you that." He set me gently down on my feet at the base of the tree. "I don't know *why* I assumed you were going to be more careful than that…"

I stuck my tongue out at him, an instinct, then felt guilty about it because he had definitely just saved my life. "You're really soft," I muttered.

"You're welcome."

"Thanks."

He chuckled—mostly to himself I think.

"Correct me if I'm wrong," he said, "but I'm fairly certain those two are supposed to be in the opposite order."

"Fair point. We can redo it—" I cleared my throat. "Thank you, Sir Barry."

"You're welcome, tiny Lilah."

My attention turned to the watch, which I held up like a dead rat by the tail. The face was cracked all the way down the middle. I glared up at the tree, directing all my grumpy thoughts toward the blue jay even though I couldn't see it anymore.

Barry hunched down, hands on his knees, head tilted to one side. I showed him the watch.

"I was under the impression that it was already broken," he rumbled.

"Not *that* broken," I sighed.

"If you were so worried about breaking that watch, whyever did you bring it with you?" Barry poked at the watch face, his thick fingernail making a *tink-tink* sound against the glass. "Either hold on to it by keeping it somewhere safe, or give the thing away and stop worrying about it."

I let out a huff of hot air, glaring at the watch face. "I can't just donate it—it's one of a kind."

"I could fix it for you," Barry offered. When I raised my eyebrows at him, he added: "I'm a bit of a tinkerer myself... I get a lot of me time when I'm working—lots of snow and lots of solitude equals lots of opportunities to learn new skills."

Slowly, like a laggy computer, I realized he was being serious. I looked down at the little watch...then I shook my head. "No, I can't— I'm leaving today, won't be back until next summer."

"I'll be here." His voice was steady.

My grip tightened on the strap. I ran my thumb over the cracked face and the sticky leather.

I held the watch up to Barry. "Deal. I'll pick it up next summer— swear."

Barry took the watch, then shook my little hand with thumb and pointer finger. "Lovely doing business with you, Small One."

"Likewise." Gradually, my arms and face begin to sting. "I should get back," I muttered. "Clean myself up... You wouldn't happen to know what time it is, would you?"

Barry sniffed the air again. "Half past seven."

I squinted at him. "How—" Then I actually registered the time he'd said. "Oh, crap—I really need to get home before breakfast or—"

"Or your parents will kill you, yes..." Barry sighed. "I'm getting the hang of your ritualistic existence..." He picked me up and set me down on his shoulders again. "I'll take you as far as my cave, but that's all. I'll give you directions from there—ones that don't involve falling down a giant hill, I might add."

I sunk my chin into the marshmallow fur on the top of Barry's head. "Sorry I ruined your vacation."

"Don't be silly," Barry drummed. "There *is* such a thing as too much solitude...but don't tell anyone I said that. I have a reputation to uphold." He laughed—it was deep and rumbly, like the metro back in Cali.

Over breakfast, my parents fussed a little over the state of me. Between the scrapes on my face, the big Band-Aid on my knee, and the little cuts on my hands and arms, I think they thought I'd been attacked by a rabid squirrel or something. As we each went to work on a plate of bacon, pancakes, and eggs, they just about interrogated me.

At last, I shrugged and told them the truth—well, part of the truth. "I fell," I said. "Twice."

My mom sighed, as she often did when I got too entangled with nature. "What were you doing?"

I shrugged again. "Just 'splorin'."

My dad stopped cutting his pancake to side-eye me. "I'm surprised you didn't take your iPod with you…"

Oh, boy, I thought, *I'm in for it.* I proceeded to break the awkward silence with the worst possible question, directed at my dad: "Do you miss the watch? The one Granddad gave me?"

"The broken one?" My dad chuckled a little. "Kiddo, I've told you before—I didn't even like that watch when it worked. Neither did my dad. You can keep it—no one will miss it."

I stabbed my pancake with my fork. "Oh." A tight feeling grasped my chest. *No one will miss it,* I thought. A picture of its busted little face and motionless hands flashed in my mind. *Even if it worked, no one would miss it?*

My mother cut in with something unrelated. "I won't miss you getting hurt," she sighed. "That's for sure."

I gave her my best suspicious glance. "What's that supposed to mean?"

She took a sip of her orange juice and looked at my dad. He looked at her and gave a little half shrug. I looked back and forth between the two of them like they were having some sort of inaudible-yet-tense debate. My mom kicked him under the table and he turned to me with a smile.

"Honey," my dad said, "this is going to be our last trip to Lake June." I nearly choked on my bacon. "What?" I yelled. "And you tell me this *now*?! On our *last day*? What's wrong with you people!"

My dad narrowed his eyes at me. "L.J., calm—"

"I'm calm." I raised my hands and sat back in my chair, taking in a deep breath.

"We would've told you sooner," my mom said, "but with the changes in mortuary expenses—" She glanced at my dad, who was staring at his plate. She smiled back at me, expression seeming a bit brittle. "It's just not in the cards to keep this cabin, honey."

"That's fine," I said flatly. "Fine." I could feel my brow knit tightly together. Then my eyes widened and I shot out of my chair. *That stupid watch,* I thought. *That stupid watch that no one will miss—dang it!* I couldn't leave it like that.

I just couldn't.

While my parents yammered at me, I darted out the kitchen door. I tripped on my way to the front porch and nearly barreled through the screen door in my fervor to get to the front steps. With my Twinkle Toes blinking like a seizing radio tower, and my little heart thundering in my chest, I pushed through the trees until I was in familiar yeti territory, retracing the path Barry had given me.

Without stopping, I burst into Barry's cave.

It was a lot bigger on the inside than I had expected. In one corner was a bathtub-shower combo, strung with a striped shower curtain. A king-sized bed sat against the back wall between two large armoires and a reclining chair. There was a flat-screen television and shag carpet, for cryin' out loud.

I was too distressed to care, though. As soon as I saw Barry—who was sitting at a thick wooden desk with a bunch of little tools, fiddling with my watch while wearing a magnifying eyepiece—I darted over to him. My eyes were burning—they felt wet and fragile.

Barry looked up, his eyebrow raised, and put the watch down.

"Small One?" he asked. "What's wrong?"

My answer got caught in my throat. It took me a few tries to get it all out in one sentence. "We're not coming back," I managed to say. "I didn't know that—they didn't—"

He patted me on the head. "It will be all right," he said softly. "The lake will always be here when you're ready to return."

"But I promised you—"

"You're very sweet, Small One," he smiled. "But it's alright. People come and go. That is the way of things." He looked down at the desk. "I only wish I had gotten your little watch properly fixed up in time."

My face felt so hot—it must've been lifeguard red. "No one cares about the watch," I muttered.

Barry laughed, which threw me off guard. "You certainly care about it," he said, "and I've rather enjoyed my time with it. It's an intricate design. Lots of 'character,' as you so aptly put it earlier." He started to pick up the pieces and hand it back to me when I suddenly yelped at him to stop. He froze, eyes wide and mouth tightly closed.

I brushed some of my fringe out of my eyes. "You should keep it."

Barry tilted his head back. "Pardon?"

"You like it, right?"

"I do, but—don't you want it?"

I paused, then said: "I do love it, but honestly—I'll just lose it, or break it again. It deserves better than that. You can fix it—and you can actually wear it. And you'd like wearing it." I took in a big breath and let it out, a smile spilling across my face like high tide. "Granddad didn't even like wearing it—best you keep it."

Barry leaned back in his chair. "I promise, little Lilah, I'll take good care of it. And," he added, "maybe one day I'll have the pleasure of giving it back to you."

I smiled and gave him a hug—though my arms still didn't fit all the way around him. "Thanks, Barry." He patted my head again.

I heard my mom shout for me in the distance: *"Lilah Jade Maxwell! Where did you go?"*

"Oh dear," Barry muttered. "Middle name—if I understand your culture correctly, that's not a very a good sign..."

I winced. "Yikes. Yeah. If I don't—"

"Yes, yes—the parents and the killing and all that—I've got that bit."

I headed towards the cave mouth. As I was standing in the entrance, I stopped and turned around. "I'll see ya around, Barry."

He tilted an invisible hat in my direction. "I look forward to it."

After lunch, once we had packed everything into the rental and hit the road, I stared out my window and watched Lake June pass by. The water shimmered and danced. I tapped at the Band-Aid on my knee as I listened to Tchaikovsky on my iPod. *Swan Lake.* Thought it was fitting. Birds chittered as we sped past them. I turned around in my seat as the lake and the cabins started to disappear with the road behind us.

Perhaps I was leaving Lake June...

But something inside said that it wasn't goodbye.

The Girl Who Lived Under the Water

BRAD PAUQUETTE

I met the girl who lived under the water when she was ten.

The island of San Jalisco sits forty miles from the mainland. Although the water is clear and blue, full of colorful fish and crustaceans but never a single shark, the island is completely bereft of beaches. The island is surrounded by low cliffs that drop off into the ocean, which is twenty feet deep for a mile out in every direction—as if God made the island with a cookie cutter and scraped away the earth that sat outside of the mold.

There were seven years between her and I when we met. I was troubled about another girl, one of my own age, who wouldn't hold my hand or look into my eyes when I said nice things, so I went and sat on a diving raft, a flat box-like wooden platform five feet square that sat just above the surface of the water. It was attached to one of the four piers of San Jalisco, presumably so swimmers could easily jump off of it into the water, though I never saw a single person do such a thing.

Other days I went and sat in the orange grove, where I could lay in the grass and let the refreshing cool of the orange trees wash over me, but that particular day there was a chill in the air. My spirit felt cold and dank in the orange grove, so I walked to the Southern Pier. I counted my way down the thirty wooden steps anchored to the cliff and ambled onto the boardwalk that stretched out into the sea. My feet slapped lazily against the pier until I reached the diving raft, where I climbed down the short ladder to sit upon it and soak up the saltwater mist and the disinfecting power of the sun.

I laid with my back flat against the raft as I thought about the girl who wouldn't hold my hand. I tapped twice on the raft whenever I had a thought I considered especially poignant. I had been on the diving raft for an hour or more, and tapped at least a hundred times already, when I tapped again. *Tap tap.* I closed my eyes and rested my head against the planks.

A moment later, from the underside of the raft, there came a *tap tap*. I raised my head, looked around, was still alone with only a gull on the pier for company.

I tapped again and watched the bird. *Tap tap.* It didn't move, just squawked aimlessly out over the ocean like a fellow dejected suitor.

A few moments later, I jumped to my feet as the tap was returned from the underside of the raft.

I rushed to the edge of the small flat platform and looked over the edge. There I saw her, sitting on the ocean floor, staring apathetically up at the bottom of the diving raft. Her eyes blinked slowly in the salt water and she seemed to sigh with every breath. I waved to her through the water, but she just stared at the bottom of the raft, waiting.

Her hair was long and black and straight and hovered gracefully about her face, fluttering in the natural movements of the ocean water. Her skin was as white as a porcelain doll, her eyes dark and listless, peering up at the raft. She sat on her bottom on the ocean floor, unassisted by any breathing apparatus and submerged without effort. She wore a white nightgown and her tiny arms were wrapped around her knees, her hands locked in front of her.

I had lived on the island for three years, working for my father at the bike shop where we rented bikes to tourists by the hour. I had heard sparse but casual mention of the girl who lived under the water, but it was always greeted by hushed tones and a half smile. The way you might mention bigfoot some place where they sell life-sized cut-outs of cryptids.

I was perplexed by the girl on the bottom of the ocean. Seemingly alive and breathing the seawater. I became frantic, at first I removed my shoes to dive in and save her, then I looked again and decided that perhaps she was a mechanical doll.

I sat back on my haunches, looking over the side of the raft, and I tapped again. Though her face never changed, the girl blinked, stood up, flittered her feet to rise from the ocean floor with the grace of a ballerina jeté-ing on the moon, and disappeared beneath the raft.

Tap. Tap.

I had nowhere to be, nothing left to think about, and the clouds were drifting across the sun at the perfect intervals that day, so I sat in the middle of the raft and we tapped back-and-forth for hours.

To this day, I cannot accurately explain exactly how, but over the course of days and weeks and even months, like the first two humans to ever speak to each other, I learned to talk to the girl who lived under the water through taps, and she to me.

San Jalisco is one of those places, like San Diego or Nairobi, that seems to magically exist between the temperatures of sixty and ninety degrees Fahrenheit year-round. Every day I went out to the raft, and I sat, and I tapped. Each of the islanders took their turn staring at me as I sat there tapping my fingers, sometimes wild-eyed and sometimes melancholy, always with bicycle chain grease on my hands. I suspected that it was becoming a sort of game to speculate in which manner I was crazy.

She told me about the mornings she spent looking far into the ocean, to the place the water turned to endless black. She told me where the lobsters had learned to hide, where they could never be caught. One day, she told me that her name was Andrea.

But I don't like that name, she tapped to me through the underside of the diving raft.

Who says that's your name? I tapped back.

She tapped a shrug.

Then pick a new one, I told her.

That was the day we learned to tap tears. It is a bittersweet thing to be able to change one's name and it not matter. She picked a name that could only be tapped and it was beautiful.

In the days and weeks that followed, she told me about the day that her parents had dropped her into the ocean—the day after she was born.

She told me that instead of postponing their long-awaited trip to the island of San Jalisco, they took their premature newborn along with them. As the tender ferried them from the cruise liner to the Southern Pier of San Jalisco, the girl who lived under the water began to fuss to be fed. As the new mother unwrapped her shawl, positioned a blanket to conceal her breast, and unbundled the newborn baby to feed her, the baby slipped from her mother's arms and fell into the ocean where she sank like a stone.

Her father frantically removed his suit jacket, but by the time he removed his shoes and eased out of his vest and removed his watch, he looked down into the water and presumed that it was a lost cause, decided she was too far gone. So Andrea drifted slowly through the twenty feet to the ocean floor, staring wide-eyed up at her parents, distorted through the surface of the water and shrinking.

She explained that she was fortunate that she wasn't older. One minute to a baby that is five minutes old is one fifth of its lifetime, and one fifth of a lifetime is a long time, regardless of one's age. So at the age of only one day old, the minute it took her to sink to the bottom of the ocean was a considerable amount of time to learn.

As she sank to the bottom, she had the better part of a lifetime to consider the ocean and its vast array of organisms and microorganisms. In her study, she came to understand the world around her, a world full of food and oxygen against which her impartial mind could not discriminate. When the time was right, she simply breathed in and never stopped.

When their vacation was over, she watched her father and mother ride the tender from the pier back to the cruise liner. When they looked overboard they saw the wide blinking eyes of the baby looking up at them, its mouth agape in wonder. This upset the woman, so the man pulled her away from the edge of the small boat and comforted her.

It took the girl who lived under the water three weeks to tell me this story one tap at a time, and then I thought she might never tap again. For four days I went and sat on the diving raft, tapping down to her, and for four days there was no response. When I looked over the side of the platform, she was nowhere to be found.

On the fifth day, I sat on the raft in silence, melancholy in my own thoughts.

I used to come above the water, the taps came frantically and suddenly. I jumped to my feet.

I missed you, I bent over and tapped back.

I used to poke my head above the water and talk, but it was uncomfortable, and no one ever had anything to say, she explained. *I could hardly breathe the air, so sharp and fast, and my skin dries and cracks in a moment.*

It's okay, I tried to console the girl who lived under the water.

It's so dark here at night. I can't feel it, but I'm certain it's cold.

As my conversations with the girl who lived under the water progressed, I began to attend work less frequently than I had before. On the days that I went, I would leave for lunch and not return. I was only repairing bicycles for tourists, and the bicycles rarely broke.

I began to ask around town about the girl who lived under the water. First I went to the police, and they just shrugged. I went to the mayor, and he shook his head.

Finally, I went to the orphanage on the island.

"We don't have any record of a girl like that," the woman who sat behind the desk closest to the front door told me, peering suspiciously over her plastic-framed glasses.

"Perhaps we could start a record," I suggested politely.

She forced a tight smile, then pulled a blank sheet of paper from a drawer and licked the tip of her pencil.

"Where on the island does the child live?" she asked me.

"I already explained, she lives on the bottom of the ocean near the Southern Pier."

"Oh, I'm sorry, sir, but this agency is only authorized to serve children *on* the island of San Jalisco." She plucked the paper from her desk and slid it back into the drawer from whence it came.

"But—but then what agency do you suggest I speak with?" I stammered.

"Children don't live underwater, sir. If you have an issue with an animal in the ocean, perhaps you should try the marina." She clicked her tongue. Then her phone rang. She picked it up and waved for me to leave.

That afternoon, I only talked to the girl who lived under the water for a few minutes. I couldn't tell her about the orphanage, but I couldn't push the topic from my mind either.

The next day I skipped work entirely and went to San Jalisco's marina. I looked out over acres of brightly-colored catamarans and dinghies, skiffs and yachts that littered the docks anchored to the Northern Pier of San Jalisco. I hopped the steps to the main office, which overlooked the water.

I finally found the man who managed the marina at the restaurant that sat on the edge of the cliff on the northwestern corner of the island. The old man was sitting down to lunch when I met him, and he invited me to join him.

He looked more like a character in a Hemingway novel than the manager of the marina at a high-end resort, but everyone plays a part on San Jalisco. A tattered and stained captain's hat sat jauntily atop his head, an unbuttoned peacoat hung limply off his shoulders, exposing a white T-shirt and silk scarf underneath.

"Aye, I know of the girl who lives in the ocean," he told me plainly after our plates were served. "A real shame."

I was taken aback by the first islander to admit the existence of the girl. Even I was beginning to doubt her existence. I could tell he registered the shock on my face.

"They're a little mum around here about it, aren't they?" he laughed, the gritty cold laugh of an old mariner. "Weren't always. But these things get set in, you know? Nobody calls a meeting, but in a community like this one, they might as well've—nobody knows about the girl, you know?"

I nodded my head and waited for him to continue.

"Son-of-a-gun sailor who was operatin' the boat bringing those folks to shore should've stopped when he learned of it, made it right. But the guests come first on San Jalisco."

I nodded again and bit my lip.

"Oh, you've noticed," he laughed from his throat again but his eyes were distant and sad. "So it was decided by the management to leave the baby until the guests—the parents—left, then we'd pursue another course." His eyes glazed over and he sighed, sat silent for a minute or more. "The sailor who saw it happen volunteered to dive in to get the baby, and he did. But when he pulled her out of the water she howled and gasped, thrashed about, all the poor babe's muscles went rigid, and she just gasped and gasped like she couldn't breathe. So, broke his heart, but he put her back down, left her there until somebody with more brains could figure it out." He stopped talking and shoveled a bite of halibut into his mouth.

"So what happened?" I finally asked. "Why didn't they save her?"

"Oh, too expensive. University said it would cost millions to build a chamber to acclimate her back to breathing air." He took a big bite of garlic toast and continued, "Company wanted to build a viewing area, tourists could come and look at the girl who lives under the water. Island said they'd issue the permits if half of the revenues went to the chamber for the girl—"

"That's great," I exclaimed out of turn. "When are they going to do it already?"

"Aren't," he grunted. "Company determined the blasted thing would save the girl before it broke even."

I shook my head, and then rested my forehead in my hands, elbows on the table.

"What happened to that sailor? The one who let it happen?" I implored.

He looked up from his meal, his eyes distant. "Sailor was too old for the job anyway. Told him he could help on the island after that. Gave him a desk job. Started work at the marina, poured hisself into his work, did alright."

"Where can I find him?"

The old man looked me in the eye and forced a weak smile.

I went back to the raft that day. There were no clouds in the sky and I'd forgotten my hat, so I sat there and roasted in the blinding rays, waiting for the girl who lived under the water. I looked out over the water as I waited, plotting the course of the sun to its final resting place beyond the horizon, watching the gulls circle and swoop.

Hello, she suddenly tapped.

Where have you been? I asked her.

Just walking, she told me. *Where did you go today?*

Nowhere, I lied. *Didn't feel very good.* There was a long pause, and I could tell she was thinking under the raft as clearly as if I could have seen the furrow of her brow.

Don't be sad for me, she finally said.

I'm not.

I can tell by the tone of your tap.

I'm sorry, I told her. *I just wish I could help you.*

You are helping me.

Later that evening, I sat at the tourist's restaurant bar and drank a soda, avoiding dirty looks from the bartender and sipping slowly.

The next morning I got up early and went to the raft. The girl who lived under the water was waiting for me.

I've got to go away for awhile, I explained.

How long? she tapped sadly.

We can fix this, I told her.

Please don't. She paused with her finger resting on the bottom of the raft. *I need you.*

The wake of some distant cruise line beyond the horizon washed against the diving platform, and a lonely gull circled overhead and called down to me.

I have to. I'll be back, promise. Without another word, I got up and climbed off of the diving raft. I walked down the Southern Pier to a waiting tender that would take me out to a commuter vessel bound for the mainland. As I walked away, I heard what sounded like a large fish break the surface of the water and gasp, but I didn't look back.

Three years later I returned to the island with a crew from the university, a special chamber, and a lawyer who represented the nonprofit I'd formed to save the girl who lived under the water. Three years was a short time to raise $4 million, but it was an easy cause to sell once they believed.

I jumped off of the tender that took us to the Southern Pier, ran to the diving raft and sat down. I tapped gently on the wooden deck and waited. As the crew from the university disembarked from the vessel, fetched their luggage, and arranged for the deboarding of the chamber, I tapped more and more urgently.

I pounded violently on the raft, hammering her name into the wood with my fist over and over again. But still there was no response. The islanders gathered along the fence that guards the cliff and watched me as I beat the diving raft with my hand. They pointed and snickered as I put my ear to the deck and listened to the water slap against the underside of the planks.

Finally, I looked over the edge, and there she was. She sat cross-legged on the bottom of the ocean floor, her hands on her knees. The eleven-year-old girl I had left had blossomed into a young woman of fourteen. The baby fat had drained from her face, and her cheekbones were prominent and proud, her nose less like a button and her eyes sharp and clear. She peered keenly up through the water at the bottom of the raft, ignoring me, one eyebrow pegged downward in vexation.

I tapped again and she didn't move. Again and again I tapped, looking over the edge at her, but she didn't move. She simply blinked and breathed and ignored me.

As the sun began to sink into the ocean beyond the horizon, I climbed off of the diving raft and headed to my old home on the island.

For five days I sat on the diving raft as the team from the university prepared the chamber, each day passed without a response from the girl who lived under the ocean.

Then I went and sat in the orange grove of San Jalisco. The team worked for weeks to collect the girl who lived under the water and place her in the chamber, a great copper contraption with valves and a window.

When I learned that she was in the chamber, I ran to the marina where they moved it. I fought through the crowd of tourists and islanders who had gathered to see the girl and finally reached the window. I banged on the window with the flat of my hand, but she sat cross-legged on the floor of the water-filled chamber with her back to me.

Andrea! Andrea! I tapped in hysterics. But she only shook her head until a member of the staff pulled me away.

I stopped at the restaurant bar on my way back home. The young bartender shook my hand, thanked me for the increased business to the island since I took the story of the girl who lived under the water of San Jalisco to the mainland, and gave me a bottle of bourbon for the road.

I wandered back to the orange grove with my bottle, lay down on the cool, dark grass, and watched the moon through the orange leaves shifting in the breeze. I pulled my hat down low over my eyes and fell asleep.

Six weeks later I was invited to a dinner at the marina restaurant.

I didn't remember much from the previous weeks, but I was able to discern through the fog that the girl would be there, that she was cured.

I bought a suit and tie, one that I could also wear to a funeral, possibly my own if the occasion arose, and arrived at the marina restaurant at the appointed time.

I sat at a table by myself in the corner. The old man who ran the marina came by and slapped me hard on the back, smiled down at me and winked. I ignored him and he sauntered away.

As I sat and ate my halibut, the girl who lived under the water came in. She stood in front of the restaurant, eyes cast toward the ground. Her parents stood on either side of her and basked in the applause of the men and women assembled there. Her father shook hands, her mother accepted hugs, and the girl who lived under the water stood there motionless, shying away from a pat on the shoulder, sighing each time another ensemble of admirers came and went.

Eventually, her parents and she sat down to eat with the rest of us. Her mother and father talked gaily with their table in loud, excited tones, and did not notice when she got up.

I watched her wander up and down between the tables, and I realized for the first time that she was short. Standing up, her head was barely above that of a tall man sitting down. She walked lightly, moving about like a ghost between the tables, unnoticed, barely touching the ground as if she were still walking underwater. I watched her go back and forth, head down, eyes always on her feet, slowing occasionally to listen, then moving on.

As she wove her way through the maze of tables, finally I could see that she was on a course to pass mine. I wanted to call out to her, I wanted to cry and shout and hug her and tell her she was alive. I wanted to squeeze her and kiss her on the forehead and hold her close to me and mess up her hair. But as she came closer, I found that I could only choke back tears, that I could say nothing at all.

She had almost passed by me when I put my finger on the linen tablecloth and I tapped twice. She stopped two steps past my table, eyes still on her feet, and waited.

I tapped again. She took a step backward toward my table. I tapped again.

She turned toward my table, but her eyes didn't leave the ground, her face didn't change. She just blinked slowly and breathed in and out.

I bit my lower lip and slowly, intentionally, I tapped out the name she had chosen, the beautiful name that could only be tapped.

Her eyes looked up to mine, then her head picked up. She looked at me for the first time in her life, dimples grew in her cheeks, and she rested her index finger on the table.

She tapped twice, and she smiled.

Acknowledgments

Thank you for exploring these magical renditions of our world and enjoying a good beach read with us!

I figure the acknowledgments page in the back of a book is about the same as credits rolling at a movie theater. Half of the people will skip it, but the other half will stay. So thanks for staying.

A lot went into this project and there are too many people to ever thank in such a short space, but I'll do my best.

To the readers, thank you for taking the time to read these stories. We did it for you. If the book made you laugh, cry, or remember a forgotten truth, please share it with friends and leave an honest review on Amazon or Goodreads. This will help other readers connect with it.

To everyone who supported the authors in the anthology—family members, friends, Internet communities—you can't imagine how big your impact is. So many of the authors are being published for their first time. You've brought them all the way to publication. Well done.

In the same vein, thank you to my family. Ya'll are awesome.

Special thanks to Alli Prince for paving the way with *Lawless* and catching copy editing errors I missed. Thanks to Edna, Bekah, and Jack for ministering to me in the middle of the stress. Thanks to Jessica Ostrander for an amazing cover.

And, of course, thanks to Brad. I never would've imagined or even seriously thought about leading a project like this before you suggested it. I definitely didn't want to take it on without your guidance. And if I had, I would've been lost before I even started.

Finally, thanks to God. Everything we've ever accomplished is from you and for you. You're too good for words.

Vella Karman
Project Manager

Author Biographies

R.J. Catlin enjoys the magic of storytelling from her home in Appalachian Ohio. When she's not writing, she's going on adventures with friends, reading, cooking up an art project, or simply enjoying God's creation. Find her at rjcatlin.com, where she shares what God's teaching her about creativity.

Lucy Grecu is a musical theater enthusiast and fiction writer from L.A. She moved across the country to attend The Company and hone her writing skills. Apart from writing, Lucy reads novels very slowly and plays Dungeons & Dragons. You can find her at LucyGrecu.com

When **K.Ann** isn't writing, you can find her touring her favorite fantasy worlds and her local libraries. You can connect with her by visiting her on Pinterest as @kannwriter and Instagram as @k.ann.writer, where she rambles on about fantasy and Jesus.

Vella Karman (*see editor biography on page 235*)

Adara King is an aspiring fiction author/illustrator from Arkansas. Her work has appeared in UCA's *Vortex* literary magazine and the 11th edition of UAMS's *Medicine and Meaning*. Her free hours are spent crafting, singing worship, or with loved ones. You can find her art on Instagram @attherosegarden23

Vannah Leblank is an overthinker and overachiever. You'll usually find her processing her questions through writing or exploring the world in as many ways as she (ethically) can. She has participated in anthologies such as *Lawless* and *Image Bearers*, contributed to various literary magazines, and published her own poetry anthology, *Shards*. You can follow her on Instagram @vannah_leblankkkk_and_stories or write to her directly at savannahl@hotmail.ca.

Noah J. Matthews is an author and aspiring filmmaker from the woods of Northern Michigan. Noah's calling is to entertain people with artful media, while at the same time inspiring them to pursue their deepest dreams. He regularly blogs about how to get serious about your dream at NoahJMatthews.com.

Juli Ocean is an award-winning author, certified ghostwriter and chai chugger. Her encouraging words have been read on six continents. When she's not at her desk, she's an avid fermentista, participates in expanded thinking, dreams of time travel, and making Aliyah. Connect with her at JuliOcean.com

Greg O'Donnell hails from Missouri, having won first place for a short story titled "Fire," he recently completed a draft for his debut sci-fi fantasy novel. He is inspired by the writings of J.R.R. Tolkien, Robert Jordan, and Terry Brooks. He enjoys woodworking, gardening, and puzzling. Follow him at gregorylodonnell.com

Brad Pauquette (*see editor biography on page 236*)

Alli Prince has been creating stories since she could form words and has been writing since long before she learned about sentence structure and grammar (her editors think she could still learn a thing or two about grammar). Check out Alliprince.com for tips on overcoming the lies of the enemy!

Sarah Sax has been storytelling since she could talk. She loves writing poetry, epic science-fantasy, and academic papers on Tolkien. "Beachcombing" was inspired by living near the beach, where she has found plenty of shells but no shark's teeth or portals. She posts fanfiction every few months on Quotev @MessianicLife

Hannah Stiff is in her early 20s, living the life of Anne in Prince Edward Island. She's won a couple provincial writing awards and hopes she'll find time for a novel soon. Ensconced in her family homestead, Hannah also teaches music, dances like Jane Austen, and loves her Savior. Shoot her a line at: hannah@peimandolinlessons.com

Faith Tevy has stardust on her fingertips and God at her side. When she's not lost in a story or laughing with her family, she is chasing her Great Dane around her garden in Arizona. She finds delight in her Heavenly Father, and when He speaks she writes.
YouTube: @wildandfree-7

Thirzah, author of *The Librarian's Ruse* and *A Traitor's Vow*, writes fantasy books with a focus on mercenaries and royal intrigue. When she's not reading or writing books, you'll find her sipping mint tea or traveling across the country. Learn more about Thirzah and her books on her website: thirzahwrites.com

Vella Karman

Vella Karman is a story addict and novelist drawing on her southern roots to craft stories splashed with color and emotion. Her writing has been read in more than forty countries so far and she aspires to write gripping, whimsical stories that keep readers up till three a.m.

Never settling with her art, she's experimenting with groundbreaking magical realism—turning intangible concepts into magical elements for heartrendingly beautiful social commentary.

She's brought people to tears with her writing, but the real question is if she can make people laugh and cry at the same time.

Vella calls herself a goofball, and she currently has more comedy essays published on *The Pearl* than any other author, not to mention the funny reels she posts on Instagram.

As an apprentice at The Company, Vella prays over every book and most of her weekly articles, laboring under the idea that if it touches one person, brings one person even the teeniest bit closer to God, it's all worth it.

As she ventures into her career as an author, editor, speaker, and social media manager, she's grateful for this project.

Read more at vellakarman.com or follow @vellakarmanauthor
on Instagram or YouTube to connect!

Brad Pauquette

Brad Pauquette is the director of The Company and the author of *The Novel Matrix*, a bestselling writing craft book.

Brad has worked in the publishing industry since 2009. He has produced over a dozen anthologies including the *Best of Ohio Short Stories* series and *Lawless*.

Brad leads the writing apprenticeship program at The Company. This full-time college alternative helps writers like Vella Karman step into real careers as professional writers. Learn more about The Company and apply to be an apprentice at Writers.Company.

Brad lives in Cambridge, Ohio, with his wife Melissa and their seven children. You can connect with him, find links to his books, and learn more about him at BradPauquette.com.

Brad welcomes invitations to speak to churches, writing groups, and podcasters. Reach out to him via his website.

About The Company

The Company provides practical training and support for world-changing Christian writers.

Writers of all ages and skill levels are invited to join us on our website, Writers.Company, where you'll find a ton of free resources and a community of writers who are excited to support you.

Our writing apprenticeship is for writers who are ready to work hard and take things to the next level. The apprenticeship is an in-person, full-time college alternative. It is the only opportunity of its kind in the world.

Apprentices refine their writing skills, learn the business of publishing, and grow in their walk with the Holy Spirit. Apprentices are fully prepared to professionally publish their work and reach real audiences with the stories God has placed on their hearts.

As part of their training, apprentices create and manage real-life projects like *Fantastical Summer.*

Learn more and get started:
Writers.Company

PEARLMAG.CO

Curiously Good Kingdom Literature

Don't stop now.

We publish great short stories every single week.

100% free. 100% worth it. All the time.

Read and subscribe today at

PearlMag.co

Hungry for more imagination?
Try this on for size:

If you make something, and then that something accidentally comes alive and destroys your entire town...would it be fair to say that you destroyed the town, or can we just blame it on the thing?

Available wherever great books are sold!
PearlBooks.co

Scan for Amazon

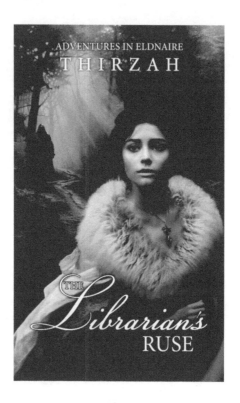

Don't stop now.
We have more short stories.

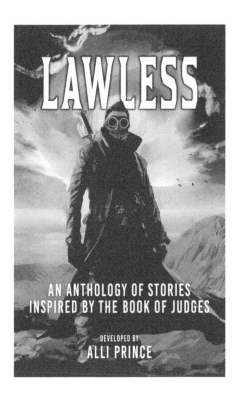

Enjoy the work of Alli Prince and Brad Pauquette,
with twelve other authors, in this gritty,
imaginative, western sci-fi anthology based on the
biblical book of Judges.

Available wherever great books are sold!
LawlessBook.com

Scan for Amazon

Made in United States
Cleveland, OH
19 June 2025

17838717R00146